S0-BBB-091

ANNE L HARVEY

SUCH A TIME AS THIS

SUCH A TIME AS THIS

By Anne L Harvey

ACKNOWLEDGE-MENTS

With humble and grateful thanks to my long-standing friend, **Judith Nisbet Lowe**, for her honest advice that completely changed the direction of the storyline. It works much better because of her fresh input.

Thanks are again due to the multi-talented **Berni Stevens** for designing the evocative cover. You can check out more of her designs on **www.bernistevens.com**

Lastly, thank you to the town of **Horwich**, in Lancashire, where I was born and where I spent my most formative years. Although I no longer live there, the town will always have a special place in my heart. Thanks for the memories!

CONTENTS

CHAPTER 1

At half past five, the hooter signalled the end of the working day and, heaving a sigh of relief, Joyce Roberts switched her looms off one by one. It had been a long day. As a towel weaver, she'd been on her feet tending her three looms since half past seven that morning. The September sun beating down on the glass-ridged roof of the weaving shed had made working conditions unbearably sticky and she was looking forward to what she hoped would be the relative cool of the outdoors. She made her way through the adjoining warp shed with its stacked warp drums of spun cotton waiting to be lifted onto the looms and out into the cobbled yard. The Beehive Mill was old, an assortment of buildings with many later additions tacked on here and there. She wondered how much longer such mills would be able to carry on. Already cheap imports and synthetic fabrics were having an impact on the once giant cotton industry of Lancashire and several of the quilt looms in her own weaving shed had remained silent as the weavers left, their jobs unfilled.

The gatekeeper's lodge where she was now

heading had probably been the manager's house though now it held the clocking-in machines and a counter for the gateman on duty. She waited her turn to clock out, doing so with a satisfying ping and joined the steady stream of people wending their way to the bus stop and home for the much-anticipated weekend. Tomorrow night she'd see Dave Yates, her boyfriend of three years and they were going to the Odeon in Bolton to see the widely-acclaimed film Ben Hur, starring Charlton Heston.

A short bus ride later, she was climbing the path that was the short cut through to the Brazeley estate where she lived with her family. In the cul-de-sac of Lancaster Avenue, a group of girls were 'dipping' to see who would be 'it' for whatever game they were playing. Her own sister wasn't amongst them; she'd be more likely to be playing with some lads somewhere. A few doors down, a couple more girls were practising handstands against the wall of a house, the skirts of their dresses falling down to reveal their navy knickers. She smiled in remembrance. It didn't seem that long since she'd been doing the same thing, though she'd never quite managed the handstand thing.

She opened the back door of the Roberts' home, to be faced with the tantalising aroma of meat and potato pie, a Friday night favourite of the whole family. Instead of playing out as she'd expected, her nine-year old sister, Lucy, was laying the table and looked up as Joyce entered the kitchen. 'Lo, Joyce.' Lucy was fair-haired and grey-eyed like their mother whereas dark-haired and dark-eyed Joyce and her elder brother Nick resembled their father. As the only two girls in the family, the sisters had always been close and Joyce hugged the young girl to her. 'Hello, sweetheart. I thought you'd have been out playing with it being such a nice day.'

Lucy pulled a face. 'I didn't feel like it today. It were hard going back to school this week after the September holidays.'

Joyce laughed. 'It won't be long till half-term.'

'I know but ...' Lucy let out a heartfelt sigh and fell silent.

'But what, love?' Joyce encouraged, hanging her coat up behind the back door.

'I've been thinking a lot about our Brian. Remembering that it were three years since he died.' A cloud passed over the young girl's face. 'Doesn't seem that long, does it?'

Thinking back to that dreadful time, when their lively twelve-year-old brother had been killed in a road accident, Joyce experienced a familiar pang of loss. Brian would have been 15 by now and would probably have been thinking about starting work in the New Year. 'I still miss him too, Lucy. Remember when he used to come charging into the kitchen in Winter Street, wanting a jam butty 'cos he were starving.'

Lucy, managed a half-hearted giggle. 'Now it's our Derek who does that.' Since 13-year-old Derek had started at the Senior School, or more properly known as Horwich Secondary Modern School, he'd

3

shot up in height and had suddenly become all arms and legs. She reached in the kitchenette for the salt and pepper, placing them in the middle of the table. 'Oh, by the way, a telegram came for you today.'

Joyce's eyes widened in shock and she gripped the back of a kitchen chair for support. 'A telegram?' A telegram spoke of urgency, a legacy from the War when they often contained bad news. She couldn't think who'd want to contact her so desperately.

'Yes, Mam had to open it 'cos the telegraph lad wanted to know if there'd be a reply.'

'In the front room, is she?' Joyce asked.

'Yes, she's just taken Dad a cuppa to keep him sweet,' Lucy said. 'You know how grumpy he is when he gets home from work.' Hands on girlish hips, she surveyed her handiwork on the table before her, gave a satisfied nod then said, 'I'm off upstairs if anyone wants me.'

Joyce lifted the lid off the old brown teapot and decided there was probably enough tea left to squeeze another cup out. Taking her tea with her, she went into the front room, where her mother was sitting on the sofa while her Dad sat in his usual chair by the empty fireplace, the belt of his work-trousers open to release the strain on his expanding belly. As usual when he got home, he was moaning about work. He was employed as a labourer at the Locomotive Works, the huge sprawling complex on Chorley New Road. It was noisy and smelly but for the men of Horwich, the main source of employment and the life-blood of Horwich.

4

Mam was sitting on the second-hand sofa they'd acquired when they'd moved in. It was shabbier now and almost threadbare in places after three years of the family sagging into its comfortable depths. When they'd moved here, much of their old stuff had come with them. There had been no money to spare for new furniture but there were some new additions too. Like the TV rented from Radio Rentals that took pride of place in one corner of the room. They still listened to the wireless occasionally but far more often the family turned to the television in the evening. Mam and Dad had their own favourite programmes like 'Dixon of Dock Green' but Joyce's preference was for 'Juke Box Jury' and the more upbeat 'Six-Five Special' with its catchy signature tune.

'Hello, Mam, Dad. Lucy said a telegram had come for me?'

Mary Roberts handed her the familiar yellow envelope, a little crumpled now after being in her overall pocket. 'Did she tell you I had to open it in case there were a reply even though it were addressed to you?'

'She did but that's OK, Mam.' Putting her cup on the mantelpiece, Joyce reached for the envelope. 'I can't think who'd want to contact me by telegram.'

Mam hesitated and Joyce saw the concern in her grey eyes. 'It's from Dave's mother, love. Not good news, I'm afraid.'

With a racing heart, Joyce pulled out the flimsy sheet, reading the contents for herself. 'Dave in Infirmary after a bad fall at work. Please come. Phyllis

Yates.' With shaky legs threatening to give way beneath her, Joyce sat down suddenly at the side of her mother. 'Oh, Mam, I wonder what's happened?'

Mam took hold of Joyce's trembling hand. 'You won't know until you get there, will you?'

'I must get changed and go straight away.' She made to get up but her mother stopped her.

'You'll do no such thing. You've been working all day and need some food inside you before you go traipsing off to the Infirmary. Otherwise you'll be ill yourself. Tea should be about ready now so I'll go and get it on the table.'

After she'd left, Joyce continued to sit, still winded by the news, her mind juggling with all sorts of possibilities. 'Your mother's right, love,' her father said, his concern obvious in the tone of his voice. 'No use fretting about it till you get there.'

Danny Roberts had mellowed a lot since Brian's death, making more of an effort with his kids. Even he and Nick, her eldest brother, got along much better now. That wasn't to say sparks didn't fly every now and then. 'Is Nick home yet?' Of all the siblings, she and Nick were the most alike in temperament and she badly wanted to talk to him.

'No. Don't expect he'll be long though. Unless he's had a job to finish off. You know what he's like.' Nick worked as a mechanic at a small garage near the Crown, loved his work and wouldn't dream of leaving until the job in hand could be left satisfactorily.

'Is he seeing Kathy tonight, do you know?' Kathy was his fiancée and she and Joyce were firm friends.

Danny snorted. 'Hardly likely to tell me, is he? Your Mam might know.'

From the hallway, they heard Mam call out at the bottom of the stairs. 'Derek, Lucy, come and get your tea. And don't forget to wash your hands first.' Then she poked her head into the front room. 'Tea's ready.'

As Joyce and Danny came out into the hall, the younger Roberts children clattered down the stairs. 'Lo, Dad, Joyce,' Derek said as he hurried past them in his eagerness to get to the table. 'I'm starving hungry.'

Mam tutted. 'Honestly, Derek, I reckon you must have hollow legs with all the food you put away.'

He knocked a closed fist against both legs while making a clicking noise with his mouth. 'Reckon you might be right, Mam.'

'Get on with you, lad!' she said, laughing and making to tousle his unruly hair. He'd become so used to the gesture now that he ducked under her arm and out of the way.

Exchanging amused glances, Joyce and her father followed them into the kitchen, where Mam was dishing up the meat and potato pie, together with mushy peas, onto plates, reminding Derek and Lucy again to wash their hands, which they did with much good-natured pushing and shoving. Peace was restored by the time they had all seated themselves and started tucking in. They hadn't been sat down long when a grimy but smiling Nick appeared in the back doorway. 'Decided not to wait for me, then.'

'Yours is in the oven keeping warm,' Mam told him, 'when you've had a wash.' She gestured to her own nose and Nick put his hand up and came away with a thick smear of grease.

He laughed. 'I wondered why people on the bus were staring at me.'

Over tea, Joyce told Nick about the telegram. He shook his head. 'Doesn't sound good, does it? Want me to come with you?' He and Dave had been mates long before she and Dave had got together. Their relationship had caused friction between the two young men to begin with as Dave had originally had a bit of a reputation with the girls, hence his nickname of Bragger. Even now the old nickname slipped out occasionally between everyone who knew him.

'Won't you be seeing Kathy tonight?'

'Aye, but I can always give her a ring from the phone box at the bottom of the hill. Or even nip over the road and tell her.' Kathy lived in one of the side streets opposite the Greenwood pub, where Joyce would be catching the bus to Bolton.

'No, I'll be all right, really. Mrs Yates'll be there anyway and you know how strict they are about visitors.'

'When's this here wedding between you and the lass going to be anyway?' Danny asked Nick now, even though he had a mouthful of food. Joyce sighed. Some things didn't change and she hated that habit of his.

'Hopefully early next year,' Nick said easily enough though Joyce had seen the hands gripping his knife and fork tense.

'Being a bit reluctant about being tied down, is she? Now she's got herself a fancy new job,' Danny teased.

'Come on, Danny, you know the lass had to finish her training as a reporter first,' Mam pointed out. 'Not to mention our Nick finishing that mechanic's course he were doing. Anyroad, I thought you liked Kathy.'

'I do, you know I do,' he blustered, 'but I reckon it's time she and Nick were wed. I'm not getting any younger and I've a fancy to have a grandchild bouncing on my knee.'

Nick burst into laughter, breaking up the tension between them. 'I'll be sure to tell Kathy that later when I see her,' he spluttered. 'I'm sure she'll be thrilled.'

* * *

On the bus to Bolton, Joyce clutched her hands together in her lap, worried about what awaited her. What could have necessitated Dave's trip to Casualty? Unless he'd hit his head when he'd fallen. His poor head! As if he'd not suffered enough after receiving a near-fatal head wound two years ago for which his attackers, Jud Simcox and his two mates, had been imprisoned. Her lips clenched tight in anger at the thought of Jud Simcox whom she hated with a passion. Dave had suffered from crippling headaches from time to time since and had even been turned down for his National Service because of it. And more recently, there'd been incidents where he'd blanked out for several seconds and seemed confused afterwards. She'd begged him to go to the doctor's but he'd refused. He was convinced it was all down to the after-effects of his injury. Perhaps this fall had been the result of one such incident.

Walking down the long green-tiled corridor to the wards at Bolton Royal Infirmary brought back distressing memories of the last time she'd been here, two years ago. Her sense of *déjà vu* was reinforced when she reached Dave's ward and saw him in bed, seemingly asleep. And to see Phyllis Yates at his side was yet another painful reminder. The plump woman in late middle-age, her eyes red-rimmed with weeping, looked up as Joyce drew near. 'Reminds you of last time we were here, lass, doesn't it?' Phyllis said, her voice faltering. During the time Dave had been in hospital recovering from his original head injury, she and Mrs Yates had bonded over his bedside even after the initial antagonism against her. That had been partly because of her youth and partly down to the fact that the family were Roman Catholics and she wasn't.

Joyce grabbed another chair and pulled it closer to the bed, facing Phyllis. 'I were just thinking that.' Dave looked normal, if a little pale, but he had an egg-sized purple lump to the right of his forehead where it had presumably come into contact with a hard surface. His blond hair, normally in a quiff, hung over his forehead, giving him that vulnerable look she remembered so well from last time. Her impulse was to reach out and push it back over his brow but she restrained herself out of respect for Phyllis. 'What happened, Mrs Yates? Do you know?'

'Apparently, he fell down some stairs at work, love. Says he doesn't remember owt ... thinks he sort of blacked out.'

Joyce hesitated, unsure whether Dave would want his mother to know in case she worried about him. In the end, she decided to mention it. 'He's been doing that a bit recently, having blackouts, hasn't he? Have you noticed?'

Phyllis set her lips in a tight gesture. 'I have that but getting him to go to the doctor's is another matter. You know how stubborn he can be. His Dad were just the same.'

'I've tried persuading him to go too.'

At the sound of her voice, Dave stirred. 'Joyce, is that you?' Dave murmured sleepily.

She reached to take his hand. It was surprisingly cool in her grasp. 'Yes, love. I came as soon as I could.'

'How did you know what happened?'

'Your Mam sent me a telegram.'

His eyes opened wide in shock and he looked towards his mother. 'Bloody hell, Mam. That were a bit extravagant, weren't it?'

'And just how did you think I were going to let Joyce know? The Roberts' don't have a phone. And I certainly couldn't have gone huffing and puffing up that hill to Brazeley.' Phyllis suffered from mild an-

11

gina and any such exertion could have caused her severe chest pains.

'Mam, I were only teasing,' he said now. Then he looked at Joyce with such open love in his eyes that she was stunned. Something had changed for she hadn't seen that look in two years. His head injury had caused all memory of their initial love for each other to disappear. With bits of it coming back to him only slowly, they had rebuilt their relationship but something of the original first flush of their love had been lost, to her regret. Now she could tell it was back and her heart rejoiced. 'I'm glad you came, Joyce love,' he said now, a catch in his voice.

'Once I knew, nowt would have kept me away,' she said, squeezing his hand. 'Now you're awake, what did the doctors have to say?'

This time it was he who hesitated, looking from one to the other, before saying, 'That's the thing,' he said, 'the doctor thinks I may have had some kind of fit.'

Phyllis jerked back in her seat. 'A fit? Did you start shaking?'

'I don't know. All I remember were being at the top of the stairs then going a bit blank. Next thing I knew, I were at the bottom feeling icy cold and very tired. Even now, I can hardly keep my eyes open.'

'Did someone ring for an ambulance, then?'

'Must have done but I can't remember.'

'Did you tell the doctor about these blank episodes you've been having?' Joyce asked.

He grinned. 'After the nagging I've had from you

two, I thought I'd better. The doc did seem to think it were important. Anyroad, they're going to keep me in for a few days, run some sort of tests. Probably summat to do with that head injury.'

Joyce and Mrs Yates looked at each other, hoping the same thing. But a fit? Surely that was more serious? Joyce didn't know too much about what caused someone to have fits apart from it being something to do with the brain. Ah well, no use worrying about it too much at this stage. If he was having tests, they'd find out soon enough.

To lighten the mood, she told him about her Dad's chance remark about being desperate for a grandchild before he got much older. He tried to laugh but winced instead. 'Ouch, that hurt. I must have bruised myself when I fell down the stairs.'

'You were lucky you didn't break owt,' Phyllis said, a look of motherly concern on her face.

'Don't fuss, Mam. I'll be OK when I get out of here,' he said, giving Joyce a wry grin.

'But you could have broken your neck,' his mother pointed out.

'Well, I didn't. Whatever happened, I'm here to tell the tale.' A note of irritation had crept into Dave's voice. It was totally unlike his usual easy-going self and Joyce guessed that the fall – and the possibility of a fit being the cause of it – had shaken him more than he was willing to admit to. 'Now let's change the subject.'

They chatted about this and that, steering clear of anything more serious, the way people do when visiting someone in hospital. All too soon, a staff nurse appeared in the doorway and began ringing the bell in her hand, a signal that visiting time was over. Phyllis rose, patting Dave's hand. 'Time for us to go, love.' She leaned over and gave him an awkward peck on the cheek. 'You take care now and do as the nurses and doctors tell you.'

He sighed. 'I will, Mam, go now and let me have a minute with Joyce.'

Once she pattered off down the ward, Dave grasped Joyce's hand with an urgency that surprised her. 'I wanted to tell you, Joyce. I've remembered.'

Joyce looked at him, puzzled. 'What do you mean, you've remembered?'

'My memory's returned.' He touched the lump on his forehead. 'This latest clout on my head seems to have brought it back, every bit of it. Even our daft plan to elope.'

Joyce's cheeks burned, recalling how they'd made tentative plans to elope in in the summer of 1957 after being forbidden to see each other. They'd planned to take advantage of the town closing down for the Wakes Week to run off to Scotland and get married there. Looking back, it had been a stupid plan but it had seemed the only thing to do, so desperate were they to be together. 'Oh, Dave, that's wonderful.' She leaned across to kiss him.

Even though he winced, he pulled her closer to him across the bed. 'How could I have forgotten all this?' he whispered in anguish. When their lips met, it was a reminder of all that they had been through together and full of promise for the future.

A voice interrupted their tender moment. 'Come now, Mr Yates, visiting time's over. You'll get me in trouble with Sister if your young lady doesn't leave now.' The staff nurse was at the side of the bed, bell silent in her hand now but she had a smile on her face.

'Sorry. I'm just leaving,' Joyce said.

Dave clutched hold of her hand as if to keep her there. 'Can you come back tomorrow night? Mam'll come in the afternoon because she goes to her Housey-Housey of a Saturday night and we'll be able to talk more then.'

She left him with a spring in her step and a beaming smile on her face, matched by that on his own.

CHAPTER 2

S ince moving to the pleasant village of Lindrick in North Yorkshire, Sally Roberts had come to enjoy the month of September. The way the lowering sun gilded the late summer flowers and edged the leaves on the trees with gold, hinting of the autumn to come, lifted her spirits and made her heart lighter. In the village, with its old cottages and abundant gardens bordered by trees, this effect was particularly noticeable.

Her husband Phil had been posted to RAF Lindrick in September 1957, two months after their marriage in Blackpool, in time for the opening of the Air Training School and she had followed early in 1958. Initially, it had been a devastating blow to discover that, as Phil was under 25, they wouldn't be eligible for married quarters. Nor would they receive a marriage allowance. It seemed that the RAF didn't approve of its servicemen getting married young and the rules had been implemented in an attempt to discourage such marriages. Instead they lodged with the elderly Mrs Harris in Pear Tree Cottage, near to the main street of the village. Sally had been to the air base many times now for various social functions and been invited back to married quarters. From what she'd seen of them, they were cheerless places with only very basic amenities compared to the cosy comfort of Mrs Harris' house with its coal fire and homely atmosphere. The drawback of living at Pear Tree Cottage as opposed to their own quarter was the lack of privacy. One blessing was that Mrs Harris was completely deaf without her hearing aids. And the small cottage had a bathroom tucked under the rafters, unlike other cottages in the village, many of which still had outside toilets. One of the advantages of having the air base close to the village was that proper sewerage had been brought to the village where previously everyone would have had septic tanks.

As she approached the cottage, she heard the roar of a Provost jet engine in the distance as someone throttled up to take off. After being here nearly two years, she had grown used to the constant take-offs and landings of the trainee pilots, 'circuits and bumps' as they were known in RAF lingo. The villagers weren't always quite so happy though. She recalled a time Phil had told her about when the training school had first started. One particular pilot had been having difficulty and the instructor had been making him do it again and again. The control room had received a phone call from an irate villager demanding to know why the pilot couldn't bloody-well land the plane once and for all. The duty Flight Lieutenant had explained what was happening and managed to calm him down. Since then, 'circuits and bumps' were restricted to certain hours and re-lationships between the villagers and the base were relatively harmonious. Unless you counted the oc-casional boom as someone broke the sound barrier. Some of the villagers even claimed the noise stopped their hens from laying.

When Sally walked in, Phoebe Harris, wearing one of her trademark hand-knitted cardigans, was sit-ting in the late afternoon sunshine, soaking up the warmth as if storing it up for the coming autumn and winter. On the edge of the North York moors, winters here could be extreme and it wasn't unknown for the village to be cut off. Sally felt sure that the village's isolation was one of the reasons the airfield, the old-est military airfield in the world, had been developed so much in the last couple of years was its proximity to Europe across the North Sea, given the Cold War be-tween the Western Allies and the USSR, a legacy from the division of Europe after the second World War.

'Hello, Sally, love.' The old lady, who suffered badly from arthritis, pushed herself up, steadying herself on the arms of the chair as she did so. 'You look tired. Come and sit down and I'll make us some tea.'

'You stay where you are, I'll do it,' Sally said, moving to the old woman's side to steady her if neces-sary.

'No.' Phoebe waved her away. 'It does me good to keep moving about. Besides, you've been working. I take it that's where you've come from?'

'Yes, I've just finished.' Sally had been lucky to find a job in the village pub, The Fawkes Arms, so named after its association with the infamous Guy Fawkes who had close family links to the area. Her job, cleaning in the morning and serving in the bar at lunchtime, took its toll on her feet by mid-afternoon, the end of the working day. Yet there was no way she could have stayed at home all day like some of the RAF wives did. It would have been different, of course, if babies had come along but so far they hadn't. A familiar tug of grief swept through her at what might have been if things had turned out differently two years ago but she firmly dismissed it. The events of that time had brought Phil into her life and she couldn't regret that.

With a thankful sigh, Sally sank onto the sofa and eased her shoes off. Phoebe appeared moments later pushing a trolley with all the paraphernalia for tea as well as a plate of delicious home-made scones, a task she still enjoyed. Being a little unsteady on her feet, Phoebe used the trolley rather than risk carrying a tray. 'Oh, lovely, thank you, Phoebe.' Sally still felt awkward about calling the old lady by her first name but she'd insisted. 'It makes me feel like a person,' she'd claimed, 'rather than being invisible which seems to happen when you get old.'

'Help yourself, love, while I pour the tea,' Phoebe said. Sally buttered herself a scone and added some of Phoebe's home-made raspberry jam while keeping an eye on Phoebe's swollen and shaking fingers in case she spilled some tea while pouring it. 'While I think on, there's another letter come for you.' Phoebe passed her an envelope from a side table.

Intrigued, Sally looked at the handwriting. 'It's from my sister-in-law, Joyce.' She and Joyce, Phil's younger sister, knew each other from working at adjoining looms in the mill where they worked and had kept in touch though not regularly. 'Do you mind if I open it?'

Phoebe, her own mouth full of scone, waved her assent. As Sally suspected, besides a short note from Joyce herself, the envelope contained another letter from her sister, Eileen, and forwarded on to her by Joyce. Since a massive falling-out with her mother after she'd married Phil, her mother had threatened to burn any letters to Sally's two sisters, so any correspondence had had to be redirected through Joyce, who like Eileen, worked at the Beehive Mill in Lostock, on the outskirts of Bolton and Horwich. Sally swiftly read the contents of Eileen's letter and her heart sank. Their mother had apparently had a stroke. It was only a mild one with few after-effects but Eileen had been warned that it could happen again at any time. Given that Mam seemed to be reasonably mobile, Eileen and younger sister May were managing at the moment but thought Sally might want to come and see her. She was, after all, Sally's Mam too. That, Sally knew, was a mild dig at her because she hadn't been near the house Mary Street West in two years.

Phoebe leaned over and touched Sally's arm. 'Is everything all right, love? Only you've gone a bit pale.'

'I'm ok thanks. It seems my mother's had a bit

of a stroke, nowt too serious, as it happens but my sister's asking if I want to go down and see her.'

'And will you?' Phoebe queried. She knew a little of Sally's background because when Phil was on duty they'd sat talking many a time over a cup of cocoa before going to bed. Both of Sally's grandmothers had died before she was born so she had begun to look on Phoebe as a replacement grandmother figure.

'I don't know. I'll have to talk it over with Phil. What worries me ...' she hesitated before continuing, '... is that I've a feeling my brother's due out of prison some-time soon.'

'The one that attacked your sister-in-law's boyfriend?' Phoebe didn't miss much in spite of being deaf.

Sally squirmed a little in her seat, uncomfortable in ways she didn't want to talk about discussing her brother. 'Yes, that's him.'

'How is the young lad he injured? Still going out with your sister-in-law?'

Giving a relieved sigh that Phoebe's attention had been diverted, she answered, 'Dave's OK in himself though he still hasn't recovered all his memory. It's frustrating for Joyce, I think. She feels they can't move forward until he does.' She put the letter back in its envelope and shoved it in her pocket.

'Oh, I had a letter from our Nancy today as well.' Phoebe produced the blue airmail letter from the small table at the side of her and waved it in Sally's direction. Knowing how much Phoebe missed her daughter and grandchildren since the family had immigrated to Australia some years ago, Sally was happy to let her ramble on about the letter's contents for a while. It left her own mind free to wander. It was still whirling with the news of Mam's stroke and whether she could get over to Lancashire to visit. And to wonder did she really want to.

Later, in the tiny kitchen, more of a scullery really, of Pear Tree Cottage, Sally was preparing tea for the three of them while Phoebe dozed in her chair. Her mind was still on the letter and its implications. What would happen should her mother have another, perhaps more serious stroke, and die? How would her sisters cope? Would they be able to keep on with the tenancy of the house in Mary Street West? And how would Jud's coming out of prison affect matters?

Then she chided herself. It was no use looking too far into the future. None of them knew what was going to happen, especially with the threat of a nuclear war, a result of the Cold War, hanging over everyone's heads. She'd heard rumours, scuttlebutt as it was known in military jargon, that the Government was installing concrete bunkers below Whitehall in the event of such a disaster happening. And the peace movement, Campaign for Nuclear Disarmament, was gaining new members every day with thousands attending the annual Aldermaston marches or demonstrations in London. Surely after the devastation caused by the atom bombs dropped on the Japanese cities of Nagasaki and Hiroshima in 1945, no-one would be crazy enough to deliberately launch the new Intercontinental Ballistic Missiles with nuclear warheads and risk almost total annihilation?

Troubled by such thoughts, she was glad when she heard the front door open and Phil's cheery greeting, 'Sally? Are you there, love?'

'I'm in the kitchen.' She wiped her hands on a nearby tea-towel and went through to the sitting room to greet him. It was clear that Phoebe hadn't heard him come in for she gave a grunt then settled herself into a more comfortable position.

He'd been on duty a lot this past week and it showed in the lines of weariness on his often-serious face. She was glad it was Friday afternoon and that for once he had a completely free weekend. 'Hello, love,' he said. 'What are we having for tea? Meat and potato pie?'

'How did you know?'

'Well the fantastic smell is a dead giveaway for one thing. For another, you've got a smudge of flour on your cheek.' He turned her round to face the old mirror over the sideboard on the back wall so that they were both reflected in the mirror.

Wiping the smudge off, she took the opportunity to fluff up her naturally curly blonde hair, mussed up from her walk from the pub. And, as Phoebe had said, she did indeed look tired, with faint shadows beneath her blue eyes. 'I look a mess,' she moaned.

'You're always beautiful to me,' he said, taking the opportunity to drop a kiss on the top of her head.

'Oh, you, Phil Roberts,' she said, giggling and escaping from his arms with reluctance. She'd enjoyed the distraction while it lasted. 'Come through to the kitchen so as not to disturb Phoebe. I don't think she sleeps well of a night with her arthritis.'

He lounged in the kitchen doorway watching her while she finished placing the pastry crust on top of the casserole dish containing the meat and potato pie and put it back in the oven. 'I had another letter from your Joyce today but it were really to enclose a letter from our Eileen.' Sally told him.

Phil shifted out of the way as Sally tried to reach the cutlery drawer in the kitchenette, the only cupboard space they had. 'Oh, what did she have to say?'

She turned to face him. 'To tell me that Mam's had a stroke.'

A look of concern came on his face. 'Oh, love, I'm sorry. Is it serious?'

'Eileen says not, apart from a slight slurring of her speech and being even less mobile than usual.'

He laughed. 'No change there then.' They both knew how lazy her mother was.

'Phil, how would you feel about me going over to see her? I know me and Mam parted on bad terms and I haven't seen her since but I feel I ought to go.'

'If that's what you want to do, love, I shan't stand in your way. As long as she doesn't turn nasty on you again, like last time.' Because she had so nearly married Nick, Phil's older brother, Sally and Phil only told their respective families after their own marriage. Phil's mother had been understandably hostile at first but had since become, if not a friend, then an ally. By contrast, Sally's mother had been particularly vindictive, saying she wanted nothing more to do with either of them and calling Sally a lying bitch. Such vitriol wasn't easily forgotten but Sally did miss her sisters, Eileen and May. If she were to visit Horwich, it would be a good opportunity to catch up with them again, Letters between them had only been sporadic, going to and fro as they did via Joyce though they had met up occasionally away from the house.

'There's only one way to find out and that's to go there. I'll make enquiries tomorrow. And see if Sid will give me a few days off.' Her boss Sid, the landlord of the Fawkes Arms, was a decent enough bloke but inclined to grumpiness especially if he thought he'd be inconvenienced. Yet underneath his cantankerous exterior, she'd often seen glimpses of a good-hearted man so perhaps he'd understand.

'Might be a bit of a tedious journey,' Phil pointed out. 'Probably York to Manchester then Manchester to Bolton by train ...'

'...Then the on the bus to Horwich, yes, I realise that,' Sally sighed. 'And I really don't want to go ... to be away from you.'

He had her in his arms in seconds. 'It'll only be for a few days, love. And I'll be here when I'm off duty to keep an eye on Phoebe. I've told you before, I don't mind where you go or who with as long as you come back here. To me.'

She knew from talking to other RAF wives that many of the husbands were a bit controlling, maybe it had something to do with ordering people about, particularly the more senior they were, but Phil wasn't like that. Snuggling into his arms, she whispered, 'I do love you, Phil.'

'And I love you,' he mouthed against her lips. 'Always will. Never forget that.'

CHAPTER 3

The late September day slid towards the night and the street lights came on, bathing the terraced houses that dominated so much of Horwich in a yellow sodium glow. In one of the houses opposite the Greenwood pub on Chorley New Road, Kathy Armstrong was curled up on the comfy old moquette sofa watching the television, lost in the world of the medical make-believe that was Emergency Ward 10. So engrossed was she in the drama unfolding on the screen that it took her a moment to realise that someone was ringing the doorbell. Before answering it, she took a few seconds to check her reflection in the mirror and run her fingers through her long auburn-tinted hair, glad that she still had some remnants of mascara showing after her day at work. Licking her lips to moisten them, she opened the front door to find a grinning Nick on the doorstep. 'You'd forgotten I was coming, hadn't you?' he said.

'Not exactly.' She pulled him inside and wrapped her arms round him, sliding them under his jacket, savouring the feeling of his lean yet muscular body against hers. 'I was watching television.'

Breaking apart after their initial kiss, he followed her into the sitting room just as the closing credits were coming up on the TV housed in the alcove by the fireplace. 'I might have guessed,' he said, nodding at the screen.

'My favourite programme,' she admitted.

'It wouldn't have anything to do with that handsome young doctor, would it?' He pointed at the actor playing one of the doctors on the TV screen.

She faced him, hands on her hips, pasting what she hoped was a beguiling smile on her face. 'Nick Roberts, why would I look at someone like Charles Tingwell when I'm engaged to the best-looking lad in Horwich?'

'Flatterer! Come here, wench!' He pulled her towards him again and kissed her again.

'Oh, I love it when you're being masterful,' she said, when she had breath to do so.

He looked around the room the by-now familiar room. 'Where's your Mam, by the way?'

'Gone to a meeting at St Elizabeth's with Mrs Westbury. You know that they're trying to raise funds to build a new church rather than the tin hut in Knowsley Grove?'

'Ah, dear old Lizzies. Yes, I did hear summat. How long is she likely to be gone, do you reckon?' he said, a mischievous twinkle in his eye.

'No more than an hour or two.' She looked at him, with her head on one side, guessing his thoughts. 'So you can take that calculating look off your face.'

He laughed. 'Can't blame a bloke for trying.'

'What are we going to do then? Stay in? Or go to the Greenwood for a drink,' she asked. They didn't get out much these days, tending to stay in or go for a last drink or two in a pub. Occasionally, they went to the pictures and it was a rare treat to go dancing now as they'd done previously. Saving up to get married was difficult, especially as Nick was on a lower wage compared to when he'd been a labourer on a building site.

'We'll go for a drink a bit later but first, there's summat I want to talk to you about.'

She looked at him with raised eyebrows. 'Sounds ominous. Do we need a cuppa to fortify ourselves?'

'Good idea, love. Want me to make it?' After courting for nearly three years, Nick knew his way round the kitchen of the house in Travers Street, something Kathy had encouraged.

Later, with steaming mugs of tea in clasped hands, the pair snuggled close to each other on the sofa. 'How's work going, love? Anything interesting cropped up?' Nick asked.

Kathy pulled a rueful face. 'No, just the usual court reports and flower festival sort of stuff.' Three years ago, Kathy had swapped from secretarial work to journalism and had finished her initial training a year ago. Since then, although she no longer had to shadow the more experienced reporters, she usually ended up with all the humdrum stuff of everyday reporting. 'I'd give anything for something I could really get my teeth into.'

'The blokes still not letting you get a word in

– literally?' As one of only two women reporters, one much older, working for the Bolton Evening News, Kathy had faced much opposition from the male-orientated thinking of the editorial staff. Despite the occasional feeling of disappointment creeping in, she'd stuck at it with grim determination, making the most of every opportunity, no matter how mundane. She still wrote occasional anecdotal pieces for the Town Topics feature and she prided herself on tracking down such stories.

'The news editor does his best to allocate more fairly,' she said, 'but more often than not, one of the blokes will butt in saying things like, 'I'm going that way. Makes sense if I do it' or 'I covered that one originally. I'd like to follow it up, if that's ok.' Usually said with a disarming smile in my direction.

'What about you? How's things at the garage? Mac OK?' Nick worked for the Scottish owner of a small independent garage near the Crown as a motor mechanic and Kathy had grown used to Nick's permanently scarred hands or grimy fingernails that copious amounts of Swarfega and persistent scrubbing could not completely eradicate.

'Busy as usual. As for Mac, I think he's OK,' he said, 'but I've got a feeling that summat's brewing,' he said, before taking another mouthful of tea. 'He's been out a lot recently and the other day he came back looking as if he'd found a ten-bob note.'

'Something to do with the garage perhaps?'

'Who knows? You know what Mac's like. Keeps things close to his chest until he wants you to know.'

He put his now empty mug down on the hearth and Kathy smiled. Her mother would have a fit if she knew but to her it wasn't that important. 'By the way, our Joyce got a telegram from Dave's Mam today to say Dave had had a fall at work and had to go to the hospital.'

'Oh, no! Could it be something to do with his head injury, do you think?' She liked Dave Yates, not only because the good-natured lad was Nick's sister's boyfriend, but also because he was Nick's best mate.

'No idea. Must have been bad enough to cart him off to hospital though. Joyce hadn't got back by the time I set off to come here so I don't know what's up with him. Anyway,' he said, taking her mug and placing beside his on the hearth, 'enough talk of other people. I'd rather talk about you and me.' He pulled her closer and she snuggled willingly into his side.

'I'm listening,' she said, loving the feel of him by her side, wishing it could happen more often.

'I think it's high time we were wed.'

She pulled herself up, stunned by his words. They'd talked about it so many times, made half-hearted plans but then usually ended up straying off the subject for one reason or another, often when Nick started kissing her. 'But I thought we decided we'd wait until we have enough for a deposit on a house.'

'Well, now I think we should make definite plans. We've been together three years now and I'm tired of waiting.' She knew what he meant. Their relationship was a strong one, based on a solid friendship, but underneath was an ever-present undercurrent of passion they had problems controlling. They had resolved to wait until they were married to make love, difficult though it was, satisfying themselves instead with heavy petting whenever they could. Although she didn't like to mention it, another of Kathy's concerns was whether she would be allowed to carry on working at the Bolton Evening News once she was married. Admittedly, attitudes were changing and more women wanted to continue working, at least until any babies came along but some places of employment still had a marriage bar meaning women had to leave on marrying.

'But where would we live?' she said, still trying to gather her thoughts.

'I'm not talking about next week, love,' he pointed out. 'Maybe next year, say in the spring? We'd have time to look around and, if the worst came to the worst, we'd have to get lodgings somewhere.'

'You know Mum would suggest we live here, don't you?'

He gave a mock shudder. 'Definitely not. I get on all right with your Mam now but I couldn't be doing with being under the same roof as her.'

'You and me both, love,' she said with feeling, thinking about the thin walls between her bedroom and her mother's.

'And there's no room at our house. We're packed in as it is. No, I were just thinking if we set a date, book the church, sort out where we're going to have the reception, it'll give us summat to look forward to, work towards. Happen somewhere for us to live'll work out too.'

And, suddenly, it made sense. They longed to be able to spend more time alone, to start to build their lives together, to become a family in their own right. 'When did you have in mind?' she asked.

'I don't suppose you've got a calendar for next year, have you?'

She shook her head then said, 'Wait a minute, I think there's one in my pocket diary.' She wriggled away from his embrace and stood up to retrieve her handbag from the sideboard at the back of the room. Together, they pored over the tiny printing, picking first one date then another, finally plumping for a Saturday in late April 1960, for no particular reason other than the weather would hopefully be better by then.

Kathy counted the months on her fingers. 'Eight months. That should give us plenty of time to book it...' she stopped, then looked at Nick warily, aware that he'd gone down this route once before. 'Do you have any objections to a church wedding?'

He laughed. 'I know what you're thinking, lass. You're remembering the time when Sally and I were having to get married.' It had been the most painful time of her life, when she'd truly thought of moving away to avoid seeing Nick with Sally on the streets of Horwich, especially pushing a pram. She'd known she couldn't of course; her father had been suffering from terminal cancer and she'd never be able to leave her mother alone. Then, after what was, for them a fortuitous miscarriage if not for poor Sally, she had released Nick from his pledge to stand by her. By the time her Dad had died the following year, Kathy and Nick had been together.

He turned her to face his, looking deep into her eyes. 'This is nothing – nothing – like what happened with Sally. With her, I refused to get married in church because to me it made a mockery of the whole thing. Which is why I insisted on a register office wedding then. With you, sweetheart, I'm happy to be married in church. That'll be the Parish Church, will it?'

The Church of the Holy Trinity stood on Church Street, close to a cluster of cobbled streets and stone-built houses, once part of a housing scheme for the workers of Wallsuches bleach works and initiated by the entrepreneurial Ridgway family in the late 18th century. 'I think so, don't you? Shall I give the vicar a ring and arrange to visit him with a view to booking the ceremony?'

'Why not? Sooner the better, I reckon, now we've made our minds up. Strange though, how things have worked out. Sally called the marriage off, fled to Blackpool, met our Phil there and now they're married.'

'I know we haven't seen much of them since he was posted to … where was it?'

'RAF Lindrick, North Yorkshire.'

'That's it. I did wonder initially if she'd married Phil on the rebound but when we do see them, it's obvious how they feel. They're totally wrapped up in each other.'

'Just think, love, that could be us in eight months' time.' He cupped her chin in his hand and kissed her hungrily. 'I don't suppose we could practice getting it right now, could we?' he pleaded.

'Nick, you're incorrigible!' she breathed under the onslaught of his kisses. 'Don't get too carried away. Remember Mum might be home any time ....'

'... Then let's not waste any more time...' He stopped her speech with another lingering kiss and then the two of them were lost to the world, consumed in an ever-rising tide of passion.

CHAPTER 4

T he trek from Lindrick to Horwich seemed to take Sally forever. How long would it have taken to do the journey across the Pennines by car? Not more than a couple of hours, she reckoned. Less than that if the talk of a motorway between Lancashire and Yorkshire came to fruition. With more and more cars on the road, the new motorways seemed inevitable. The first one, the Preston bypass, had opened last year and was apparently well-used. And the first stretch of the North-South M1 was due to be opened some time later this year, November, she seemed to remember. In any case, Phil had never had the opportunity to learn to drive. And on Phil's pay and with her only working part-time, they couldn't have afforded to buy let alone run a car.

As she got off the bus at the Crown, she wondered what waiting her at the house where she had lived for the first twenty years of her life. She could no longer call it home; home was where Phil was. She knew already from Eileen's letters that their mother wasn't an easy patient. Even when well, she was lazy and inclined to complain about her lot. Nothing was ever right for her and, when Sally was living at home she had been the recipient of most of Mam's criticism. She knew why that was. Jud was the closest to their mother's heart and when Sally had come along, a mere ten months later, Mam had resented having to give her the attention she would far rather have given to Jud. Eileen and May had both been born later with about eighteen months between them and hadn't faced the same problem.

Dragging her feet and with her suitcase getting heavier by the moment, Sally trudged along Hope Street and although the sight of Rivington Pike in the distance was a welcome one, it was with a heavy heart, that she turned into Mary Street West. It appeared to be much the same, a row of terraced houses backing onto Catherine Street West with neat net-curtained sash windows and donkey-stoned doorsteps. Their house had always stood out by being the exception, with grimy net curtains and a grubby doorstep. Approaching the house, she saw that that hadn't changed. She didn't blame her sisters. They had enough on their hands with looking after their Mam as well as working. Taking a deep breath, she opened the front door, never locked except at night, and called out, 'Hello? Anybody home?'

A frazzled looking Eileen came through into the lobby, wiping her hands on one of Mam's previously seldom used aprons. 'Sally! I'm that glad to see you.' She rushed forward and pulled her sister into a hug. Sally was always surprised at how tall and slender Eileen was compared to the rest of the family. But then, their father had been tall so Eileen must have got her height from him. She and Jud were both on the small side, as was May, who, in addition, was on the dumpy side like their Mam.

From the front room, where Eileen had said they'd put their mother so she didn't have to climb the stairs, came the shrill call, 'Who's that I can hear, Eileen?'

'How is Mam?' Sally asked, deliberately keeping her voice low and indicating the front room.

'What do you expect?' Eileen's tone was bitter. 'I'll be honest, our kid. She's driving me mad. I know she gets frustrated being stuck in that armchair all the time but she's so demanding. It's always 'do this, fetch that.''

As if on cue, another shout came from behind the closed door. 'Are you there, Eileen? I need a wee!'

Eileen threw her hands up in the air. 'Best get her seen to before she wets herself and I've to change her. Again. I reckon she does it deliberately sometimes to get attention.'

Sally raised her eyebrows. 'She needs that much help, does she?'

'You know Mam. She's always been a lazy sod. She sees this as an excuse to do less than ever and be waited on hand and foot.'

'Well, I'm here now, for a bit anyroad. I can help you with her.'

Before Eileen opened the door, she put a hand on Sally's arm. 'Before we go in, I didn't tell her you were coming. She'd have said she didn't want you here and, honestly, I need your help for as long as you can manage.'

Sally gave her a rueful grin. 'Best go in and get it over with then.'

As soon as Sally appeared in the doorway, behind Eileen, colour suffused their mother's pudgy face and her mouth set in a hard line. 'What's she doing here? She can get out now,' she said, pointing a shaking finger at Sally.

Sally bit back the words that were on her tongue. 'I've not come for you, Mam. I've come to give Eileen and May a bit of a break. You've worn them both out.'

Her mother flapped her hands in Sally's direction, the mottled hands of an old woman, she noticed. 'I don't want you anywhere near me, you lying bitch.'

'You wanted a wee, didn't you?'

The older woman wriggled in the chair as if reminded of her need. 'Yes, but you're not helping me.'

Sally stood her ground, hands on her hips. 'Well, it's either me or you sitting in wet clothes, which is it to be?'

'Eileen can help me.'

'She's got other things to do, haven't you, Eileen?' Sally waved her sister, who'd been hovering in the doorway, away.

'Er, yes, I need to do some potatoes for tea.' Eileen sidled out of the door but not before Sally had seen the smile on her face.

'Now, come on, Mam, let me give you a hand.'

With some difficulty because of her size, Sally man-oeuvred her mother upright and onto the commode, which she noticed desperately needed emptying. The task wasn't a pleasant one particularly as her mother grumbled constantly and kept trying to push her away. 'You can stop that, Mam, I've better things to be doing than looking after you.'

'Rather be with that Roberts lad, I suppose, liv-ing it up on that fancy air base,' her mother sneered.

'If you mean Phil, he's my husband and yes, I should be with him. And life as an RAF wife is far from easy.' After straightening her mother's clothes and ig-noring the obvious hostility, Sally took the chamber pot out of the commode and holding it away from her as far as she could, went into the kitchen. 'That's Mam sorted. At least for the time being.'

Eileen wrinkled her nose as she came over to inspect the contents of the chamber pot. 'I thought so. She says she can't manage on her own, but it looks to me like she's been using it when I've gone out.'

'That's exactly what I thought. I think she's playing on this stroke to get out of doing owt for her-self.'

Eileen grimaced. 'I reckon you might be right.'

'I'll just get rid of this little lot then I'll give you a hand with the tea.' She made for the back door and the outside lavatory. 'Milady can wait for a while.'

The outside toilet was cold and damp, and while it was reasonably clean, the walls could do with another coat of whitewash and the strips of news-paper they used to wipe themselves on needed replenishing. And here they had flushing toilets rather than the tippler system with a wooden seat across the width of the cubicle as some houses in Horwich still had. As she emptied Mam's chamber pot into the bowl, it dawned on her that she'd have to get used to using this lavatory and washing at the kitchen sink over the next day or so. She'd find that hard after the comfort of Phoebe's little bathroom.

While they were preparing the tea, Eileen filled in the details of what had happened when Mam had had the stroke. May had gone in to her bedroom to bring her an early morning cup of tea and seen instantly that something was wrong. She'd called Eileen, then run to the phone box to ring for the doctor. When he came, he confirmed that she'd had a stroke and, in view of the fact that her blood pressure was very high, had said she could well have another. It was that that had prompted them to move Mam's bed downstairs and make her comfortable there.

Sally gaped at her sister. 'How did the two of you manage that?' Mam's bed was a solid brass one and weighed a ton.

To her surprise, Eileen blushed. 'I asked Ken to help us.'

Sally quirked her eyebrow. 'And who's Ken?'

'Ken Poole. He's my boyfriend. He lives in one of them council houses higher up Hope Street.'

Sally gave Eileen a dig in the ribs. 'You little madam, you never said owt in any of your letters.'

'Well, it's not been very long, only three months, and I didn't want to presume too much early

41

on but he's been absolutely brilliant.'

'What's he like then, this Ken?'

'Tall, dark, handsome – well, I think so – a bit like Nick Roberts only without the Teddy boy suit and Tony Curtis quiff. And he's doing an apprenticeship at the Works.'

At that moment, May came through the door, gasping with surprise when she saw Sally, and launched herself at her older sister, almost knocking her over in her eagerness. 'Sally! Am I glad you could come! Me and Eileen have done our best but we desperately need you to sort us out.' Although she'd been christened Mary, she could never say that when she was little. 'May do it,' she'd say and so May was how she had been known ever since.

'You do know I can't stay long, don't you?' Sally looked from one to the other of her sisters, immediately seeing the disappointment on their faces. 'Phil's been good about letting me come for a few days but I need to get back as soon as I can.'

'Did you manage to get time off work then?' Eileen asked.

'Yes, my boss was OK about it but that's another reason I must get back as soon as possible. I won't get paid while I'm not working and we need the money.'

'Course not, we understand, don't we, Eileen?' May said.

Eileen nodded in agreement. 'Tell you what, let's get our tea over with, settle Mam for the night then we can sit down and work out a plan of action.'

'Thankfully, she's not much trouble at night, now she's got the telly,' May said. Sally knew the two girls had managed to rent a television for their Mam a year or so ago and she loved it. She wouldn't let anyone talk while it was on so it would be easy for the three young women to chat in the kitchen, hopefully not interrupted too much with demands from the front room for a cup of tea or to use the commode.

* * *

To the sound of the 'I Love Lucy' and their mother's laughter coming from the front room, the three sisters sat around the fire in the kitchen after washing up and clearing away. 'What I want to know,' Sally said, 'is how you've been coping with Mam like this when you've had to work.'

Eileen and May looked at each other. 'With difficulty,' Eileen said finally. 'We took it in turns for the first few days to have time off but then, as she's improved...' Here May snorted, making the other two giggle. 'Well, we needed the money so we've just had to leave her.'

'Fortunately, Mrs Pritchard ... do you remember her, from across the road? ... she offered to come in morning, dinner-time and afternoon to make Mam a cup of tea and to see she's been alright. One of us makes Mam a butty before we go to work.'

Sally struggled for a moment to remember Mrs Pritchard then said, 'Oh, yes, I know who you mean.

Tall lady with grey hair and glasses. I seem to remember she goes to church a lot.'

'Can't fault her for that. At least she's living out her beliefs,' May said, giving Sally a stern look. 'We'd have been stuck without her.'

'Oh, I'm not being critical, honest. She's always seemed a really sweet person, very gentle.' Sally was reminded of Reverend Marchant who'd been so kind to her when she'd been living and working in Blackpool.

'We've been doing our best to cope but as you can see, the house is a bit of a mess,' Eileen said, sweeping a hand to take in their untidy surroundings.

'Well, I can stay a few days and help out, give you both a bit of a break,' Sally said. 'Whether she likes it or not, we'll try to get Mam more mobile.'

'You know what she's like, won't do owt if she can help it,' May pointed out. 'She won't like that.'

'Well, she'll have to lump it. We'll have to be a bit hard on her.'

'Might work,' Eileen mused. 'Worth having a go anyway.'

'Nowt to lose,' May agreed.

'By the way, how've you been managing for money?' Sally asked.

Eileen laughed. 'We've actually managed better. You know we had to hand our wages over to Mam each week? Well, she seems to have forgotten about that so we've been pooling our resources and sorting it out between us. You know what she were like, wasted most of it on muck and cigs. She's even stopped smoking. Did you notice?'

Sally gaped at Eileen. 'No, really?' Mam had always smoked like a chimney previously. Now that she thought about it, the house did smell a lot sweeter.

'Aye, and she seems more forgetful since the stroke but the hospital did warn us that might happen,' May added.

'She didn't forget that she hated me,' Sally said.

'And she doesn't forget that our Jud's due to be released sometime soon,' Eileen said. 'She keeps asking us when. Except that we don't know. I reckon he's keeping it quiet deliberate like so he can catch us out.'

Although Jud no longer had the power over her that he once had, Sally couldn't stop a shiver going through her. 'That sounds about right. He always did like to be top dog.'

'Now that we've moved Mam downstairs, Jud can have her bedroom when he comes home,' Eileen said, 'rather than have to share our bedroom.'

Something in the tone of her sister's voice made her look up quickly and, seeing a dark look in Eileen's eyes, she said, 'Do you mean ... he ...' she stopped, not knowing how to continue.

Her two sisters exchanged a knowing look. 'Oh, aye, he tried it on with both of us at one time or another. Fortunately, we had each other and ganged up on him,' Eileen said softly. 'From what Mam told us, you weren't so lucky.'

Colour flamed in Sally's face. 'I didn't realise you knew,' she whispered.

Eileen reached over and clasped Sally's hand in her own. 'Mam let it slip one day, what you'd said. Oh, she said you were lying but we knew you weren't, didn't we, May?'

May nodded. 'You should have said.'

'Well, I were only 14 at the time. Not the sort of thing you talk about to your younger sisters.'

'Does it bother you now?'

'No. Not once I'd got it in the open, explained to Phil.'

May gasped. 'So he knows. What did he say when you told him?'

Sally giggled. 'That he wanted to give him a good hiding.' Then she sobered. 'The worry is, that he might still do that when Jud gets out.'

'Worry about that at the time. What about you and Phil? You enjoying married life?' Eileen asked.

'Oh, yes, though it'd be better if we had our own quarter and we can shut the world out.' Her sisters already knew the situation regarding not being eligible for married quarters or the marriage allowance.

'Any sign of a baby yet?' Eileen asked, wiggling her eyebrows suggestively.

Sally sighed. 'I had a miscarriage early on. It would have been a honeymoon baby.' She could recall, with a slight tightening of her inner parts, she and Phil making urgent love on the rug in front of the fire in the Lake District cottage loaned to them for their brief honeymoon. It was then, she was convinced, that she'd conceived. When she miscarried after only a few weeks, they were quite relieved because money would have been impossibly tight.

'A second miscarriage? Could there be a problem, do you think?' Eileen asked, dragging Sally back to the present.

Sally looked at her sister in bewilderment. 'What do you mean, a second one?'

It was Eileen's turn to look puzzled. 'Miscarriage. You lost Nick Roberts' baby, didn't you?'

Colour once more flooded Sally's face. 'Oh, I'd forgotten about that. It seems so long ago.' She hadn't forgotten. How could she? She had indeed told her family she'd had a miscarriage hoping they'd never find out the truth. That she'd carried Nick's baby full-term, only to lose him to a complication when he was born. Although her initial grief had faded, the pain of it cropped up again occasionally and she could see again, that tuft of dark hair that so reminded her of Nick.

She pushed herself up out of the armchair. 'I need the lavvy,' she said to her sisters, hoping they hadn't seen the tears gathering in her eyes.

As she was disappearing out of the back door, she heard her mother calling, 'Sally, are you there? I need the po.'

Eileen waved her away. 'Go on, I'll see to her.'

It was only as Sally was sat on the toilet that she realised that Mam had called for her, not Eileen or May.

CHAPTER 5

K athy and Nick, bubbling with excitement, emerged from the Edwardian vicarage on Church Street in Horwich into a gloriously sunny October morning that had more than a hint of autumn. 'So we've finally booked our wedding,' breathed Nick, taking in a gulp of fresh air.

'I know. Hard to take in, isn't it?' she said, a quiver in her voice.

Nick swung her round to face him. 'You'd better believe it, Kathy love, because it's really going to happen.' On the gravelled drive, he gave her a lingering kiss, not caring about a couple of passers-by. 'And I can't wait. It's been a long three years.'

Her face became serious. 'It's not always been easy, has it?'

'No, but we've got through those times and we will face whatever we have to face in the future,' he said. 'Look what's happened to poor old Bragger.' He'd already told her what had transpired following Joyce's visits to the Infirmary.

'Has he had results of the tests yet?' she asked.

'Not as far as I know but he's due to go back

some time in the next week or so.'

Holding hands, they walked down the hill towards the centre of Horwich. As they reached the Black Bull pub opposite the Police Station, Nick said, 'What do you think to having our reception here? It's pretty central for everyone and I've heard they've got a big function room upstairs.'

She looked up at the stone built exterior of the large pub standing a little way off the road. 'I don't think I've ever been inside. What's it like?'

'I've only been in for the odd pint with the lads but there's only one way to find out. Let's go and have a look.'

'It's not opening time yet,' she pointed out. 'It's all locked up.'

'We're asking about a wedding reception, not calling for a drink. Good business for them, I reckon.' With that, he rapped sharply on the solid entrance door.

Within another half hour or so, they'd looked over the function room and booked their wedding reception, though the decisions about the actual meal and confirmation of numbers would be discussed nearer the time. It wasn't cheap but her mother had assured her months ago that she and Kathy's Dad had saved up for years to give her 'a good send-off' as she'd called it, making it sound as if she were going on a long voyage. As they were shown off the premises, accompanied by the genial landlord, Kathy took a deep breath and, gripping Nick's hand, said, 'Now I feel even more giddy.'

'How about telling everyone at the weekend? Would you and your Mam come up to our house on Sunday afternoon? Then we can all have a bit of a discussion about arrangements.'

She laughed. 'Oh, my Mum'll love that. She'll be able to put on her best organising hat. She's become even bossier since she started going to St Elizabeth's.'

'Aye, I doubt we'll get a word in edgeways when our Mams get together. I'll ask my Mam if it's OK for you both to come for tea then let you know.'

By this time, they'd reached the Palace cinema, looking ever more shabby and run-down as the years had passed. Kathy couldn't remember the last time she'd been here. Nowadays they either went to the Picture House or one of the Bolton cinemas.

'Do you remember coming here when it rained and you couldn't hear the film because of the noise it made on the tin roof?' Nick said.

'Who could forget? And did I tell you about the time I was sat on the toilet when a mouse ran between my feet and disappeared under the door?' she said, laughing.

'You did. Good job you're not afraid of mice. People might have thought you having hysterics was part of the film.'

'Still, it did give me a bit of a shock.'

'Now there's only the Picture House left since Johnny's closed down too. I've heard rumours that they're going to demolish the Arcade,' Nick said, mentioning the long-neglected Prince's Arcade where the cinema, fondly called Johnny's after a long-dead owner, and the run-down dance club known as the Fling, very much a part of their tempestuous early days, had been located.

'Well, it's been derelict for years,' she said. 'Odd to think that there used to be three cinemas in a small town like Horwich, now there's just one.'

Nick shrugged. 'Not as many people go to the pictures as they used to now that everyone's getting televisions.'

By this time, they'd reached the junction of Winter Hey Lane with Lee Lane. 'I'll have to leave you here, love, get back to work. With calling at the Black Bull, I've been a bit longer than I told Mac I would be,' he said.

'I've one or two errands to do for Mum anyway.' They kissed lingeringly and she watched him stride away up Lee Lane in the general direction of Mac's garage, a tall handsome figure in tight trousers and his favourite leather jacket, looking shabbier now than when she'd first seen him in it. It was soon after Nick had completed his National Service when he'd intervened to stop Jud Simcox who'd tried, along with Bill Stephens, to grab her in Coffin Alley. She and Nick had known each other before that when both had attended St Catherine's Youth Club and she'd had a massive crush on him. There'd been an instant attraction but she'd fought against it because she'd been going out with middle-class charmer John Talbot at that time. Then there'd been that sorry business with Sally, Jud's sister ...

'Kathy?' said a voice nearby. Startled, she

turned quickly to find herself face to face with the young woman herself, an uncertain look on her face.

Unnerved by the fact that she'd just been think-ing about Sally, Kathy laughed nervously. 'Oh, hello, Sally. What are you doing in Horwich?' then could have kicked herself. It sounded like Sally had no right to be in Horwich anymore.

Thankfully, Sally herself seemed to think noth-ing of it. 'My Mam's had a bit of a stroke and I've come over to give my two sisters a bit of a hand.'

'Oh, I'm sorry to hear that. I hope it wasn't too serious.'

'No, she doesn't seem to have been affected too badly, though she does get a bit confused.' She gave Kathy a rueful look. 'She's still as difficult as ever though.'

Kathy remembered Phil telling her about the altercation when they'd been to tell Mrs Simcox they were married. Choosing to change the subject, Kathy said now, 'Is Phil with you?'

Sally shook her head. 'No, not this time. We couldn't have stayed at Mam's anyroad. She still doesn't want to have owt to do with him.'

This whole conversation reminded Kathy of all that had gone between them previously. They'd never been friends; if anything they'd been enemies at that time for Sally had believed herself to be in love with Nick. Kathy couldn't help thinking back to the time soon after Nick had been beaten up by Jud Simcox and his mates and they had been surprised by the unexpected arrival in Mac's flat of an irate

Sally. She'd caught them out in a passionate embrace, soon after they'd declared their love for each other but, back then, Nick had been promised to Sally. Now that they were to be sisters-in-law, a kind of uneasy truce existed between them on the odd occasion they had met at the Roberts' home, usually when Phil had some leave and they managed to make the trek over from Yorkshire. Maybe it was time to rectify that. On impulse, Kathy said, 'Do you have to dash back for your Mam immediately?'

Sally looked wary and hesitated before saying, 'Not right away. One of our neighbours is keeping an eye on her while I get few errands done.'

'Then why don't we get ourselves a bottle of pop and a meat pie or something and nip into the park from an impromptu picnic.'

Sally looked at her, eyes wide in surprise. 'Are you sure?'

'Why not? It's not as if there's a decent café in Horwich and I didn't think you'd want to go to Harry Stockers,' Kathy said. Harry Stocker's Temperance Bar was where the youngsters of Horwich, too young to go in pubs or the Billiard Hall, tended to congregate.

Suddenly, they were both laughing. ''No, I think my Temperance Bar days are over,' Sally said.

'Mine too.'

They grabbed a couple of bottles of Tizer from the newsagents on Winter Hey Lane and a pie each from Cases, before making their way through the back way to the park, where they found a convenient bench. Taking a drink from her bottle, Sally said, 'To be honest, I somehow never thought of you doing owt like this.'

Wiping her mouth of the juice from her meat pie with her handkerchief, Kathy said, 'I'm sure my mother would be horrified to see me so I shan't tell her but since I've been reporting for the Bolton Evening News, I've learned to take advantage of every opportunity for a tea or a wee.' Sally spluttered into her bottle of pop and suddenly they were both laughing. 'I know I sometimes give the impression of being stuck-up, perhaps a bit snooty, but I'm not, not really,' Kathy said when she had breath to speak.

'I realise that now,' Sally said, wiping her own mouth.

'So, do you think we might be friends, after all, in spite of all that's happened in our past?' Kathy asked, feeling diffident because of their shared history.

'I'd like that, really I would,' Sally whispered. To Kathy's amazement, there were tears in Sally's eyes. 'I still feel a bit like a bit of an intruder with Phil's family, to be honest.'

'Because of what happened with Nick, you mean?'

Sally appeared to hesitate before saying, 'I suppose so. I mean, it isn't going to go away, is it?'

On impulse, Kathy reached out for the other young woman's hand and said, 'Sally, we've all got to put it behind us. After all, we'll be part of the same family soon.' She stopped, wondering if she should confide in Sally, then decided to carry on. 'In fact, if I tell you something, will you keep quiet about it for a few days?'

Sally gave her a questioning look but then made a zipping movement to her mouth. 'My lips are sealed.'

'Nick and I have just booked our wedding for April next year. We haven't told our families hence the need to say nothing yet. Apart from Phil, of course, you can tell him.'

'He'll be so pleased for you. As I am, genuinely,' she said, as if realising she should emphasise the point. 'I realised a long time ago that what I felt for Nick was a sort of hero-worship, you know, with the whole Teddy boy thing. What I feel for Phil ... what he feels for me ... is the real thing.'

'And you're making a new life for yourselves at Lindrick, aren't you? Are you in married quarters? How's that working out?'

Sally shook her head. 'Unfortunately, with Phil being under 25, we weren't eligible. Instead, we're lodging with a dear old lady in the village. It would be lovely to have the privacy of a quarter but I've been told it's not all plain sailing. There's a lot of petty rules and regulations. And you wouldn't believe the snobbery among the wives. We do go to the base for various social functions though ... and there's certainly plenty of those. They're a right boozy lot.'

Sally soon had Kathy laughing at some of the shenanigans that went on at the camp and before they realised it, time had passed and they had to part. Reluctantly, in the end.

* * *

The following Sunday afternoon, Kathy drove her mother up Brazeley where the Roberts family lived. She'd been driving about 18 months now and, with her job taking her all over the Bolton area, having the car had been a godsend. It meant, too, that she could take her mother out and about; otherwise she'd have been limited in her outings to where she could get to by bus. The driving had been her lovely Dad's idea, once they knew his illness was terminal, and had meant she'd inherited the car. From the amount of traffic she came across these days, it was obvious that more and more people were buying cars.

'What's this little get-together in aid of?' Vera Armstrong said, her irritation at having her Sunday afternoon disrupted obvious. A little on the plump side, she was a woman of late middle age with tightly permed hair under the obligatory hat, gloved hands firmly gripping the handbag on her lap.

'You'll just have to wait and see, won't you?' Once her mother knew the reason behind this visit, Kathy knew she'd be thrilled. She'd long wanted Kathy to settle down with, as she'd often been in the habit of saying, a suitable young man. In no way had her mother initially considered one-time Teddy boy Nick Roberts being that person. Over the past couple of years though, as Mum had got to know him, she'd warmed to him, especially as he was always willing to help out with little jobs in the house that neither Kathy nor her mother could do.

'You're not pregnant, are you?' Vera asked now.

Kathy's fingers gripped the steering wheel tightly. Why did her mother always have to think the worst? After 23 years, Kathy ought to be used to it by now. Now though, instead of retaliating as she would once have done, she merely sighed and said, 'No, Mum, I'm not.' Then she couldn't resist adding, 'But if I had been, I'd have told you in private not blurted it out in front of the Roberts.' Her mother gave a deep sigh and pointedly looked out of the window.

In the cul-de-sac that was Lancaster Avenue, she could see Lucy standing by the gate waiting for them. As the Morris Minor pulled up outside the Roberts' house, Lucy opened the gate and came flying down the path towards them, flinging herself into Kathy's arms once she'd locked the car. She and Kathy were old friends. 'I'm right glad you're here, Kathy. For some reason, everyone's getting on each other's nerves today.'

So the tension wasn't just in the car between her and her mother. 'Say hello to my mother, Lucy,' Kathy gently reminded her excitable young friend.

'Oh, sorry, I forgot. Hello, Mrs Armstrong,' said Lucy, looking contrite, even while pulling Kathy towards the front door which stood open.

Then Mary Roberts, a still-slender woman in her mid-forties, was there to greet them, giving Kathy a kiss on the cheek then shaking Vera's hand. 'So glad you could come, Mrs Armstrong.'

'Please, do call me Vera.' The two women had met before on the occasion of Kathy and Nick's engagement party but that had been a more formal occasion.

'And I'm Mary.'

From the upstairs came the sound Derek belting out, 'My Old Man's a Dustman.' She couldn't help smiling though Mrs Roberts didn't look so pleased. 'Stop that racket this minute, Derek. We've got visitors.'

'Sorry, Mam. Be down in a minute.' This was followed by the sound of the toilet flushing then thirteen-year-old Derek hurtled down the stairs. 'Lo, Kathy, Mrs Armstrong.'

Nick appeared in the doorway between the kitchen and the hall. 'Hello, love.' He gave her a hug then turned to her mother, giving her a peck on the cheek. 'Hello, Mrs Armstrong. Are you well?'

'You asked me the same question last night, young man,' she said, 'and nothing's changed since then.' It wasn't meant to be a rebuke if the glimmer of a smile hovering on her mother's lips was anything to go by.

Nick looked sheepish. 'Sorry, Mrs A. I'm a bit nervous to tell you the truth. Come and sit down.'

As they followed Nick into the front room, Vera turned to Kathy and whispered, 'Are you sure you're not pregnant?' From the teasing look on her mother's face, Kathy knew that this time she wasn't being serious.

Laughing, she shook her head and took hold of Nick's hand. With the whole family, plus Kathy and her mother, the small front room was crowded. Greetings were exchanged with Nick's Dad, who'd vacated his chair so that her mother could sit down, an honour indeed, and his sister, Joyce, who'd been curled up on the settee but now made room for Kathy. Mr Roberts, looking tidier than she'd ever seen him, went to stand at the back of the room, where, being a big man, he took up a lot of space. 'So what's all this about then? Can someone please tell me?' he said now, looking from one to the other of them. 'I know that summat's brewing.'

Nick perched on the arm of the settee and put his arm round Kathy's shoulders. 'Me and Kathy have got summat to tell you.'

'You've not gone and got the lass in the family way, have you?' Mr Roberts boomed. 'Not that I'd have minded,' he was quick to add.

Nick gave his father a look of annoyance. 'No, Dad, nowt like that. The exact opposite in fact.' He gave Kathy a questioning look to which she nodded. 'We wanted you all to know that we've fixed a date for getting married.'

To gasps of excitement and astonishment and cries of 'when, when?' from Lucy and Joyce, Kathy said, 'Next year. Saturday, 30th April at the Parish Church.'

'But that's a long time off,' Lucy said, pouting her lips in disappointment.

'Unless you get married in a register office,

Lucy love, you have to book these things well in advance,' Nick explained. 'Oh, and we've booked the reception too. At the Black Bull on Church Street.'

Vera was beaming at them both, her now-gloveless hands held out to Kathy. 'Oh, how lovely! But why didn't you tell me, Kathy?'

'We thought it would be a nice surprise for everyone.'

'Well, you've done that, right enough,' Nick's Mum said, her face showing her delight. 'I'm that pleased for you both. And it'll give us all summat to look forward to.'

'Well, I'll be buggered!' Mr Roberts said, heading towards the door. 'I reckon that calls for a celebration. What do you say, Nick? I think we've got some whisky left from last Christmas.'

His wife gave him a warning glance. 'Not just now, Danny. We'll be having our tea shortly.'

Kathy turned to Joyce at the side of her. 'I'd like you and Lucy to be my bridesmaids. My friend, Carole, too.'

'We'd love to, wouldn't we, Lucy?' Joyce said. The young girl herself was jigging up and down with excitement at the side of Kathy.

'Oh, yes, please.' Then, as the implications dawned on her, she said, 'Does that mean we'll have to wear fancy dresses?' These days, Lucy preferred dressing in dungarees or shorts and playing football with the lads in the street to playing with dolls.

'Fraid so, love,' Kathy said, 'but we'll make sure it's nothing too frilly or flouncy.'

The girl gave a mock shudder. 'I should hope not. All me mates would laugh at me.'

'I hope you weren't thinking of me being a page boy,' chimed in Derek, making everyone laugh at the look of horror on his face.

Nick ruffled his hair. 'Wouldn't dream of it. What about being an usher instead?'

Still looking wary, he said, 'What's an usher have to do then?'

'Showing the wedding guests where to sit. And perhaps Dave Yates'll be an usher too.'

Derek's jiggled his mouth from side to side as he contemplated the idea. 'OK then. Sounds a sort of grown-up thing to do but what about Phil?'

'He'll be my best man, of course.'

Lucy turned to Kathy. 'Are you going to ask Sally to be your bridesmaid too?'

A momentary silence pregnant with hidden meanings fell on the group until Kathy spoke. 'I think three bridesmaids are enough, don't you? I'm sure Sally will understand.'

Mary Roberts jumped up and, giving a small cough, said, 'I reckon it's about time we had our tea. What do you say, Vera?'

CHAPTER 6

I t had been a difficult day for Joyce. Knowing that it was today that Dave had been due to go back to the hospital to get the results of the various tests he'd had, she hadn't been able to concentrate. To the detriment of her weaving. She'd had a huge 'smash' where a broken thread had tangled with others, breaking even more and ruining the towel. The loom had then been out of action for most of the day while the tackler sorted it, no doubt cursing her under his breath. And as they were paid on piece work, she'd lose money too. Heaving a sigh of relief as she came out of the mill gates, she didn't see Dave waiting for her. It was only when he spoke her name that she looked up and saw him.

'Dave, what are you ...?' Her voice faltered as she saw the grim look on his face, took in the set lines around his mouth, the haunted look in his eyes. She reached out a hand to touch his cheek, finding it chilled. 'What's up, love? Bad news at the hospital?'

'Let's say it weren't good.' His voice was dull and lifeless.

Her heart sank with his words. 'Tell me then.'

'Not here, too many people about.' He indicated Joyce's workmates all piling out of the mill gates, laughing and joking with each other at finally getting out. Their light-hearted and carefree attitude jarred with the cold fear clutching her heart. The worst of those fears was that it was a brain tumour. That thought had been at the back of her mind along with other possible causes for his problem. 'Can't you tell me now?' she pleaded.

'No, but can you come home with me now and help me break the news to my Mam? It's something we all need to discuss together,' he said, then, as if realising that he'd sounded harsh, he continued, ' Sorry, love ... it's just that ... there might be ... implications for the future.'

'All right then, but we'll have to find a phone box so's I can leave a message with one of our neighbours. She'll send one of the kids round to our house to tell Mam I won't be home for tea.'

'Happen we can get some fish and chips later though I have to be honest and say I don't feel much like eating at the moment.'

On the short bus ride into Horwich, Dave was silent but held her hand with what Joyce felt was a quiet desperation, his fingers wrapped tightly around hers, his other hand on top of both of theirs. And he would not be drawn about what he wanted to talk about with her and his mother. From the phone box outside the Post Office in Winter Hey Lane, she managed to get through to their neighbours. Even as she was saying goodbye to Mrs Brown, the woman was calling for one of the children to take a message to Mrs Roberts.

The Yates' house in Wright Street was similar to every other two-up two-down terraced house built for the workers who'd flocked to the town in the late 19th century to work at the Locomotive Works. With dated décor and furniture, it was no worse, no better than any other house of its kind. It was, as always, spotlessly clean and, with bright cushions and floral curtains, cheerful and welcoming. Mrs Yates greeted them warily as they walked into the house, casting glances between the pair as if waiting for one or the other of them to speak. Joyce guessed that she too had spent the day wondering what the news was going to be. Eventually, sensing she wasn't going to get an answer, Mrs Yates said, 'Do either of you want a drink? Or can you wait awhile?'

Still clutching Joyce's hand, Dave said, 'We'll wait, Mam, if you don't mind. I'd rather get this out of the way.'

Mrs Yates leaned towards him, worry written deep around her eyes, her hands clasped tightly under her bosom. 'What is it, son? What did they say at the hospital?'

'I'm sorry, it's not good news,' he said, then turned to each of them before continuing, 'it's epilepsy and there's no cure for it.' Joyce was stunned. Even though that was one of the things she had considered, it was still a shock to hear the word in relation to Dave.

Mrs Yates' hands shot up to her mouth and she

let out a cry of anguish. 'Oh, dear Lord, no! They'll lock you away in one of them institutions.'

Dave clasped his mother in a close embrace. 'No, Mam, they won't, not now. They've recently passed a law that means they can't put you away like they used to.'

Despite these reassurances, Mrs Yates was sobbing now and it took several more minutes to calm her down. Over his mother's shoulder, Dave cast Joyce a despairing look, a question in his eyes. Although there was no longer the same antagonism and mistrust towards anyone who suffered from the disease, it was still very much something of a stigma, particularly among older people. Mrs Yates' reaction was typical. And what of her? She didn't know what to feel. She still loved him, of that there was no doubt.

As if reading her mind, Dave, his arms still holding his mother, said, 'Joyce, love, if you want to call the whole thing off between us, I will understand.'

She didn't hesitate in replying. 'Don't be daft! No question of that, not after what we've been through already.'

Dave flashed her a quick smile. 'In that case, would you mind making a drink? I think we could all do with one now, while we talk about it some more.' He guided his mother to one of the fireside chairs and pulled up a kitchen chair to sit at her side. 'Come on, Mam. It's not as bad as it seems.'

While Dave reassured his mother, Joyce set about making a pot of tea in the adjoining scullery. She'd been to the house loads of times now and, from helping Mrs Yates clear away after the teas they'd shared, she knew roughly where everything was. By the time she took three mugs of tea through to the kitchen, Mrs Yates had calmed down and, although she still clutched tightly on to Dave's hand, she was listening to what he was saying.

'So you see, Mam, it's not as bad as it sounds. All being well these tablets I've been given will help to control the fits and I've been told that I'll be able to more or less live a normal life.'

'You're sure they won't lock you away like they used to?' The fear was still in her voice as she took the mug from Joyce with shaking hands.

'No, Mam, this new Act – it's called the Mental Health Act – came out earlier this year and it means I won't have to be institutionalised.'

'It's just that ... I've never told you ... but your Uncle Bob used to have fits when he were a lad. Our Mam would never tell anyone for fear he'd be locked up.' Her voice faltered as she said this and it was obvious where her fear for Dave was coming from.

'I didn't know that. I'll certainly tell the specialist next time I go to see him. He did ask me if there was a history of epilepsy in the family.'

'Is it hereditary then?' Joyce asked. Irrespective of the uncertainty of the future, she was thinking of any children they might have.

'Apparently not though the doctor did say there were more of a chance of it occurring if it had happened to anyone else in the family.'

'What about work, love? How will they take

it?' Joyce asked now, sitting in the fireside chair opposite Mrs Yates, her own mug cradled in her hands. Dave worked at the sprawling De Havilland Propellers site, not far from the Beehive Mill, in the Drawing Office.

A look of uncertainty flitted across his face. 'I don't rightly know at this stage whether it'll affect my job or what De Hav's will have to say about it. No doubt I'll find out tomorrow when I tell them. It's not like I'm dealing with machinery so there's no risk in that respect.'

'Did the doctor confirm that it were as a result of the injury?' Mrs Yates asked now.

'He thought so though there's no definite way of knowing.'

'That Jud Simcox has a lot to answer for,' Mrs Yates said, her hatred for the young man in question clear in the tone of her voice. 'I'd like to get my hands on him.'

A grim smile flitted across Dave's face. 'You and me both, Mam.'

'You aren't the only ones,' Joyce said. 'Both my brothers feel exactly the same. Even the mention of his name gives me the creeps.' She remembered all too clearly how he and his mates had lunged at Dave in that back alley in Bolton, felling him to the cobbles, seeing the blood pouring from the resultant wound to his head. And feeling guilty that she had been a cause of it. Jud Simcox had been mithering her for months to go out with him and had even made the disgusting suggestion that he and Dave share her. It had been that remark that prompted Dave to defend her honour. She couldn't help an involuntary shudder. She hated the man even if he was Sally's brother.

Dave brought her back to the present by saying, 'Isn't he due to come out of prison about now?

'I would think so though Sally might know more than us. Pity I didn't think to ask her when she came up to see us the other week.'

Mrs Yates jumped up. 'Look at the time. I should think about getting us some tea. The truth is, I never gave it a thought. I were that worried about what the hospital would say.'

'Why don't we have some fish and chips, Mam? That'll save you bothering.'

'But it's not Friday,' she protested.

'You don't just have to have fish on a Friday, Mam,' Dave teased, thus lightening the mood. 'It's not a sin. You'll have some fish and chips with us, won't you, Joyce, love?'

The warmth in his tone reminded her that the pattern of their love had never been easy and she was determined that this epilepsy would not come between them. She made her mind up that she would find out all she could about this disease that was threatening their future together.

* * *

They were to find out over the following weeks how much prejudice still existed about epilepsy. The managers at De Havilland's were wary initially and insisted on a letter from the specialist at the hospital confirming that it could be controlled with drugs. Once that had been received, they seemed reassured though that didn't stop the prejudice creeping in from his work colleagues, who'd started avoiding him. He'd tried to carry on as normal but Joyce knew he'd been deeply hurt by their attitude.

She and Dave had gone up to tell her parents a couple of days after receiving the news. They had reacted in much the same way that Mrs Yates had done. Her Dad sat stunned, for once with nothing to say, while Mam's face reflected the shock she felt at hearing the news. 'Don't they lock people away with that?' she said in a small voice.

'Not any more, Mrs Roberts,' Dave said, then explained about the new Mental Health Act.

Her Dad found his voice and Joyce noticed it was deep with sympathy. 'But what does it all mean for you, lad?'

'It means that it's been classified as a physical illness not a mental one like it used to be and one that can now be controlled reasonably successfully with drugs.'

'I'm sorry to say this but old habits die hard, Dave. You'll face a lot of prejudice,' Mam pointed out.

Dave sighed. 'I already have, Mrs Roberts. Some of the older factory workers have called me 'loony' or made gestures signifying that I'm mad.' He made a circling movement with his forefinger at his temple.

'Who's mad?' came a deep voice from the doorway. It was Nick late home from work as usual.

'According to some people, I am,' Dave said.

'Because of the fit you had?' Nick queried.

'The results of the tests I had show that I have epilepsy,' Dave said quietly.

'Bloody hell, Bragger!' The nick-name tripped off his lips easily. 'That's not good news.' He came to perch on the arm of the sofa next to Joyce. While Mam went to make a cup of tea, Dave told Nick all he'd told the Roberts and the reactions he'd had from some people.

'Well, nobody had better call you 'loony' in my hearing,' Nick said, 'or they'll have me to reckon with. You're an honorary member of the Roberts' family, Brag, always have been. Anybody messes with one of ours, they'll know about it.' That was certainly true from the time he and Dave had been best mates, knocking around the pubs and dance halls.

'Thanks, Nick. Much appreciated.'

Just how deep the prejudice against epileptic sufferers was brought home to Joyce with a vengeance a couple of days later. They'd been to the Picture House to see 'Idol on Parade,' a comedy about National Service, with Sid James and Anthony Newley and were making their way through the crowd to the exit when Dave stopped suddenly, his eyes blank, causing the man behind to say, 'Get a bloody move on, lad, you're blocking the way.' Before she could say anything to the man, Dave had fallen to the floor where he lay, shaking violently, his hands clenched claw-like, his face in a grimace, his knees drawn up in a foetal position. A woman nearby screamed and people started to back away. Feeling icy cold, Joyce knelt and went as if to comfort him.

'Don't touch him, lass, just make sure there's nowt nearby he can hurt himself with,' came a quiet voice nearby and a calming hand came down on her shoulder.

Joyce looked up into the sympathetic eyes of and older woman. 'What do I do?' she whispered. 'I've never seen him like this before.'

'You can't do owt, lass. He'll only be like this for a few minutes. Likely as not he'll be a bit confused afterwards. And he'll be tired. Best get him home as soon as you can.'

'How do you know all this?'

'My brother had it,' she said quietly. 'We all kept quiet about it in case he got locked up and we learned how to cope with it.'

The shaking had stopped now and Dave was un-curling himself, his fingers, face and knees beginning to relax. Joyce became aware of murmurings around her and looked up to find a few people still standing around gawping and muttering. Then, louder than all the rest, she heard a woman say, 'Freak! He ought to be locked up.'

Joyce rose to her feet, fury in her eyes and voice. 'Shut up, you stupid woman! You know nowt! It's a disease, like any other illness.'

The woman walked away, followed by a man who looked decidedly uncomfortable especially when she said. 'Well, at least, he should be kept at home where decent folks can't see him.'

'And what about if he'd been your son?' she called after the woman's retreating back. 'Or yours?' she said to a man who was hovering nearby. 'Or your boyfriend?' she said to a young girl, giggling and pointing a finger at Dave. She flapped her hands at them. 'Go home, all of you. Show's over.'

Finally, it was just herself, Dave and the older woman, her husband who'd been hovering sympathetically in the background. It was he who helped Dave stagger to his feet. So limp was Dave that Joyce had to support him with her shoulder. 'Did it happen again, Joyce?' he said, in a voice that quavered.

'It did, love, but don't worry about it.'

'I'm sorry you had to see that.'

She touched his slightly-sweating cheek with her hand. 'Don't think about it. It had to happen sometime. Now let's get you home. And remember that I love you, no matter what.'

CHAPTER 7

Sally woke, as she often did, to the distant drone of a Provost overhead, as yet another trainee pilot on the basic jet training course took to the skies. With new recruits arriving every seven weeks for the 28-week course, there was a constant flow of them. Phil, who was on duty later, still slept beside her, his face in repose looking much younger than his twenty-three years. His fair hair stuck up in wayward spikes reminding her of his younger brother, Derek, who had the same colouring. He slept, as he always did, with one arm exposed and lying on top of the bedspread, making her long to reach out and stroke the smooth skin. She took in every contour of his face, from cheekbone to chin, loving every inch of him.

As if reading her mind, his eyes flickered open, started in surprise for a second then he smiled. 'What are you looking at, wench?'

'My lovely husband.'

He rolled closer to her, his hand snaking round her waist, looking deep into her eyes. 'Might you be just a bit prejudiced?'

She giggled. 'And why not?'

He leaned over her and began nibbling her ear. 'That's enough talk for now. Let's enjoy this rare lie-in together.'

She pretended to be shocked. 'What will Mrs Harris think?'

'Bugger what she thinks! Don't we have a right to some time to ourselves? Anyroad, you know she toddles off to the village in the mornings.'

As if to reinforce the point, they heard the front door bang and Mrs Harris on the doorstep having a word with her next-door neighbour then her slow footsteps fading into the distance. 'In that case ...' she said, snuggling even closer to him.

A little later, while Phil enjoyed a post-breakfast cigarette and shared a leisurely second cup-f-tea, Sally looked round at the cluttered sitting room of Pear Tree Cottage. Sometimes she did wish they had the privacy of their own quarter. In talking to other RAF wives on the base, she knew there'd have been drawbacks. Anyone living in quarters was issued with a leaflet several pages thick with regulations on what they could and could not do on moving in. And it was said to be even worse when moving out, when every speck of dust or dirt had to be eliminated, where even the oven had to be taken to pieces, meticulously cleaned, then reassembled.

'Penny for them, love,' Phil said, cigarette in his hand.

'I were just thinking how nice it would be to have the privacy of a quarter, no matter how basic they are.'

'I know, love, I wish it too. The old lady's lovely but it is a bit ...' he waggled his eyebrows suggestively, '... restricting living here.'

She tutted at him. 'You've got a dirty mind, Phil Roberts.'

'I've not heard you complaining,' he said, leaning across to kiss her.

Laughing, she pushed him away and, hearing the letter box rattle, went through to the tiny lobby to pick up the letter that lay on the mat. 'That's funny,' she said as she examined the handwriting. 'It's from our Eileen. I only had one last week and she doesn't write that often.' Since Mam's stroke had rendered her dependant on others for much of the time, she and Eileen had been corresponding direct instead of through Joyce.

'Hope that doesn't mean your witch of a mother's taken a turn for the worse, love.'

Sally skimmed the contents of the letter quickly and, putting a hand to her mouth, she gasped. 'No, nowt to do with her. It sounds as if she's being as troublesome as ever. It's our May.'

Eighteen-year-old May was the quietest of the three Simcox sisters, on the shy side and with a more reserved nature. 'Oh, what's she been up to then?' Phil asked, gathering their cups together and taking them over to the sink.

'Only gone and got herself a boyfriend.'

'Nowt wrong with that, is there? She might be a bit on the dumpy side, like your Mam, but her heart's in the right place.'

'No ... but it's a coloured lad, come over from the West Indies.' Although there'd been a steady influx of immigrants coming in from the West Indies, mainly Jamaicans, since the end of the war, Horwich and Bolton had seen few of them. Mostly they had seemed to gravitate towards the industrial centres like Manchester or Birmingham, where they'd been forced to take low-paid jobs, usually the ones no-one else wanted, in factories and mills in order to exist. She knew that the idea to encourage immigrants from Britain's colonies from the late 1940s onwards had not been without its problems. The immigrants themselves had experienced much prejudice and it was well known that many houses offering lodgings, now had signs in the window stating 'No coloureds, no Irish, no dogs.' There'd been numerous episodes of racial tensions and clashes, particularly where relationships with white girls were concerned. There'd been similar trouble during the war, she seemed to remember, with the black GIs, who'd been seen by many white women as glamorous.

Phil turned to face her, shock on his face. 'Bloody hell, your little sister's full of surprises, isn't she? How did she meet him then? Does Eileen say?'

'He's works in the dyeing shed at Victoria mill and apparently one of the older blokes in there were giving him a hard time when May, who were about to brew up, heard him and stood up for the coloured lad.'

'I'll say this for your sister, she might be quiet, but she's a gutsy little madam.' Over the past couple of years, she and Phil had met up with Eileen and May occasionally, always meeting in pubs, so they'd got to know and like each other.

'His name's Norman and he came over with his elder brother about three years ago,' she said, tapping the letter. 'Apparently, she's kept quiet about it until now for obvious reasons but one of the other lasses from the mill saw them together in Bolton a week or so back and has been tormenting her about it ever since. Knowing what Horwich is like for gossip and that Eileen might get to know about it, she decided to confess. Now our Eileen wants to know should she do anything about it.'

'Well, the way I see it, there's not a lot either of you can do if that's what she wants,' he said, 'and it's early days yet.'

'Yes, it's only been a month or so but Eileen's worried about repercussions if Mam gets to know about it.'

Well, as she isn't up to going out, that's not likely to happen, is it? Though there is your Jud to consider,' he said, giving her a meaningful look.

Sally went cold at the thought. 'You're right. He'd definitely lay the law down, trying to forbid her to see him,' she said. 'If only we knew when he were being released then we could prepare ourselves, but as usual, he's saying nowt.'

'In the meantime, what are you going to tell your Eileen?'

'To do nowt for the time being, see how things go. You never know, it might fizzle out.'

'And if it doesn't all either of you can do is point out the difficulties they would face as a couple in the future,' Phil reasoned. 'One of the current intake of trainee pilots is an Indian, who came here with this parents after the Indian Partition in 1947. Brought up here, well-educated, a clever bloke, otherwise he wouldn't have been selected for pilot training but even for him there's been a bit of trouble, name calling and such like.'

Sally sighed. 'Change is never easy, is it?'

* * *

Sally had rampant butterflies in her stomach as she dressed later that evening. Shortly, she and Phil were due at the base for a reception to welcome the new Station Commander. They'd been to a few such events since she'd been here and it was always the same; with it being such a close knit community, she always worried about putting a foot wrong and this was the biggest occasion she had attended so far. She knew that Phil would do his best to guide her through the protocol but he couldn't be with her every step of the way. With little money to spare, she was wearing the rose pink taffeta frock she'd bought to attend her first dance at RAF Kirkham three years ago. She felt the pink dress, with its full skirt, was dated especially with the new slim-line dresses coming into fashion.

'You ready, Sally? We really ought to be going,' Phil called up the stairs. She recalled what she'd been told, one must never be too late and that arriving after senior officers was simply not on.

Fluffing up her naturally blonde curls, she checked her lipstick one last time. 'Coming, love.'

Phil, dressed in his number one dress uniform, was waiting for her at the bottom of the stairs, his appreciative eyes watching her descend. 'You look good enough to eat, love. Wish we didn't have to go tonight.'

'Not more than I do. I'm always so scared of making a mess of things.'

'If anyone's going to blunder it'll be me, mixing with the higher-ups.' Now that he mentioned it, she could see the anxiety in his eyes. As one of the youngest Flight Sergeants and the lowest rank that would be seen at the reception, he had more to lose than her. It was more important than ever that she didn't let him down.

As if sensing Sally's anxiety, Phoebe, sitting in her usual chair close to the fire, said, 'You look lovely, Sally, so you've nothing to worry about.'

She crossed the room and planted a grateful kiss on Phoebe's warm pink cheek. 'Thanks, Mrs H. You're a dear.'

They walked, hand in hand, to the base thankful that the October night wasn't too cold, Sally carrying her high heels in a bag. Above them, in this more isolated spot, the night sky appeared in all its glory. When she'd first come to North Yorkshire, Phil had taken his time in pointing out various constellations and she could now recognise The Plough and

Anne L Harvey

Orion's Belt but had never grasped the others. Living as she had in Horwich with all its street lights, she'd never taken much notice of the skies before.

'Reminds me of that night on the North Pier in Blackpool, when we first started to realise how we felt about each other,' Phil said, the pressure of his hand tightening in her own.

'I were just thinking the same thing,' she whispered.

'No regrets?'

'None at all,' she said, as they approached the brightly lit entrance to the Mess where the reception was to be held. They looked at each other, drew in a deep breath and stepped into the foyer, where a chirpy Senior Aircraftsman checked their names off his guest list. 'Cloakrooms to your left, Sir, Madam, then through to the Mess Room.'

'Remind you of Chipper, Sally?' Phil said in an undertone. Chipper had been one of Phil's best mates at RAF Kirkham and best man at their wedding.

Sally laughed. 'Yes, he does. How's he doing, by the way?'

'As far as I know, he's still at Cosworth and according to him, practically running things.'

'That sounds like Chipper. Have you heard from Fred recently?' Welshman Fred had also been part of the threesome who'd formed a deep friendship while stationed at Kirkham.

'Not since that last letter when he told us he'd had to quit on compassionate grounds to run the family business after his father had that stroke.'

The main room held only a few of the more junior ranks but Sally guessed that the other ranks would start to arrive soon, with the new CO making a grand entrance last of all. They accepted a drink from a passing waiter and went to stand in a quiet corner where they could watch proceedings. Gradually the room began to fill up with the more senior ranks. 'Better make some sort of a move to circulate,' Phil said, the bobbing of his Adam's apple betraying his own nervousness.

She gave his hand a reassuring squeeze. 'I'm ready.' Around them was a steady flow of conversation, the tinkle of laughter, the clink of glasses, the guffaw of men's laughter. Sally resisted the urge to giggle; it was all such a far cry from the Fling, the shabby, run-down dance club that had been so much a part of her life a few years back, in Horwich.

'Ah, there you are, Sergeant Roberts,' boomed a man close to them. Sally hadn't yet learned to differentiate between the different markings on uniforms so had no idea of the man's rank, only that the uniform belonged to a senior officer. 'Is this your good lady wife?'

Phil saluted and stood to attention. 'Yes, sir, my wife Sally. Sally, this is Squadron Leader Thompson.

'At ease, man.' The man beamed at her, his moustache quivering at both ends as he did so. 'Pleased to meet you, Mrs Roberts,' he said, taking her hand. In his large fatherly hand, her own felt tiny.

She resisted the urge to curtsey. 'Likewise, Sir.'

'May I introduce you both to my wife, Mrs

Thompson?' He indicated the tall elegant woman, wearing a deep turquoise cocktail dress, by his side.

For such a senior officer's wife, she had a surprisingly friendly face and, as she shook first Phil's hand then Sally's, she said, 'Ignore the formality, you two. My name's Jenny and I'm pleased to meet you both.'

'Come with me, Roberts, I'd like you to meet ....' With that, Squadron Leader Thompson bore Phil away. Over his shoulder, Phil gave her a helpless shrug. Without him by her side to guide her, she felt the panic begin to rise.

As if guessing what she was feeling, Jenny said close to her ear, 'Don't worry, Sally, he'll be back shortly. Is this is your first time at such a big event?'

'Is it that obvious?' she whispered back.

'Only to someone's who's already been there,' Jenny said, patting her hand. 'Stick by my side and I'll do my best to guide you.' Taking her arm, Jenny led her towards a nearby group of women, talking as they went. 'One of the first things to learn at big events such as this is that most wives tend to introduce themselves with the rank of their husbands. Like me saying 'I'm Squadron Leader Thompson's wife.' Don't! You soon lose your individuality that way. Having said that, it is a fine line you have to tread,' she added.

Under Jenny's guidance, Sally was soon feeling more relaxed, even when being introduced to more wives. She found them, by and large, a friendly bunch. When, eventually, there was a stir at the entrance, Jenny excused herself. 'Oh-ho, looks like the big-wigs have arrived. I'll have to re-join Brian and you should do the same with that lovely young man of yours.' With a cheery grin, she was gone as Phil arrived at her side.

'I've been tipped the wink to re-join you so it looks like the formalities are about to begin,' he said, his face much more relaxed now than it had been. 'How've you been? OK with the Squadron Leader's wife?'

'Jenny,' Sally prompted. 'She was really helpful, kept making me laugh at some of the remarks she made about ... certain of the officers' wives.'

'I can imagine,' Phil said, with a lift of one eyebrow, as one of the more senior officers rapped his fountain pen against the side of his glass.

'Ladies and gentlemen, may I have your attention please? I'd like you to join with me in welcoming our new Station Commander, Group Captain Bingham.' A tall, distinguished man, maybe in his late thirties, entered the Mess, at his side, his wife, a surprisingly small woman, dressed in a fussy green cocktail dress, to resounding applause.

The new CO acknowledged the applause by raising his hand. 'On behalf of my wife and myself, thank you for the warm welcome.' He had a deep, reassuring sort of voice, Sally decided, and thought he might be a good CO. 'I can't tell you how much I've been looking forward to this new posting. I recognise, of course, that life on a bleak North Yorkshire airfield under the cloud of the Cold War won't be easy but I am looking forward to the challenge, especially in the light of the advances of jet propulsion.' He continued in much the same vein for a few more minutes to enthusiastic applause, before waving his hand as if to say that was all he was going to say. A couple of the more senior officers, including Squadron Leader Thompson, followed with official words of welcome and within a short time, the formalities were over and everyone was free to move around again and partake of the finger buffet laid out on trestle tables and presided over by Mess staff in pristine whites.

The whole thing took no more than a couple of hours and soon enough, both heaving a sigh of relief, Phil and Sally were strolling back to the village, arm in arm, through the now cold night air. 'I don't know about you, love, but I'm right glad that's over,' Phil said. 'Fortunately, we won't have to attend too many of those. More often than not, such do's are confined to certain ranks and mostly we'll be mixing with other NCO's.'

'It weren't as bad as I'd expected,' she admitted, 'and being introduced to Jenny certainly helped. I couldn't help thinking though ...' she stopped.

'What, love?'

'How did an ordinary mill girl like me come to be mixing with such exalted company?'

Phil laughed. 'Or me, a working class lad, born in Winter Street, Horwich. Makes you think, doesn't it?' He stopped and turned to look at her. 'Tell you what though. I were proud of us both tonight. I reckon we did right well.'

CHAPTER 8

By the end of November, Kathy was beginning to panic about finding somewhere to live after she and Nick were married. With the Conservative government having won a resounding third term in office in October, the economy was on the rise and house prices were going up accordingly. Many of the terraced houses they'd looked at required considerable work doing to bring them up to more modern standards, putting the cost far beyond anything they could possibly afford. Nick had even contemplated quitting his job and going back into the building trade. So far, Kathy had convinced him not to do so. He loved tinkering around with engines, a skill he'd first learned while doing his National Service, but on returning to Civvy Street had discovered his Army qualifications didn't count. He'd bravely gone to Horwich Technical College, even though he was older than the other students, so as to become a fully qualified motor mechanic and had finally completed the course in the late spring. Even though more people were buying cars, Mac's garage was still only a small business and he couldn't afford to pay Nick much.

She often found herself contemplating the problem during the monotony of the bus journey to and from work and tonight was no exception. Consequently, her head was aching and, after a busy if somewhat tedious day, she was looking forward to getting home, having her tea and relaxing. So she groaned when her mother met her in the hallway and said, 'Before you take your coat off, love, Nick's phoned. He said could you meet him at the garage as soon as you can. Apparently, his boss wants to talk to you both.' As if sensing her hesitation, Vera Armstrong smiled. 'Go on, get off with you while you've still got your coat on. I'll keep your tea warm. Sooner you go, the sooner you'll be back.'

The buses into Horwich at that time of day were frequent so before long she was alighting at the Crown. Crossing Chorley New Road, she made her way to the small but busy garage tucked away to the side of a row of terraced houses. The double doors of the workshop were open, in defiance of the damp chill of November, revealing a begrimed Nick bending over the engine of a car. Even after three years, her heart gave a lurch of love at the sight of him. 'Hello, Nick.'

So engrossed was he in his task that he looked up too quickly and cracked his head on the propped-open bonnet lid. 'Bugger!' he said, wincing as he rubbed at the side of his head.

She laughed. 'Sorry, love. I thought you'd heard me. Anyway, what's all this about?'

Nick wiped the worst of the oil on his hands on a filthy cloth, looked at it doubtfully, then wiping the remainder off on his already grease-stained overalls. 'Search me. All I know is that Mac's been like a big kid today, dead excited about summat.'

'Where is he, anyway?'

'Up in the flat. He said we'd to go up when you came,' he said as he pulled the double doors to and locked them.

Kathy had only been to the flat above the garage a couple of times when Nick had been badly beaten up and somehow made his way to Mac's. Then she'd been so concerned about Nick's injuries that she hadn't taken too much notice. She did recall that, not surprisingly for a man living alone, it had seemed dusty, shabby and untidy. This evening, she was pleasantly surprised. Mac seemed to have made a bit of an effort and tidied up in preparation for them coming.

'Come in, come in,' Mac said, beaming at them. He was a Scot in late middle-age with a slight paunch and thinning hair. After a traumatic incident in his life after the war, he had somehow drifted to Horwich and settled there. He'd bought the then run-down garage and become a mentor to Nick, taking him on as a mechanic even though he only had an Army qualification at that time. Neither had Mac, come to that, but he at least had served time as an engineer in the Navy. 'Will you have a cup of tea?'

Shortly after, sitting at the small table with a mug of tea in front of them, Mac said, 'Now, you must be wondering what all this is about, why I wanted to speak to you both together so I'll come straight to the point.' He looked from one to the other, anticipation in his eyes. 'I know you've been having difficulty finding somewhere to live, especially as the wedding is getting nearer. So,' he said, taking a deep breath, 'how would you like to live here?'

Kathy and Nick exchanged puzzled looks and seeing their confusion, Mac continued, 'Fact is, I've bought a house in Beatrice Street so as soon as it goes through, you can have this.' He waved his arms around the room to make his point. 'If you want it, of course.'

'Is that what all the coming and going recently has been about?' Nick said. 'I knew you'd been up to summat, you crafty sod.'

Mac grinned in obvious delight, then continued, 'It's not a huge flat but it'll be better once a lot of my clutter has gone.' He indicated the piles of newspaper, car magazines and books piled on every surface. 'I'd only charge a nominal rent because it would be useful you being on the premises.'

'What do you think, love?' Nick asked, reaching for her hand. Kathy looked round the sitting room, trying to see beyond the grubby walls and smeared paintwork, looking instead to the high ceiling, the window to the side, another one overlooking Chorley New Road, letting in a lot of light into this room in particular. It showed promise and would certainly give them the start they needed.

With a surge of excitement, she said, 'I think it's a wonderful idea, Mac, and it's very kind of you. I'm OK with that, if Nick is.'

Mac turned to Nick. 'What do you think, Nick?

You'd have the advantage of being on the doorstep.'

Kathy laughed. 'That might be a bit of a disadvantage, Mac. I can see him saying, "I'll just nip down and finish that little job off."'

Nick had the grace to look sheepish and gave her a smile. 'Not too often, I promise.' Then, turning to the older man, said, 'Mac, I'm touched that you should think of us this way and we'll gladly accept. When do you think it might be?'

'My solicitor thinks the sale'll go through fairly quickly as the house I'm buying is empty and there's no chain involved. About six to eight weeks, he said. Course I'll want to get the new house decorated, which'll be another two to three weeks, then this can be yours.'

'Should give us enough time to get the flat decorated and furnished in good time for the wedding,' Nick said.

On an impulse, Kathy leaned across to give Mac a hug. 'Thank you so much, Mac. I hope you know how much we appreciate the gesture.'

The older man looked uncomfortable but responded by patting her on the back. 'Least I can do, lass. Nick brought me to back to life again and I've seen how happy he is since he got together with you.'

After looking round the rest of the flat, the trio talked over details for some time until Kathy looked at the old-fashioned clock on Mac's cluttered sideboard realised how long she'd been gone. 'Oh, I'd better go. Mum's keeping my tea hot.'

'Aye, Mam'll think I've got lost as well. I'll have

a quick clean-up then we can both go together,' Nick said, rising to his feet. 'Tell you what, Kathy love, let's treat ourselves tonight, go out for a drink and we can talk over what we're going to do.'

'Good idea,' she said. 'In any case, I'm too excited to settle to anything else.' Miraculously, her headache and former weariness seemed to have vanished.

* * *

Under normal circumstances, Kathy loved working in the cluttered Newsroom of the Bolton Evening News, feeling a part of the chaos that often surrounded her. Battered desks arranged close to each other to maximise space, scarred wooden chairs in various stages of stability, an assortment of aged typewriters, overflowing wire baskets and ashtrays, mugs of tea long since gone cold. And over all, the heavy fug of cigarette smoke.

Today though, she sat at her own desk tucked away in a dark corner, as befitted a junior reporter and a woman at that, feeling more than a little disillusioned and disenchanted. At the time, she'd been so thrilled to be accepted onto the journalism training scheme for the Bolton Evening News, looking forward to when she could really get her teeth into a good news story. It hadn't worked out that way; the male reporters still managed to get the best of the jobs. It was inbuilt prejudice, she knew, though why that should be especially after the magnificent role played by women in two world wars. She still seemed to be allocated the run-of-the mill jobs, reporting on council meetings, court cases, and the ubiquitous community fetes and fairs. And there was only so much enthusiasm she could muster for bonny baby competitions and flower festivals. It simply wasn't fulfilling enough.

Making a sudden decision, she rose and, making her excuses, she went to see if Matthew Bleakley, the Features Editor and her mentor, was in his office. Luckily, he was. She knocked and popped her head round the door. 'Can you spare me a minute, Mr Bleakley?'

The older man looked up and, taking the ever-present pipe from his mouth, smiled. 'For my favourite Town Topics contributor, of course I have a minute.' He grabbed the ever-present pile of papers from the chair adjacent to his desk and indicated she should take a seat. 'Now what can I do for you?'

She hesitated, not knowing how to explain what she felt without sounding ungrateful. Finally, she settled for, 'You know how thrilled I was when I was accepted for training, thanks to your recommendation, but it hasn't quite worked out as I'd hoped.'

'From what I hear that you're doing an excellent job with the day-to-day stuff that makes up the bulk of the paper,' he pointed out.

She sighed. 'I appreciate that but it's not ...'

He gave her a knowing smile. 'Not what you'd hoped? Not fulfilling enough?'

'Exactly. So, I wondered if there was anything you could think of that I could get my teeth into.'

'Mmm, let me think.' He stuck the pipe in his mouth again and puffed on it for a few seconds before scrummaging through a few old newspapers hanging off the corner of the desk. He flicked through the pages quickly then, finding what he wanted, folded it and handed it to her. 'Tell me what you think about this, it's a review of the Little Theatre's recent production.'

She knew of the Bolton Little Theatre, a purpose-built theatre at the back of the Market and used by several of Bolton's amateur dramatic societies though she'd never been to see any of their productions. On the few occasions she'd been to the theatre it had been to either the Hippodrome, home of the Bolton Repertory Theatre who put on regularly-changing plays or the Grand, often the venue for visiting productions or variety shows. She read the review briefly then said, 'It hardly inspires me to go and see the show.'

A look of what could be satisfaction passed across his face. 'Why do you think that is?'

She read it through again more thoroughly then said, 'It's dull and plodding ... 'the leading role was admirably filled by etc ...' and there's no critical element to it.'

Matthew Bleakley relaxed back into his chair and breathed a sigh of satisfaction. 'Exactly so. Yet I had to let it go because I needed to fill the space. So,' he drew in a breath, 'how about you having a go at a review?'

A thrill ran through her at the thought. 'I'd love to, if you think I could do it.'

'I have every confidence in you. There's a new production coming to the Grand next week, Noel Coward's 'Blithe Spirit.' Go and take that young man of yours. Remember it's not just the acting, it's the whole production. Any problems you mention them, but try to keep it positive and light-hearted if possible.'

Filled with anticipation and not a little anxiety, she was making her way back to the Newsroom, when she bumped into an old adversary, Rita, one of the news typists. The latter had been slightly diminished since her old ally, Pauline, had left the Bolton Evening News but on the odd occasions when she came across Kathy, she always managed to make some cutting remark. Today was no exception. 'Well, if it isn't our star journalist, Kathy Armstrong, queen of the flower show and the summer fayre.'

'Well, someone has to do them, I suppose, and,' Kathy said, bearing in mind what Matthew Bleakley had said, 'the grass roots stuff does make up the bulk of the paper and it's what a lot of readers buy the paper for.'

Rita gave a mocking laugh. 'Very appropriate, then, that you get paid considerably less than the male reporters.' At her words, hot anger filled Kathy, making her head throb and her heart pound. She ought to have realised of course. It was the norm after all. But she simply hadn't thought that part of it through. And, after finishing the training, she'd only recently gone on what she'd thought was the full rate.

Seeing the look of shock on Kathy's face, Rita continued, 'You mean you didn't know? That male reporters get paid a lot more than you although you're supposed to be doing the same job?'

Forcing herself to smile at the other young woman, she said, 'No, I didn't know, so thanks for doing me a favour for a change.' Changing direction, she headed for the Personnel Office. She had to wait a few minutes before the Personnel Officer could see her but she sat quietly marshalling her thoughts.

'Miss Armstrong, isn't it? Now what can I do for you?' On the few occasions she had spoken to Miss Murphy, the Personnel Officer, Kathy always thought of her as a typical middle-aged spinster, tall, thin, bespectacled, dressed in a brown tweed skirt and beige twinset. It only needed pearls at her neck and ears to complete the picture. Yet she couldn't have been more than forty.

'Is it true that I'm being paid considerably less than my male colleagues?' she burst out.

Miss Murphy seemed surprised by her question then said, 'Well, of course, I cannot divulge actual salaries but, yes, you are paid less.'

'That hardly seems fair when I'm doing the same job. Can you explain the reason why?'

The older woman seemed puzzled at Kathy's question and took a moment before answering. 'Well, of course, it's only right that a man earns more because he has to provide for his family. Whatever a woman earns is considered secondary to that of the man.'

'I don't think that's fair when we're doing the same work,' Kathy said, as reasonably as she could. 'I happen to live with my widowed mother and my salary goes to support her.' It wasn't strictly true as her Dad had left her mother well-provided for although Kathy did pay her mother board for her upkeep.

'That's as may be, my dear girl, but nationally that's how it is and it's not likely to change any time soon,' Miss Murphy said, obviously accepting the status quo herself. 'In any case, I understand that you're getting married early next year so it will hardly matter, will it?'

Kathy reeled with shock at her words. 'You mean I'll be expected to leave when I get married?'

'Well, er...' Miss Murphy blustered, 'I thought that's what you would want to be doing. And surely you'll be wanting to start a family soon after?'

'No, I will not – not that it's anything to do with the job I'm doing. And provided I'm allowed to, I shall keep on working. My fiancé is only on a low wage and we will need my salary to supplement our income, at least for the time being.'

Miss Murphy seemed to collect her own senses. 'Of course things have changed since I was your age. Then, if I had married, I would have been forced to leave work.' Kathy caught a note of wistfulness in her voice and wondered if she'd had a fiancé or boyfriend killed in the war. 'Now, the attitude has relaxed a little although I believe some companies, particularly the banks, do enforce the rule more than others. As far as this newspaper is concerned, there is no reason why you may not continue working after you marry though should you fall pregnant, then you will be expected to leave.'

'Then I shall just have to make sure I don't fall pregnant, won't I? At least I have some control over that.' Kathy rose, noting with some satisfaction, the shocked look on the older woman's face. 'Thank you for your time, Miss Murphy.'

CHAPTER 9

Although the Clean Air Act of 1956 was beginning to have an effect on the previously evil-smelling sulphurous fumes emanating from the Works, a faint whiff still hung around Horwich if the wind was in a certain direction. As it was on the gloriously sunny but cold December day when Joyce and Dave decided to go for a walk 'up Rivi.' This affectionate term roughly described the area around Rivington village though it was officially called Lever Park. Going for a walk 'up Rivi' was a favourite pastime for the people of Horwich and surrounding areas for families pushing prams, serious walkers wearing heavy walking boots, older couples out for a Sunday drive and, of course, gangs of lads and lasses eyeing each other up. Seeing them now, Joyce felt older than her nineteen years. So much had happened since she'd been like them, a carefree young lass. She recalled one such time when, with her friend Sheila, she'd seen Dave with a pretty blonde girl and had confronted him, only to find out that the girl had been Dave's American cousin come over for a family funeral. Remembering the incident with a smile she realised that she hadn't seen Sheila for some time and resolved to get in touch soon. The last she'd heard, Sheila was courting a lad called Mike from Chorley, whom she'd met at the Tudor Ballroom.

Though they were well wrapped-up and had kept up a steady walking pace, by the time they'd reached the Great Barn, Joyce's face, fingers and toes were tingling. As if reading her thoughts, Dave turned to her and said, 'I don't know about you, love, but I'm bloody frozen. Do you fancy a hot drink in the Barn?' She noticed that his nose was red and suspected hers would be too.

Almost too cold to speak, she nodded, and they made their way into the 14th century Tithe Barn that had served the people of Horwich for generations. Although there was the odd paraffin heater dotted about in a vain attempt to heat the cavernous space, it really wasn't much warmer than outside but the urn steaming gently on the serving counter and the cups and saucers lined up looked welcoming enough. Minutes later, with her cold hands wrapped round a cup of tea, she was feeling much more comfortable.

'Even though Horwich is a dirty smelly industrial town, it always amazes me that we have such a building like this on our doorstep,' Dave said now, indicating the ancient cruck beams above their heads.

'Not to mention Rivington Hall Barn,' she replied. The Hall Barn, situated behind a Georgian Manor House, half a mile or so up the road, was a venue for dances on a Saturday night with people coming from miles around in buses laid on specially.

Like the Great Barn, it opened its doors to passing visitors on a Sunday, serving teas, coffees and snacks.

'Do you know, I haven't been to the Barn since I used to go to the dance there with your Nick and the other lads,' Dave said. 'Odd to think you and I have never been to together.'

'Well, to begin with, we were meeting in secret,' she reminded him.

'Then it all blew up around us when Jud ...' he stopped, as if unable to carry on.

She put her cup down on the scarred table and, sensing his distress, placed her hand over his. 'It isn't important, Dave.'

'Not been much a life for you though, has it?' he continued. 'For the last couple of years, our lives seem to have been dominated first of all by my recovery, then by this latest news.'

'The diagnosis you mean?'

'Yes, this bloody epilepsy,' he groaned. 'On the face of it, I seem to be coping OK, but it's always there, hanging over my head.' He tapped the side of his head three times.

'You haven't had any more fits though, have you?' She couldn't help worrying that if he had, he wouldn't tell her in order to spare her.

'Not since the one at the Picture House, no. So far, these Zarontin tablets I'm taking seem to be working but ...' He stopped, as if unsure how to continue.

'But what, love?' she prompted him.

'What the tablets won't cure is the feeling of

being less of a man.'

She couldn't help it, she giggled, thinking of their many necking sessions when they were hard-pressed to keep their desires in check. 'I haven't noticed.'

'Hussy!' Instantly guessing her meaning, he grinned at her. 'Seriously though, I hate this feeling of not being normal. In company, I want to shrink into myself for fear of being ostracized. People are so damned judgemental. Remember that woman at the Picture House? Said I should be locked up.'

Joyce was horrified. 'I didn't realise you'd heard her.'

'Oh, I did, but only vaguely, as at a distance.'

'I could have slapped her. What a thing to say?' Even now, she felt a spurt of anger at the woman's conduct.

'But that's it, isn't it? Ignorance – and left-over attitudes from the days when people like me were locked away.' He fell silent, a bleak look on his face before saying hesitantly, 'Look, Joyce, I know I've said this before but if you want to call it off between us, I will understand.'

She looked at him as if he'd lost his mind. 'Why would I want to do that?'

'Because ... well, I've been told I'll always be like this ...that there's no cure ...,' he said, stumbling over his words, '... and in that case, what sort of future do we have? Uncertain at best. I can't ask you to share that.'

She stared at him aghast. 'Dave Yates, I've loved

you since I were barely sixteen and nowt's happened to change that. The only time our future were in doubt was when you couldn't remember us being together after the accident.'

'Aye, I remember wondering what the heck my best mate's sister were doing there when I came to,' he said, with a cheeky grin on his face. 'Seriously though, love, do you really believe we can hack it? Together?'

'I don't see why not.' She was uncertain where this conversation was going.

He leaned across the table to her, his eyes full of the love he felt for her, taking both her hands in his. 'In that case, will you marry me?'

She realised, in that moment, that he'd been building up to this, working out how she really did feel about him and her heart pounded in her chest. 'Of course I'll marry you.'

He gave a shout of joy, to the surprise of their near-neighbours, a young family, and half-rising in his seat, reached over to kiss her. Then he sobered. 'You are sure? Even with all the problems?'

She laughed. 'Just what will it take to convince you?'

He didn't hesitate before saying, 'Come with me to Bolton to buy an engagement ring. I've been saving up for one for ages.'

'As long as it's from Preston's,' she said. That was by way of being a joke, since almost everyone bought their engagement and wedding rings from the iconic jewellers, Preston's of Bolton, with their distinctive corner shop, dominated by an impressive clock tower, often a meeting point before going on to a cinema.

They talked away the rest of the afternoon, discussing plans, some of them crazy, some of them practical. They decided not to tell Joyce's parents or Dave's mother but to surprise them by showing up with Joyce wearing an engagement ring at some point. She was glad that they didn't belong to the kind of society where Dave would have had to ask her Dad for her hand in marriage. Neither her father nor Dave would have been able to handle that without collapsing into laughter. They knew they'd not be able to marry for a good while yet as they'd need to save up, as Nick and Kathy had been doing, but it was good, after all the uncertainty of the last couple of years, to know that they would have a future together.

The excitement and anticipation lasted most of the following week, Joyce hugging the precious secret close to her both at work and at home. Then, on Thursday evening, as she was leaving work, Dave was waiting for her in his usual place outside the mill gates. As soon as she saw him, she knew there was something wrong. He had a stricken look on his face and his eyes were haunted.

Ignoring the curious looks from the millworkers were giving them, she ran up to him and tugged at his arm. 'Dave! What's up? Have you had another fit? Been sacked?'

He pulled her into his arms, holding her fiercely, regardless of the bystanders. 'Worse, much worse,' he groaned.

'Tell me, what is it?'

'We won't be able to get married. Epileptics aren't allowed to get married.'

With the starkness of those words, her breath went, her knees began to buckle and, had Dave not been hold of her, she would have fallen. 'What? Say that again?'

'It's apparently against the law for epileptics to marry.' His voice was harsh as if he was finding it hard to say the actual words.

'That's barbaric,' she gasped, trying to take in deep breaths to control the racing of her heart. 'What law? Who told you?'

'One of the senior draughtsman ... he's never liked me ... takes every opportunity to knock me down,' he said. 'He took particular delight in telling me today.'

Still struggling to take in the news and endeavouring to shed some light on the situation, she said, 'What did he actually say?'

'Came up to me on the pretext of inspecting a drawing I was doing, and said, "I understand you've got a girlfriend. You do know, don't you, that as an epileptic you'll never be able to marry her?" Seeing as I were gobsmacked, he went on, "There's a law forbidding it."'

'What did you do?' she said, knowing from her own reaction, what he must have felt like to hear those words.

'What I wanted to do were smack him in the

mouth. What I did were make my excuses and go to the toilet. Later on, I went to my boss and said I weren't feeling well and could I leave work early. He agreed instantly, happen scared I were on the verge of a fit.' He sighed deeply. 'I've been wandering round the estate ever since, trying to come to terms with the knowledge, waiting for you to come out of work.'

Inside, she was railing against the unfairness of it all, especially as epilepsy was a neurological disease that no-one had any control over. Instead, she said, 'Do we know what the law's called?'

He gave a rueful grimace. 'Hardly the sort of thing that comes up in normal conversation, is it?'

'Then I think we need to try and find out exactly what the law says.'

'That was my first thought but I've no idea how to go about it. Have you?'

'Not a clue but if we can't marry, what about living together?'

He stared at her aghast. 'You can't mean that! It'd break your parents' hearts. Not to mention my mother's.'

'Then we'll move away somewhere, pretend we're married.'

'No!' That single word was so emphatic that several stragglers from the mill turned to look at them and Joyce herself reeled from the coldness of his tone. 'Stop dreaming, Joyce. It's not going to happen. If I can't marry you, I won't settle for less. You deserve better than that.'

'You don't mean that,' she said, at the same

time recognising that he meant every word.

His face had taken on a determined look that she wasn't familiar with. 'I do. I'm not the man I was nor am I ever likely to be. Besides,' he added, 'there's summat else I've not told you. People can actually die from epilepsy, for no apparent reason ... sudden unexplained death, they call it. And, as it happens, it's more common in men.'

Stunned anew by his words, she tried to gather up the arguments that were rattling round her brain. 'I'm willing to take the chance,' she said eventually. 'I'd rather have a few years with you than not at all. Some people don't even get that.'

'No, Joyce. Better that we should finish this now rather than face more heartache in the future ... for either of us. Let me walk away from you now. It's the only way.'

Recalling what he'd said only moments before about feeling less of a man, she could do no other but agree. To keep persisting would only demean him. 'If that's what you want,' she said, though the numbness creeping around her heart told her that it was well on the way to breaking.

'It is.' Though the tone of his voice was firm, she could see that his eyes were welling up with tears. As were her own. 'Goodbye Joyce, love,' he said. 'Try to forget me.'

With that, he walked away with a determined stride, in the general direction of De Havilland's, while she stood watching him. 'That's impossible,' she whispered to his retreating back. 'I'll never forget you as long as I live.'

CHAPTER 10

Sally and Phil were walking up the steep path from Chorley New Road to the Roberts' home on the first day of Phil's Christmas leave. Somewhere up ahead of them on the estate, they could hear a rag and bone man with a horse and cart calling out something undecipherable but which might have been a long-drawn out 'Bo...ones.' 'You're very quiet, love,' Phil said as he swapped their shabby suitcase from one hand to the other. 'What's up?'

'Nowt really ... well, the truth is I still feel a bit uncomfortable whenever we come to stay at your Mam and Dad's,' she said.

'There's no need, not after all this time,' he chided. 'And Mam and Dad always make you welcome.'

She sighed. 'I know they do. Take no notice of me, I know I'm being silly.'

'Besides, we couldn't stay at your house, could we? Your Mam would have another stroke if we were to do that,' he pointed out.

'And can you imagine Jud's reaction if he turned up and you were there,' she said with a slight shudder.

'Aye, that'd be ... interesting,' he said, a grim note in his voice. 'Anyroad, you know our Nick usually stays at Kathy's when we do come. There'd be no room otherwise,' he pointed out. As it was, Sally would be sharing a bed with Joyce in the girls' bedroom, with Lucy on an old army-issue camp bed. Phil would sleep in Derek's bed in the tiny third bedroom with Derek, who reckoned he could sleep on a clothes line, on the floor beside him. But, oh, she would miss going to sleep in Phil's arms.

Phil's Mam was in the kitchen stirring a large pan on the cooker when Phil opened the back door. 'Hello, Mam,' he said. 'By heck, summat smells good.'

His mother whipped round, dropping the wooden spoon in the pan as she did so. 'Oh, I were miles away,' she said, wiping her hands on her overall. 'Come in, both of you, you look frozen to death.'

'Aye, it's cold out there,' Phil said, stowing the suitcase out of the way of anyone tripping over it.

'Hello, Sally, love,' Mary Roberts said. 'Did you have a good journey here?'

'Not bad, thank you,' Sally said, thinking of Kathy's wise words about putting it all behind them and the both of them becoming part of the whole family.

'Well, tea'll be ready shortly. Or do you want a cuppa to warm you up? Danny'll be wanting another one any minute now.'

A cup of tea was just what she needed. 'Yes, please, if it's not too much trouble.'

While Mary bustled about with the kettle, teapot and cups, Phil said, 'What's for tea, Mam? It smells bloody good.'

'It's only mince and chips,' she replied, 'but there's plenty to go round.'

'And mushy peas?' Phil grinned at his mother.

'Of course. What a daft question,' she said, slapping him on the arm with the tea towel she had in her hand.

Phil pretended to wince and rubbed his arm. 'Where is everyone? In the front room?'

'Your Dad and Joyce are. While I think on, don't say owt to our Joyce about Dave.'

'Why's that, Mrs Roberts?' Sally asked. She and Joyce had been friends from the time they'd worked next to each other in the mill and asking about Dave would have been the first thing she would have done.

'They've only gone and finished,' she said, passing them each a mug of tea. 'And before you ask, we don't know why. Joyce is being very tight-lipped about it.' She said this almost in a whisper as they could hear Joyce's voice calling out, 'Is that our Phil and Sally?' as she came towards the kitchen.

When Joyce walked through the door, it was as if some vital spark had gone out of the young woman. She looked to have lost weight, her face was wan and even her usually abundant mop of hair hung limply. Taking one look at their faces, her eyes filled with tears. 'Mam's told you then?' Sally didn't hesitate. She went towards the younger girl and hugged her. 'Please don't say owt,' Joyce whispered into Sally's shoulder as her Dad followed her through the door.

'How do, Phil lad, Sally,' Mr Roberts said, hitching his trousers further up his middle and nodding in their direction. 'Any chance of another brew, Mary, love?'

Mary turned to Sally and, giving her a knowing wink, said, 'What did I tell you?'

Over tea that evening, the atmosphere was a little strained but Sally knew it wasn't down to her presence this time. Everyone was being careful what they said because of Joyce. Even Mr Roberts, not usually known for his tact, was quieter than usual.

As Phil was going for a pint with Nick that evening, Sally took the opportunity to visit her own family. She was particularly interested to see how May's friendship with the coloured lad was progressing. If she was honest, she had mixed feelings about that. Daft really, because she'd never actually met a coloured person. She was worried that if the friendship continued, the couple would face considerable heartache and opposition, not to mention downright hatred. With May being the quietest of the three sisters, did she have the strength of mind to stand firm in the face of such prejudice?

As, she stepped into the hall of her former home, she could hear snoring coming from the front room so she didn't call out. No point in waking Mam. It would only put her in a bad mood and, from what Eileen had said in her letters, they tried to avoid that wherever possible. The door was ajar and as she passed she could see Mam slumped in her armchair in what looked to be an uncomfortable position. She'd probably wake with a crick in her neck but short of waking her up there was nothing she could do. She paused, taking stock of how much her mother had changed even since she'd last seen her. Her hair was thin and straggly, she'd lost her usual ruddiness, and she appeared thinner. The room was stuffy with a faint body smell, as if the windows hadn't been opened for some time, but then Mam had never been a fan of fresh air, complaining she couldn't stand the draughts.

Her mother stirred, snorted, briefly opened her eyes, then slumped even further into her chair. Not sure if she'd been seen, Sally darted into the large kitchen at the rear of the house. Eileen and May, still in their work clothes, were both there, each nursing a mug of tea, while in the doorway of the adjoining scullery, lounged a young man of about Eileen's age in navy blue work overalls, also with a mug in his hand. Eileen, on seeing Sally, put her mug on the adjacent hearth, and jumped up to give her a hug. 'Sally! Now you're here you can meet Ken.'

The young man straightened and came to shake her hand. He was tall, on the lanky side, and she guessed he still had some filling out to do. He wasn't handsome by any means but he had a friendly and open face with warm brown eyes, topped by unruly dark hair. 'How do, Sally,' he said, shaking her hand. Sally liked him immediately. He'd do nicely for Eileen, she thought.

May rose to give her a hug too but Sally noticed that she seemed a little guarded. "Lo, Sal. Want a cuppa? There's some in the pot.'

'That'd be lovely.' She sat down in the chair vacated by May. 'So, how's Mam?'

Eileen pulled a face. 'Much the same, bad-tempered and determined to make life difficult for all of us.'

'Sorry I can't be here more often to help out.'

Eileen shrugged. 'You can't do owt about that. It could as easily be you stuck here.' Sally looked at Eileen keenly. Was she venting her resentment that Sally wasn't around more? But no, Eileen's face was an open book.

Ken planted a kiss on top of Eileen's head and said, 'I'd better be off, love. See you later tonight?'

'You sure you don't mind staying in again?'

'Course not. And, for some reason, your Mam likes me so, if necessary, I can help you with her.'

Eileen gave him a loving look and blew him a kiss as he waved on his way to the back door. 'Mam's really taken to him, Sally. Thinks I could do a lot worse.'

Unlike Phil, whom Mam hated because he was a Roberts, she thought. 'He seems nice. It's going well, then?'

'It's only been a few months but yes, it seems to be.'

May passed a mug of tea to Sally and sat on the shabby pouffe at the side of Eileen, the one that Mam used to rest her feet on while Sally took the chair opposite Eileen. 'What about you, May? Anyone on the horizon?' she said. Eileen had stressed in her letter

112

that she hadn't told May that Sally knew about the West Indian lad. They'd agreed between them to pretend she didn't know.

May blushed and started fiddling with her nails. 'Well, I have met someone but ...'

'But ...?' Sally urged.

If anything, she went a deeper shade of red but, to her credit, she looked Sally straight in the eye and said, 'He's a West Indian lad.'

'Oh, I see,' Sally said, keeping her voice neutral.

'We've only known each other a few weeks, Sal, but we really like each other. Please don't say we mustn't see each other again.'

'May, love, I've no right to say owt like that. It's your life, your choice. But,' she said, 'Mam might not think the same. I take it she doesn't know?' As May shook her head, Sally continued. 'And I daren't think what our Jud'll say about it.' The sisters all fell silent, remembering only too well Jud's bullying ways. 'Do we still not know when he'll be out?'

'No, he's deliberately keeping us guessing,' Eileen said, 'though by my reckoning it should be sometime early next year.'

'So tell me a bit more about this lad – what's his name?' Sally urged.

'Norman. He's not very tall, quite stocky but muscular with it. Ordinary looking but ... he has a lovely smile, twinkly eyes and a laugh that makes you want to laugh with him.'

Sally had to smile at May's enthusiasm. 'He sounds wonderful,' she said. 'What do you think about all this, Eileen?'

'I'm like you, Sally, a bit wary. Especially as ...' she hesitated, then continued in a rush, '... you know what girls who go out with coloured lads are called.'

'Common, cheap tarts,' May flashed back. 'But I hope you know I'm not like that.'

That made them both smile. Small, on the dumpy side, but with a sweet face and trusting eyes, May was far from either description. 'Nobody's implying you are, love,' Eileen reasoned, 'only that you might get called that.'

'I've already experienced the prejudice out there,' May said, with some bitterness in her voice.

Sally looked at her younger sister with concern. 'Why, what happened, love?'

'We were just coming out of the Lido,' she said, naming one of the dozen or so cinemas in Bolton, 'when there were a bit of name-calling from some lads. Nowt too bad, a bit of jostling, broken up easily by the manager. As he ordered them to leave, he said to me, in a kindly sort of way, "What's a nice lass like you doing going out with a n...?"' May couldn't continue, her embarrassment and humiliation showing in the tears filling her eyes and the vivid red suffusing her face.

Sally rose to give the younger girl a hug. 'Oh, May, love, how horrible. What did Norman say?'

'He were upset on my account. He asked me if I wanted us to finish.'

'What did you say?' Eileen asked though Sally guessed they both knew the answer.

'I told him not to be so daft,' she said, a fierce look in her eyes

From the front room came a low moan then a querulous voice calling, 'Eileen, are you there?'

Seeing the look of dismay on Eileen's face, Sally said, 'I'll go. I'd have had to have had a word with her anyway.'

In the front room, her mother was weeping, sobs tearing from her throat. From the spreading stain on the bottom half of her clothes to the fresh smell of hot urine, Sally knew what had happened. From her mother's distress, it was obvious that she hadn't done it deliberately and Sally knew instant pity.

Her mother registered that it was Sally and said, through sobs, 'Sal? What you doing here?'

'I've come to see you and the girls, Mam.'

'Don't shout at me, will you? I didn't mean to do it. I knew I wanted to wee but I must have fallen asleep before I could shout out.'

Sally couldn't help feeling sorry for her and leaned down to give her a hug. 'Don't worry, Mam. We'll soon get you washed and changed,' she said. 'Might as well put your nightie and dressing gown on at this time of night.' As she and Eileen did what was necessary, Sally came to realise that the pathetic woman before her was only a shadow of her former belligerent self and her heart was saddened.

* * *

The following night, lying in the bed she was sharing with Joyce, Sally was finding it difficult to fall asleep. It hadn't been a problem last night as she'd been tired after the long journey and seeing her family. Tonight though, with it being Christmas Eve, they'd all stayed up late playing cards and chatting, and her head was buzzing. She thought Joyce had dropped off some time ago and was surprised when her voice came out of the gloom. 'You asleep, Sally?'

'No, I can't sleep. You the same?' she whispered back.

'I'm not sleeping much at the moment anyroad,' came the reply. 'If I tell you the reason me and Dave split up, will you keep it a secret?' There was so much heartache in the younger girl's voice that Sally groped for her hand under the covers.

'Course. But are you sure you want to tell me?'

'I can't tell anyone else – not yet anyway'

Sally raised herself on one elbow and looked down at Joyce, barely visible in the semi-darkness of the room. 'You're not pregnant, are you?' It seemed sad that it was always this possibility that sprung to the front of everyone's mind in these circumstances.

'No, nowt like that. A couple of weeks ago, Dave asked me to marry him. We'd planned to go and buy a ring then surprise everyone at Christmas.'

'What's happened since then to cause things to change?'

Joyce let out a deep sigh that was almost a sob. 'Someone told Dave that epileptics weren't allowed to marry.'

Sally had thought that May would face difficulties if she continued her relationship with the coloured lad, but Joyce's news was disastrous. 'Oh, no! Is it true?'

'I don't know. I've been to the library to try and find out but I can find nowt written down. Perhaps Dave's consultant at the hospital might know but now that his medication seems to have stabilised his fits, he doesn't have to go again for another few months or so. In any case,' she continued, her voice thick with unshed tears, 'Dave can't see the point in us carrying on. He thinks it's better for us to part now rather than later. He said that I should forget about him and find someone else. As if I could!'

'Oh, love, that's terrible. Is there any chance he'd change his mind?'

'Possibly, but only if we can find a loophole in the law or summat.'

It all seemed so unfair when the young couple were so obviously in love. Sally's brain went into overdrive. How could they find out? Then, into her head popped a name. Reverend Marchant, the chaplain of the Mother and Baby Home she'd been in. As an Anglican minister, surely he'd know who could and who couldn't marry. But how could she mention him to Joyce without explaining how she knew him and she couldn't do that without giving away the fact that she'd actually given birth to Nick's baby? She'd have to go over to see the man but maybe she could combine it with a long-overdue visit to Betty and Bob

Parrott, her former employers and dear friends. 'I do know someone who might be able to tell me but it might be a month or so before I can find out. Are you OK leaving it with me for a bit?'

Joyce leaned over to give Sally a quick hug. 'I could wait a lot longer than a month if it meant that we could go ahead.'

Joyce dropped off to sleep soon after but Sally lay awake much longer, her mind busier than ever, with both May's and Joyce's problems and the sad decline of her mother.

CHAPTER 11

The evening before Christmas Eve, Kathy and her mother were watching the quiz show 'What's My Line?' on the television when the telephone rang. 'You go, love,' Vera said, not moving her eyes from the screen where the panellists were trying to guess the occupation being mimed by one of the contestants. 'It'll probably be for you anyway.'

In the small space at the bottom of the stairs that passed for a hall, Kathy picked up the phone and said, 'Horwich 626.'

'Is that Mrs Armstrong?' came a woman's disembodied voice.

'No, it's her daughter, Kathy. Can I help you?'

'It's Cissy Parker, a neighbour of Mrs Drummond, your mother's sister. She's asked me to give your mother a call.' The woman on the other end sounded agitated and Kathy could hear shrieks of childish laughter in the background.

'Hold on please, I'll just get her for you.'

Back in the sitting room, Kathy said, 'It's Auntie Liz's neighbour, Cissy Parker.' Auntie Liz was Vera's elder widowed sister whose only son lived down south somewhere. 'She wants to speak to you.'

Vera rose at once. 'Oh, dear, that sounds like bad news. I hope she's alright.' She came back some minutes later, a troubled look on her face. 'Our Lizzie's had a nasty fall outside, no bones broken fortunately. She's badly bruised and shaken up and wonders if I can go over to give her a hand. Cissy said she'd have helped out under normal circumstances but she's got family staying and wouldn't be able to do much more than pop in occasionally.'

That explained the childish laughter in the background. 'Why hasn't she gone to stay with Barry this year?' Kathy asked though she guessed the answer before her mother answered. Her cousin Barry had put on considerable airs and graces since he'd married the boss's daughter and rarely seemed to put himself out for his mother.

'Apparently, he and his wife have a lot of social events planned and didn't feel able to invite her this year.'

'Typical!' Kathy said. 'Does that mean you're going to have to go and stay with her over Christmas?' Kathy said.

Vera plumped down in her chair. 'Looks that way but I'm not happy about leaving you on your own over Christmas. Why don't you and Nick come with me?'

Kathy's heart dropped. She'd been so looking forward to spending more time with Nick over Christmas even had her mother been there. She thought carefully before answering. 'Sorry, Mum, but that won't work, it wouldn't be fair on Nick. Or me, come to that.'

Vera gave a resigned sigh. 'I suppose so. It's, well …' she hesitated then said in a rush, her voice betraying her fears without the need to spell it out, '… the two of you will be on your own for a few days.'

'Mum, I'm 23 years old and old enough to look after myself. Besides Nick and I are getting married in a few months' time.' Seeing her mother juggling with her concern for her sister and her worries about the two of them being alone, she continued, 'If you're concerned about us sleeping together, don't be. Nick's going to be sleeping down here on the sofa, mine's only a single bed and there's no way I'd sleep with him in your bed.'

Vera looked faintly shocked at the thought. 'I should think not. Though I do realise that things have changed a lot since your Dad and I were courting,' she added.'

Kathy smiled remembering that her Dad had once hinted that her Mum hadn't always been so straight-laced. 'Look, I'm only working tomorrow morning. Why don't I take you over to Cheshire in the afternoon? It'll be a lot easier for you than catching buses and trains, especially as the timetables may be different with it being Christmas Eve.'

Her mother's face cleared. 'That would be lovely if you're sure you don't mind. I must admit I wasn't looking forward to the tedious journey.'

'Mum, that's what Dad suggested I learn to drive for, so's I could run you about when you needed me to.' They both fell silent thinking of dear, dependable Ron Armstrong, who'd died of lung cancer two years ago. Although Kathy and her Mum got along better these days, Kathy in particular missed him for his soothing intervention in the arguments she and her mother still had occasionally.

The following day, before she left Horwich to take her mother to Cheshire where her Auntie Liz lived, she'd managed to ring Nick at the garage to tell him what was happening and that she'd leave a spare key under the old brass posser stick that lived outside the back door. 'She's actually leaving us on our own together for a couple of days?' Nick had said, a hint of laughter in his voice.

'I know. Amazing, isn't it?' She'd heard the closing of her mother's wardrobe door followed by a click as she closed the small suitcase she was taking with her. 'Look, I can't linger. Mum'll be coming down in a minute ...'

'... And you can't say owt because she can hear you.' The laughter was quite definitely in his voice now.

'Bye, love,' she'd said as her mother came downstairs, suitcase in hand.

Because of heavy traffic around the outskirts of Manchester, Kathy was late getting back to Horwich after dropping her mother off. When she opened the door to the sitting room, she could see that Nick, his hair rumpled and his shirt half hanging out of his trousers, had nodded off on the sofa. Asleep, he looked just like the young lad she'd had a crush on at

St Catherine's Youth Club all those years ago. So much had happened since then but he was the one she knew she wanted to spend the rest of her life with. He was the other half of herself, her soulmate. Lost in her thoughts, she hadn't realised that he was awake until he said, 'What's that look for, love?'

'I was just thinking how much I love you.'

'Is that all? I'd hoped you were thinking of what we can have for tea.'

Laughing, she pulled her scarf off her neck and made to throw it at him over the back of the sofa but before she could let go of it, he'd grabbed the other end and pulled her over the back of the sofa and on top of him. Her weight on top of his over-balanced them both and they fell onto the floor, laughing helplessly, limbs entangling. 'You're mad, Nick Roberts,' she said, trying to free herself but finding that her coat was trapped under his body.

'Mad maybe, but not daft. I knew what I were doing,' he said and kissed her. Perhaps fuelled by the knowledge that they were completely alone, with no chance of being disturbed, passion flared between them. Long moments passed as they kissed and kissed again. Eventually, Nick said, in a shaky voice, 'Kathy, love, maybe this isn't such a good idea.'

She looked down at him puzzled. 'What do you mean?'

'Being alone over the next couple of days. Maybe I should go back home, flop down on the sofa or summat.'

'You'll do no such thing. We get so little time

alone together, let's make the most of it.'

He groaned. 'Knowing we're going to be on our own, I don't honestly know if I can restrain myself.'

She'd been thinking about this over the past 24 hours and took a deep breath before saying. 'What if I said maybe we shouldn't?'

'Not sure what you're getting at, Kathy.'

She tried to make herself look serious but guessed that she'd failed. 'I told Mum that we wouldn't sleep in her bed and my bed's too small but that doesn't mean that ...'

He stopped her words with another kiss before saying, 'Are you trying to lead me astray?'

'No, merely that ...' She was interrupted by the front doorbell ringing. 'Oh, hell! Who's that?'

'You'd better go and find out.' He pulled her up and wriggled back on to the sofa, adjusting himself as he did so. 'Better straighten your blouse, love. It's come adrift from your skirt.'

Giggling, she shrugged off her coat and hung it on the old-fashioned coat-stand in the hall. The caller was their notoriously nosy neighbour, Mrs Westbury, from over the road. 'Hello, love, your Mam get off all right, did she?' she said brightly. 'She asked me to call to see if you're all right.'

Kathy didn't open the door any wider than necessary. Any encouragement on her part and Mrs Westbury would be in the house like a shot. 'I'm fine, thanks. I've not been back long from dropping her off.'

'Your young man here, is he?'

'Yes, we're just about to have some fish and

chips for our tea.' She didn't really know if they were, they hadn't discussed it, but it was the first thing that came into her head.

'I'll let you get on, then, but just let me know if you need anything.'

'I'm sure we'll be fine, thank you,' she said, as she made to shut the door.

Back in the sitting room, she collapsed against the door frame, laughing. 'That was Mrs Westbury from over the road. Trust Mum to ask her to keep an eye on me.'

Feigning a look of devastation, he said, 'Is she likely to pop over again?'

She went to sit on the arm of the sofa. 'Afraid so. And she'll probably do it at the most unexpected times. Trying to catch us out.'

'Then we'll just have to behave ourselves.' He pulled himself upright, straightened his shoulders and sat with his hands demurely folded on his lap.

'On the other hand,' she said, 'she's hardly likely to come across with her rollers in and in her nightie and dressing gown, is she?'

He grasped her meaning immediately. 'What time does the old bat go to bed?'

'About half-ten, I think,' she said, trying not to laugh.

'Then we'll just have to take advantage of her early nights, shan't we?' he said, pulling her onto the sofa with him. All thoughts of something to eat were banished from their minds for some considerable time.

* * *

Normally, the Newsroom of the Bolton Evening News was a hive of activity with people coming and going and telephones ringing. Today, though, the Newsroom was quiet, the normal buzz of the place missing. Kathy assumed everyone must be out on their morning rounds prior to the deadline. She should have been writing up a review of the pantomime she and Nick had seen at the Grand over the Christmas period. Since the first review she'd done for Matthew Bleakley, she'd done a couple more and both had been published, much to the annoyance, she suspected, of some of her male colleagues. It still rankled that they were being paid so much more than her but at least she had more job satisfaction now. Yet today the words wouldn't come.

Instead, she found her mind wandering back to the wonderful Christmas she and Nick had shared, a foretaste of what she hoped their married life would be like. Every moment had been filled with love and laughter. And yes, they had made love, not once but several times, and it had been every bit as wonderful as she'd imagined. Nick had been a caring and considerate lover and he'd taken her to such dizzying heights as she'd never imagined possible. She was sure she'd never feel the same about that old brown moquette sofa. Their time together might have only been two days but they had made the most of every moment. It was going to be hard over the next few months knowing there would be so little opportunity for them to repeat the experience.

At the other end of the Newsroom, she became conscious that the News Editor was speaking to someone on the phone and from the tone of his voice, she guessed it was urgent. 'How long? Where is it exactly? Right I'll get someone over there right away.' He put the phone down and, looking round the room, saw that Kathy was the only one there, then called her over.

With a surge of excitement, she grabbed her notebook and a handful of pencils and shoving them in her bag, she dashed over to his desk. 'What is it, Eric?'

'There's a fire at the bottom of Bank Street, one of those old warehouse buildings overlooking the River Croal. Get yourself over there and report what's happening.'

Her heart tripped with excitement. This would be the first big job she'd been offered. Then self-doubt hit her. 'Are you sure you want me to cover it?'

He quirked a sardonic eyebrow at her. 'You're a reporter, aren't you? Besides,' he said, waving his arm round the empty room, 'everyone else is out.'

'Thanks, Eric. I'm on my way.'

The top of Bank Street was cordoned off by a police car and in the background she could hear the clanging of the bell as another fire engine from the Fire Station on Marsden Road raced to the scene. Although she couldn't see anything at this stage, a pall of smoke hung over the area. The policeman on duty at the top of the street wouldn't let her through, even though she showed him her Press card but, as he waved the latest fire engine through, she slipped past him and raced after it, a trick she'd learned from a seasoned reporter. She turned to give the policeman a wave which he acknowledged with a shaking of his head and a grin. 'OK then but mind you keep clear,' he shouted after her.

As she approached the bottom of Bank Street, she could see no flames as yet but thick black smoke was pouring out of an unloading hatch on the third floor of the building, a relic from Bolton's industrial boom in the late 1800s. The area was dominated by such old buildings, many of them now looking the worse for wear, as well as a few shops and the odd pub. Several people in work clothes stood on the opposite side of the street, workmen, she guessed, evacuated from the building. Others stood in doorways, all being held in check by the vigilant police. When Kathy approached one of them, to ask if she could get a little nearer saying she'd been sent from the Bolton Evening News, he said, 'Best not, love. Just let the firemen get on with their job, eh?'

Firemen were aiming their hoses at the third floor where the unloading hatch was, when she noticed the first flames appear, not on the third floor as she'd expected, but on the fourth. A couple of the workmen saw the flames too. 'Bloody hell, that's the paint store,' one of them said while his mate dodged the nearest policeman and dashed across to one of the firemen. Whatever he said galvanised the firemen into frenzied activity amid much shouting, although with the roar and crackle of the flames, the noise of the engines and the hiss of water, she couldn't hear what they were saying. One of them waved at the two policemen, indicating that everyone should move further up the street. The small crowd didn't need much urging, they could sense the urgency of the situation and they'd all heard the workmen mention the paint store. There could be a very real risk of an explosion. Kathy hoped everyone who worked in the building had got out safely.

Then, she saw someone she knew walking down the street, Edwards, the senior reporter. He was one of the worst offenders for patronising her and her heart sank. As she'd expected, he spotted her and came over to her. 'You can go back to the office now, Kathy. I'll take over from here.'

'But Eric specifically sent me as everyone else was out on other jobs,' she pointed out. Even as she said it, she knew she was wasting her breath. This was only one of the ways her role was undermined.

'Well now I'm back, he's asked me to take over.' With that, he turned his back on her and started quizzing the policemen, scribbling in his notebook as he did so and, she saw, getting more response than she'd had.

Kathy, having no way of knowing whether Eric had actually said that, gritted her teeth at having yet another opportunity snatched away from her and was determined that she wasn't going to go quietly.

Shoving her notebook back in her bag, she began to walk back up towards Deansgate as if she really was leaving but stopped in an empty shop doorway further up Bank Street, from where she had a clear view of the proceedings. Taking out her notebook again, she began to jot down her impressions of the scene, the measured movements of the firemen, the shouting, the gesticulating, the haphazard tangling of the hosepipes in front of the building, the awed reactions of the small crowd on the opposite side of the road, the over-powering smell of burning and a whiff of some chemical or other. On sure ground with this kind of writing, her pencil flew over the page. Then, there was a deafening bang, making her wince, and the windows on the third and fourth floors bulged outwards, showering firemen, policemen and, to a lesser extent, the watching crowd with glass and debris. Fortunately, most of them were wearing flat caps and escaped injury. Even Edwards was wearing a trilby. She was glad she'd moved now. With nothing on her head, she would have been much more vulnerable.

It was only when the sky started to darken that she realised that she'd been there for what seemed like hours. Her legs were stiff with standing and she was desperate for the toilet. For most of that time she'd been writing down the scene as she interpreted it and she'd filled many pages of her notebook. Whether she'd ever be able to use any of it, she didn't know. In any case, the scene was quietening down now. One of the fire engines had been stood down and the fire seemed to be well on the way to being under control. It was only when she made a move that she realised how cold she was. But she had a deep satisfaction, knowing that what she'd written had the making of a good article, more of a feature, she thought. If Eric didn't want to use it, she'd maybe have a word with Matthew Bleakley.

As she packed her notebook away in her handbag, she became aware that there was renewed shouting and gesticulating from the firemen and a couple of them ran into the smouldering building. She looked around to see if Edwards was still there but realised he must have disappeared some time since, probably to file his news report, which meant that she was the only reporter still on the scene. Ignoring her urgent need for the toilet, she knew she had to stay where she was to report on this latest development, whatever it was. In the distance, she heard the clanging of another bell, an ambulance this time, she thought. Sure enough, an ambulance careered round the corner from Deansgate and raced down to the front of the building. Such was the urgency surrounding the firemen now that she was able to get closer to the scene, closer even than she'd been before.

From the disjointed speech of the firemen, who'd been joined by a couple of policeman, she gathered that they'd realised that two of the fireman hadn't made it back outside before the explosion, the reason for their colleagues rushing back inside the building. At that point, they staggered out, each carrying a colleague over this shoulder. Even from this distance, she could see that the injured firemen's uniforms were blackened and smouldering and her body went even colder. Surely they weren't dead? The ambulance attendants bent over them and, for the moment, she could see no more. Then one of the attendants lifted his head and shook it. From that, she had to conclude that the poor man was dead and she had to gulp a sudden nausea back down her throat. From the gestures she could see, it would appear that the second one was still alive and, with the urgency that the ambulance men were seeing to him, gathered that he was at the least, seriously injured.

It was at that point that one of the policemen came over to her. 'You shouldn't be here, love. It's not a pretty sight.'

'I've been authorised to come from the Bolton Evening News,' she said. 'I'm a reporter.'

'That's as may be, miss, but it's still time you got out of the way so that cleaning up operations can get under way.'

'Am I right in thinking one of the firemen is dead and one badly injured?' she ventured.

He gave her a reproving look. 'You know I can't confirm that one way or another.'

She gave him what she hoped was a warm smile. 'I thought not but thanks anyway.' She knew that whatever she'd seen latterly would have to be worded speculatively. 'It is thought that there were some casualties etc...' but she was sure Eric would sort that out. If he even used it.

As she made her way up the street, she couldn't

help smiling. Edwards would be furious that he'd missed this. Then she caught herself. What was she thinking? This was the lives of two people, one possibly dead, one seriously injured, and their families. Her attitude of moments before smacked of cynicism, prevalent among many of her world weary colleagues, and she'd sworn she'd never let that happen to her. It was in a more introspective mood that she entered the Mealhouse Lane premises housing the Bolton Evening News.

CHAPTER 12

The canteen of the Beehive Mill was, as always at dinnertime, noisy. The sound of 'Worker's Playtime' relayed over loudspeakers was almost drowned out by the tide of chatter and laughter, cutlery scraping against plates, the banging of pans from the kitchen area behind the hatch, the occasional jeer as someone dropped a plate. Joyce had chosen to sit alone, something she often did these days. She had friends among her work-mates but with all that was going on in her life at present, she chose instead to isolate herself from them. Dave was never far from her thoughts. After the revelation that they wouldn't be able to marry and his rejection of her, she'd not seen him. She felt like a part of her, an arm or a leg, not to mention her heart, had been ripped away. Perhaps even more hurtful perhaps was his belief that she'd be better off with someone else. She knew she'd never love anyone else, no matter what he said.

Deep in her thoughts, she didn't see anyone approach until a voice close to her said, 'Joyce?'

Startled, she looked up. In front of her was the slim, blonde-haired Eileen Simcox, Sally's sister.

They'd known each other vaguely with both attending the Senior School though not well as Eileen was slightly older and in the year above her. With Eileen working in another department of the Beehive Mill, they didn't come across each other in the course of their work but since Joyce had been acting as a courier between Sally and her sisters, they'd had a friendly few words over the exchange of letters. 'Hello, Eileen. Got another letter you want me to post on?'

'No, there's no need now. My Mam's had a stroke and doesn't know what's going on half the time so me and our Sally have been corresponding direct,' the other girl said, juggling the tray containing her dinner in her hands.

'Come to think of it, it has been a while since you asked me,' Joyce said. 'Sorry to hear about your Mam though. Has she been much affected?'

'She tends to get confused and she's not too good on her pins but her speech is OK.' Eileen indicated a place at the table. 'Is it all right to join you? Everywhere else seems to be busy.'

Joyce looked around her, noted that the canteen did seem busier than usual. Even the other end of her table was taken by two lads who were leaning over to chat to a couple of lasses on an adjoining table. 'Be my guest,' she said, indicating the chair opposite.

'Thanks,' Eileen said, sitting down and preparing to tackle her sausages and mash. 'My supervisor were having a go at me about summat I'd missed so I were late getting here.'

'You work upstairs in the Warehouse, don't

you?'

'Yes, I'm a Cloth Picker. You know, picking all the bits off the finished towels and checking for quality. It's a boring job but someone has to do it.'

'Weaving's boring too once you've got used to it. Half the time, I find myself day-dreaming to pass the time then end up with a smash,' Joyce said. 'And being on piece work, ruined towels don't count.'

'Round here, there's not a right lot of choice of jobs for women, is there? It's either shop work or going in the mill,' Eileen said, between mouthfuls. 'And that's only supposed to be to fill in time till we get married.' The click of her Eileen's tongue and rolling of her eyes made Joyce smile.

She found herself liking the other girl. She had the same easy-going friendly manner as Sally, whom she'd worked alongside until Sally had taken herself off to Blackpool. 'How come we've not properly got to know each other before, you and I?' she asked now.

Eileen shifted uncomfortably in her seat. 'Well, relations between our two families haven't been close, have they, what with all that to-do with our Sally and your Nick ...' her voice tailed off in embarrassment as she realised what she was saying. 'Then our Jud beating up your boyfriend. How is he, by the way?'

'He's doing ... OK, I think,' she said, careful with her words. Word had not yet got round about Dave's epilepsy, a deliberate decision with so much prejudice about, another reason for her voluntary isolation. And she certainly wasn't telling anyone about them splitting up. 'When's your Jud due for release? Do you know?'

The other girl hesitated a little before replying. 'We reckon it should have been some time around September or October but knowing Jud, he probably got into some sort of bother and had his sentence extended.' She gave a derogatory snort then said, 'All he tells us on the rare occasion when he does write home is that he's due out soon.'

As Eileen was scooping up the last of her sausage and mash, the hooter sounded for them to make their way back to their various places of work and as both girls rose to leave, Eileen said, ' In of spite what's passed between our families, I'd like it if we could be friends, Joyce. What do you reckon?'

Joyce gave her a smile. 'I'd like that too. I've really enjoyed today. It's made the time pass ...' She didn't finish the sentence, not wanting to give away her loneliness.

That lunchtime chat was to set a precedent for an almost daily get-together. With Mrs Simcox no longer capable of running a home and Sally living away, Eileen and her sister May had had to shoulder much of the responsibility for their mother and looking after things at home. Talking to Joyce, she said, was an opportunity to unburden herself. Similarly, with all that was going on in her own life, Joyce felt she no longer had much in common with her workmates. All they seemed to want to talk about was boyfriends, films they'd seen and pop songs they liked, subjects Joyce now found trivial. In Eileen, she felt she had discovered a friend.

As the days passed, both girls found themselves more able to talk about matters close to their heart with the mutual agreement that what was said was simply between the two of them. It seemed natural eventually to tell Eileen about Dave's epilepsy and what it had meant for them. And that Dave had called if off between them rather than either of them suffering more heartache.

Eileen gasped and put her hand to her mouth. 'Not allowed to marry? Oh, no, that's awful. Are you sure?'

'As sure as we can be. When she came at Christmas, your Sally did say she knew someone who might be able to confirm whether that's the case but she hasn't come back to me yet.'

Eileen shook her head in sorrow. 'It doesn't seem fair, does it, to deprive two people of happiness because of an illness?'

Joyce went on to explain about sufferers being locked up in asylums until fairly recently and Eileen was shocked anew. 'I'd no idea such things went on,' she said.

'That's because families tended to keep quiet about their loved ones to avoid them being locked up,' she said, thinking of what Phyllis Yates had said about her brother. 'It just weren't talked about. If anyone said owt at all, they might cover it up by saying that the person were suffering from nerves.'

'Oh, I've heard people say that but I never thought owt about it.'

On another occasion, Eileen told Joyce about her concern for her younger sister, May, going out with a coloured lad and how she'd already experienced racial abuse. 'I haven't met him yet but from what May says he seems a nice lad, well brought up and all that but I can't help worrying about what's to become of her if the relationship continues. You know what people say about girls who go out with coloured lads.'

'That they're common, no better than they should be,' Joyce agreed. 'But from what you've told me and what Sally's said in the past, your May's not a bit like that. Oh, why can't people just live and let live?' she said, with some bitterness, her own situation never far from her mind.

'We all know there's been a lot of West Indians – and Indians come to that – coming into the country since the war, but legally they're British citizens and have a right to come here and work.' With a glance at the clock, Eileen gathered their empty plates together and put them on a tray. 'But I think part of the problem is that white people resent them, as they see it, taking their jobs.'

'You're right,' Joyce agreed. 'It's mistrust of change, I think, particularly among the older generation who remember what Britain were like before the war.'

'But even then, it weren't all roses, were it? You only have to think of the Depression, the General Strike, the Jarrow March.' Their discussion ended, as it usually did, when the hooter went for them to go back to work.

A couple of weeks later, Eileen appeared at what they had come to think of as their table looking a bit peaky. 'Is summat up, love?' Joyce asked.

'I'm OK, thanks,' Eileen said in a low voice and concentrated on the plate of shepherd's pie in front of her. Then, abruptly her knife and fork clattered to her plate, and when she looked up, Joyce could see tears in the other girl's eyes.

'It's not your Mam, is it?' Joyce said, concerned. 'Is she worse?'

'No, she's just the same but ...' Eileen's voice broke then she whispered, 'Oh, Joyce, I think I might be pregnant.'

Joyce reached across and touched her friend's hand. 'Oh, love, I am sorry. How late are you?'

'A week now. And I'm hardly ever late, possibly a day or two, but never a week.'

'How does Ken feel about it?' By now, Joyce knew that even though they hadn't been going out for long, Eileen and her boyfriend were serious about each other.

'He's as devastated as I am. He thought he'd been so careful. But it couldn't have come at a worse time, with all that's going on with our May and having to look after Mam.'

'Not to mention your Jud coming back home at some point,' Joyce reminded her.

She shuddered. 'He'll go mad. And look how he and his mates beat your Nick up when Sally fell pregnant. I don't want that happening to Ken.'

'Is there any chance of the two of you getting married?'

Eileen nibbled at her lower lip. 'I don't think that'd be a problem but the trouble is that Ken's still an apprentice at the Works and won't be on full money for at least another year. If I had to pack in work, I don't know how we'd manage.'

'Try not to worry about it at this stage, love. It might just be a false alarm,' Joyce said, though even she thought the situation wasn't looking good for the couple.

A month later, Eileen still hadn't started her period and it became obvious that she and Ken would have start making plans soon. Any action they might have taken though, was pre-empted when, one Monday dinner-time, Eileen came looking for her in the canteen not even stopping to pick up her dinner. Across her cheek-bone was a vivid red weal. 'Eileen, love, what's happened?'

Eileen sat down heavily. 'Jud's back.'

'He did that?' Joyce asked, pointing to the mark on her face. 'What for?'

'I stood up to him when he accused me of neglecting Mam. I weren't having that. The old besom is hard work but I would never neglect her. She's me Mam.' She sighed. 'Our May stood up to him, too. Told him straight that if he started knocking us about like me Dad did with our Sally and him, we'd leave home. Not that we could. Who'd look after Mam?'

'You haven't told him about the baby, have you?'

'Oh, Joyce, I daren't. He'll go mad. Nor have we mentioned May's chap.'

They both fell silent, in agreement as to what Jud was capable off. 'Did he give you any warning he were coming?' Joyce said eventually.

'Not a word. Just turned up out of the blue. Came strolling into the kitchen over the weekend as if he'd just gone down to the shop for a packet of fags, instead of being away for over two years. Full of himself, as usual,' Eileen said bitterly.

'Oh, love, I'm so sorry. What'll you do?'

'There's nowt we can do. Except ride out the storm when it comes. Which it will.'

'If there's owt I can do, you know I will. In the meantime, go and get yourself summat to eat. You need to keep your strength up, what with the baby and everything.' Though she tried to reassure Eileen, Joyce was concerned herself. Jud Simcox's reappearance in Horwich was bad news for everyone concerned.

CHAPTER 13

Stepping from the train at Blackpool Central Station brought back so many memories for Sally, of the time she'd fled to the seaside town at the back end of 1956, alone, pregnant, with no job in the offing and no place to stay. It had been Phil who'd come to her rescue after she'd fallen in the station concourse. Phil who, seeing how shaken she was, had taken her for a cup of tea. In the café, she had recognised, with a sinking heart, that her rescuer was Nick's younger brother and, panicking, she'd fled. Later, she'd managed to get herself a job as a chambermaid at the Moncrieff, a large hotel on the Promenade. Until, following an unwelcome visit from Jud, she'd been forced to flee again, only to bump into Phil and his two RAF mates. He'd introduced her to Betty and Bob Parrott who'd taken her on to help out in their boarding house on Central Drive. Once the secret of her pregnancy had come to light, Betty and Bob had become surrogate parents and she'd grown to love them dearly. They, and Phil, had helped her through the difficult time after losing her baby. Only looking back did she become aware of what a madcap scheme had it been. It could have gone so disastrously wrong.

The plan was to stay with the Parrotts for a few days, during which time she hoped to get over to Preston to see the Reverend Marchant to quiz him regarding Joyce and Dave's predicament. If anyone would know the truth, she was confident it would be him. On her way back home, she intended to pay a brief visit to Horwich to spend time with her sisters and see her mother. On the day before she'd left, she'd received a letter from Eileen with the unwelcome news that Jud was home and, from all accounts, as full of himself as ever. The news had blighted her anticipation about this trip but she knew she'd have to face him some time. It might as well be now.

At the height of the holiday season, the front door to the Shangri-La boarding house would be, in line with landladies' policy throughout seaside towns, firmly locked against guests until it was teatime. At the end of February and with no guests at the boarding house, Sally had no option but to ring the doorbell, shivering in the icy wind that blew straight off the sea down the length of Central Drive. Betty, when she opened the door, had on what Bob called her landladies' face, business-like and purposeful, but she broke into a smile when she saw who her caller was. 'Sally, love, come on in. You must be frozen.' Inside the hallway, with its small reception area, the tall angular woman pulled Sally into her arms and gave her a hug. 'Oh, it's lovely that you could get time off work to come and visit us.'

'You do know I can only stay a couple of days, don't you?' Sally warned.

'It doesn't matter. Better that than not at all. Come through to the kitchen. Bob's just brewed up.' Still holding on to Sally's arm, she led the way down the familiar hall. 'And there's fruit cake. I've made an extra one too for you to take some back for Phil.'

Betty's fruit cake was legendary. 'He will be pleased. He sends his love, by the way.'

'Oh, bless him. How is he?'

'He's fine, doing well, I think. He seems to be well-thought of among the higher-ups.'

In the warm and welcoming kitchen, always with the smell of something newly baked, a Bob was sitting at the well-worn kitchen table and, as Betty ushered Sally in, he put his newspaper down and rose to give her a hug. Sally couldn't help noticing that Bob was becoming more portly than ever, probably a result of Betty's baking. He always did like a piece of fruit cake or a scone fresh from the oven. 'Sit yourself down, lass, and I'll pour you some tea.' She looked with fondness at the big brown teapot which always dominated the kitchen table, scrubbed almost white. 'Did you have a good journey?'

Sally did a see-saw movement with her hands. 'It was all right, a bit tedious, the usual combination of trains and buses.'

'I've heard talk of one of them there motorways being built right across the Pennines but I don't envy them with that. It's not the most hospitable place up on the tops.' He passed her a cup of tea. 'They'll have to be doing summat soon though, there's that many cars on the road now. There's no fun in driving these days.'

As she busied herself with cutting the fruit-cake, Betty quirked her eyebrows knowingly at Sally who had to smile. Bob had learned to drive at a time when one had to double de-clutch and wrestle with clunky steering and had driven a huge wagon in the war so his driving skills weren't the best in the world. Sally could see that Betty was on the point of saying something, the kind of teasing banter that this couple's marriage seemed to thrive on so, to change the subject, she said, 'Have you heard from your Peter recently?'

Peter was the son that they'd had before they were married and who'd been forcibly taken away from them and adopted but they'd managed to locate him a couple of years before. After some initial tension and difficulty, an easy friendship had developed since and when Peter had married his girlfriend Rosie last year, the Parrotts had proudly been part of the wedding. 'Oh, he's fine. And we're going to be grand-parents! Rosie's pregnant, expecting around the end of July.'

'Oh, that's wonderful news,' Sally said.

'What about you, love?' Concern was etched on Betty's face as she said it. She knew, of all people, how Sally had mourned the loss of her baby and how she yearned for one with Phil.

'No signs yet but there's plenty of time.'

'Did you know that the Queen's had another

baby? Andrew they're calling him,' Bob said now, tapping his newspaper.

'Yes, I saw it on the billboards at the station.'

'How's that smashing young man of yours?' Bob said. 'Doing OK, is he?'

'I think so. With the Cold War, there's always a feeling of tension around the camp which seems to involve a lot of admin so he's kept busy.'

'Is he likely to get posted to Germany or Cyprus, do you reckon?' Bob asked.

'There's always that possibility but not as much as if he was involved in the front line of things, like being ground crew or a pilot.' All the West German air bases were on constant alert in case of attack by the Soviets with at least two aircraft on each base kept at Quick Action Alert. Not that they'd be much use against one of these new IBCMs. Sally shuddered at the thought. It had become a very real threat and everyone lived in fear of it.

As if sensing the worry at the back of all their minds, Betty said, 'How's your Mam, love, since she had that stroke? And your sisters?'

'She's much the same, Betty, a bit forgetful and it doesn't take much to confuse her. Eileen and May are coping much better now they've got into a routine of looking after her. Eileen's courting, a nice lad called Ken and our May's ...' Sally's voice tailed off, unsure how Betty or Bob, being of an older generation, would react if she told them.

'May's what, love?' Betty prompted.

'Well, to be honest, I'm worried about her. She's

taken up with a West Indian lad.'

Betty pursed her lips while Bob shook his head sadly. 'Well, I don't know how you feel about it but in my opinion, it doesn't do to mix with people like that,' Bob said. 'I've nowt against them personally but everyone should stick to their own, don't you think?'

Recognising that they were of a generation who'd probably never come up against a problem like this, Sally said, 'I've mixed feelings about it myself but mainly because of all the prejudice that they'll face if they continue seeing each other.'

'Does she seem keen then?' Betty asked.

'Rightly or wrongly, yes, she does. But ...' she drew in a deep breath '... what our Jud will have to say about it when he finds out, I don't know.'

'Will he need to know?' Betty had learned of Jud's bullying ways, his possessiveness and jealousy, during long chats over the brown teapot and the kitchen table.

'Horwich being what it is, a place where everyone knows everybody else's business, someone's sure to tell him at some point.'

'Is he out of prison yet?'

Sally grimaced. 'He arrived back home a few days ago, Eileen said.'

'So you'll be seeing him then?' Betty asked.

'It has to be faced some time, Betty,' Sally said, with resignation in her voice.

The three of them spent the rest of the evening catching up, easily familiar with each other even after an absence of so long. Sally loved the couple dearly and wished she could see more of them.

The next day, Sally took the two-bus journey to a suburb of Preston to see the Reverend Marchant, a visit she'd arranged in advance by telephone. Fortunately, it wasn't anywhere near Heywood House, the Church of England Mother & Baby Home, where'd she given birth to her baby. Still, the vicarage was adjacent to the church where she and the other inmates of the Home had been expected to attend morning service, walking there two by two and enduring pointed looks and behind-the-hand comments from some of the locals.

It was a harassed-looking Mrs Marchant, with a toddler hanging on to her skirts and a baby in her arms, who answered the door. An older boy was peeping around the edge of a door, clutching a mechanical toy. 'It's Sally, isn't it? Luke said he was expecting you,' she said. 'Would you mind going along to his study, you know where it is, don't you?' She indicated the baby in her arms, wrinkling her nose. 'I need to change this little one's nappy.'

To her knock on the study door, Mr Marchant called, 'Come in.' The tall, spare-framed man with Brylcreemed-hair rose to shake her hand. From the direction of what she assumed was the sitting room, there came the sound of a child crying, and his wife's voice admonishing one of the children. 'Good to see you again, Sally. Excuse the racket. It's a bit of a madhouse here these days. We had another child, did you know?' He waved her over to a chair at the side of his desk.

With the untidy familiarity of the room, she was again transported back to a previous visit. 'I saw that your wife had a baby in her arms.'

'You remember how desperately we wanted children and, because we never thought it was going to happen, had adopted our eldest boy then found out my wife was pregnant herself?' At her nod of assent, he went on, a huge smile on his face. 'Well, as you saw, our prayers have been answered, twice over.'

She shifted a little on her chair and, as if sensing her unease with his talk of prayer, he said, 'Enough of that. What brings you all this way, Sally? What can I do for you?'

'My sister-in-law, Joyce, and her boyfriend were planning to get engaged but he's been told that because he has epilepsy, they won't be allowed to marry. I wondered if you might know if it were true.'

He stroked his chin. 'I can't say that's something I've come across before. There are certain prohibitions in the Book of Common Prayer but they're all to do with consanguinity.' At her blank look, he smiled and said, 'That's to ensure that no close relations marry.' He rose and went over to a bookcase crammed with books, all in higgledy-piggledy fashion, tilting his head sideways to read the spines. He pulled one book from the shelf, scanned the index quickly, shook his head then replaced it, doing the same with several others. Coming back to his desk, he said, 'I thought I might have something to help us, but it appears not. If there is such a prohibition, I suspect it might be buried in an obscure law, perhaps even an outdated one. Can you leave it with me? My brother's a solicitor and he should be able to check for us.'

Thinking of the constantly poor state of their finances and knowing that Joyce and Dave would have no way of meeting any cost either, she said, with apprehension in her voice, 'Would we have to pay him?'

'I shall let him think that I need the answer in the course of my ministry,' he said, his warm brown eyes twinkling. 'After all, who knows when I might actually need such information? I do know that epilepsy sufferers have often suffered unjust treatment in the past. Has your sister-in-law's boyfriend much experience of that?'

She thought for a moment before answering, not knowing if she wanted to reveal that it had been her own brother Jud's thuggish behaviour that had probably brought on Dave's epilepsy. Still, from the time Sally had confessed to Mr Marchant what had happened to her when she was fourteen, he knew what Jud was capable of. Haltingly, she told him what had happened two years before, which the doctors thought might have triggered the epilepsy.

'Oh, my dear, that poor young man!' he said. 'Was he ... your brother ... arrested?'

'Yes, he was convicted of GBH. He's just been released.'

'And how do you feel about that?' he asked, eyebrows raised in query.

'Not good but it has to be faced some time. In fact, on my way home, I'll be calling in to visit them all.'

'Did you go to see him while he was in prison?'

'No, none of us girls did. Mam went a few times but she had a stroke a few months ago and hasn't been since.'

A look of concern passed across his face. 'I'm sorry to hear that. Was it a bad one?'

'Not really but she needs a lot more help these days. It's mostly my two sisters who do that, with me living away.'

'And how is that husband of yours?' He steepled his hands and rested his chin on them. 'And how are you finding life on an air base?'

Once more she explained that they weren't eligible for married quarters or a marriage allowance but that they did go the base for various social events. She ended up making him laugh at some of the more ludicrous elements of being a serviceman's wife as related to her by other servicemen's wives.

After a relaxing couple of days with Betty and Bob, she was back on the long familiar streets of Horwich, wondering what would have happened to her had she not fled to Blackpool. She'd probably still have been working in the mill, possibly married to someone else by now, maybe even with a child. In the past, she'd seen young women of her own age who she'd been at school with, several of them with a couple of kids in tow and almost all looking older than their years. And last time she'd been here, she'd noticed how much Horwich was changing. The old Princes Arcade, once home to Johnny's Cinema and the Fling Dance Club, was derelict and Eileen had said that it was due for demolition to make way for one of the new supermarkets. She wondered how that would affect the Co-op grocers, a few doors higher up, and the remaining smaller grocer shops.

Mary Street West remained unchanged except for the fact that the odd couple of cars were parked on the road now. Once she reached the house, she expected the same dim and dreary exterior but to her surprise, she saw that the net curtains had been washed, the windows were no longer grimy and the doorstep was clean, if not donkey-stoned. Eileen's handiwork, she guessed, with a rush of fondness for her younger sister, touched that even with all the hard work involved in looking after their mother, she'd found the time to do that. In an attempt to overcome the faintly sick feeling, the racing heart, the dread at seeing Jud again, she drew in a deep breath and pushed open the front door. 'It's me, Sally,' she called out.

She could hear raised voices in the kitchen but ignoring that she went into the front room to see her mother, surprised to see her looking a little livelier than last time. 'Oh, it's you. Did you know Jud's home?' her mother said. 'He'll sort you all out now, stop all this nonsense.'

Anxiety curled in Sally's stomach but she kept her voice level as she said, 'What nonsense are you talking about, Mam?'

'You and that Roberts lad for a start, him what's in the RAF.'

'In case you'd forgotten, Mam, Phil and I are

married.' Confusion filled her mother's eyes and again, Sally felt a rush of compassion for her. 'Don't worry about it, Mam. Just get better, will you?'

'Oh, I will now that our Jud's home,' her mother said, an almost girlish tone in her voice.

Sally doubted Jud could look after himself let alone their mother but knew it was no use saying so. Sally walked into the kitchen into the middle of what appeared to have been a full-scale row. Eileen was in one of the shabby armchairs in tears while Jud stood over her, hands on hips, and May cowered in the door leading to the scullery. Her heart sank but in an attempt to sound normal, she said, 'What's going on here?'

When Jud looked up, she realised, with a sense of shock, that she hadn't seen him now for over three years, not since he'd surprised her by searching her out in Blackpool when she'd been working at the Moncrieff Hotel. What youthful looks he'd had, few in the first place because of his acne scars, had gone. He had become leaner, harder in the face and body and his mouth was set in mean lines 'Well, the wanderer returns,' he said.

'Hello to you too, Jud.' She kept her voice deliberately steady, reminding herself that he no longer had any power over her.

'You don't belong here, you're a Roberts now,' he jeered.

'I've a right to see Mam and my sisters. And you now you're here.'

'Well, you're not welcome so you can piss off.'

'Nice to see you're still the same Jud Simcox since you've been in prison,' she said. 'May, love, as you're standing in the scullery doorway, put the kettle on, will you?' Relieved, the younger girl did as she was told. Sally went over to put her arms round Eileen. 'What's up, love?'

'I'll tell you what's up,' Jud snorted. 'She's only gone and got herself in the family way.' That explained the thunderous look on Jud's face.

Eileen clung to her. 'It's true, Sally. I'm expecting.'

'Oh, love, I am sorry. Is it Ken's?'

At Eileen's nod of agreement, Sally said, 'Then you'll have to get married. How far along are you?'

'About two months, I think, though I haven't been to the doctors yet to get it confirmed.'

'She's not getting married. She's needed to stay here and look after me and Mam.' There was no mention of May, she noticed.

She looked over to where he stood. 'Don't be stupid, Jud. As long as Ken's willing, she has no other choice. And, if I know our Eileen, she can still look after everything.'

'I'm not having it, I tell you,' he said, belligerence in his voice and stance.

'Who do you think you are, Jud? You're not our father,' Sally said.

'If I was, I'd have beaten some sense into you all long before now,' he retorted.

She looked him in the eye. 'You tried threatening me with that, remember? And don't think you can intimidate me now by revealing what happened when I was fourteen because it doesn't matter anymore.' She nodded to Eileen who'd risen to stand at the side of her. 'Both Eileen and May know.'

Shock and something that might have been shame flickered across his face for he shrugged and said, 'I'm off out. Don't know when I'll be back so don't wait up for me.'

From the scullery came May's voice. 'Before you go, there's summat else you should know, Jud.' She came to stand in the kitchen doorway. 'I'm going out with a West Indian lad.'

'What?' he bellowed. 'Whoever he is he's not getting his filthy black hands on one of my sisters.'

She came and stood before him, her hands on her hips, a defiant look on her round face. 'His skin might be brown but underneath he's the same as us. He's kind and gentle and treats me like a lady, which is more than you ever do. And if you try to stop me seeing him, I'll run away with him.'

Sally, who'd been expecting a full-blown rant from Jud, was taken aback by the look of surprise on his face at May, of all people, standing up to him. She realised then that by putting up a united front against him, he crumpled, like all bullies.

With a disgusted, 'Huh! We'll see about that,' he said. 'A right lot of cows you all are, letting every Tom, Dick and Harry into your knickers.' Then he was gone, leaving all three girls gazing after him in amazement.

'What's all the shouting about? I hope you're

not picking on our Jud,' came the whiny voice of their mother from the front room. The idea of anyone picking on Jud set the three of them giggling.

'Trust Mam to have the last word,' Sally said.

CHAPTER 14

On a cold March day with the winds whistling down from the West Pennine moors above Horwich, Kathy and Nick were immersed in decorating Mac's flat in readiness for moving in after their wedding. The sound of Elvis Presley's 'It's Now or Never,' coming from Kathy's record player, brought from Travers Street, echoed round the empty rooms.

They'd been coming for some weeks now and only now were their efforts beginning to make a difference. After Mac had moved his own furniture and effects to his new home and the flat was stripped bare, they'd been daunted by the amount of work needing doing to make it habitable. Most of the paint-work had been a dull brown which meant stripping it right down to the bare wood, a painstakingly laborious job which both of them hated. The faded wallpaper had not been replaced since well before the war and, once they'd started stripping it, had found that there were several layers of even older wallpaper underneath. Now though, the walls were stripped down to bare plaster, the woodwork had been painted white throughout and everywhere was looking much brighter, much lighter.

Kathy straightened up, both hands on her lower back, trying to ease the strain she felt there, and looked at the door she'd just finished painting with critical eyes. 'It's starting to feel like our flat rather than Mac's,' she said.

Nick, who'd been lying on the floor while painting the skirting, pushed himself upright and stretched his own aching limbs, his gesture mirroring Kathy's. 'So it should. It's taken long enough.' They'd been coming here a couple of nights a week and most of the weekends throughout the cold weather of January and February and they were both exhausted. 'Just the papering to do now.'

'Can you believe that in just a few weeks we'll be living here?' she said, a tone of wonderment in her voice as she looked round their combined handiwork, proud of what they'd achieved.

Nick rubbed his forehead with paint-smeared fingers leaving a smudge of paint on a lock of hair that had flopped down. 'Buying some of the stuff we needed has helped to make seem more real.'

'Speaking of which, I wonder what time the delivery men will be here.' They were both conscious that the item that would play a most important part of their lives, their new double bed, was due to be delivered today.

Nick massaged the backs of his legs in an attempt to restore circulation. 'Just that it were to be some time this morning.'

Kathy looked at her wrist watch, splattered now with blobs of paint. 'Well, they're going to have to hurry up. It's nearly dinnertime.'

'What about having a break then? I'm starving and I could do with a pee.'

On the way to the flat this morning, they'd queued at Cases for a meat pie and a vanilla slice and even thinking of her teeth sinking into the tasty juices of the pie made Kathy's mouth water. 'Good idea,' she said. 'I'll put the kettle on.'

They'd no sooner settled themselves on the floor, the only place they could sit, to eat their dinner when the doorbell rang followed by an impatient knock and they both laughed. 'Bloody typical!' Nick groaned. 'I'll go and let them in.'

'And I'll put the pies back in the oven for a bit,' she said, wrapping both of them up in newspaper, not just to keep them warm, but to protect them from the accumulated grease and splashes of the oven that she hadn't yet had chance to clean properly.

One of the delivery men turned out to be a well-built young West Indian, a sight that was becoming more frequent on the streets of Bolton but this was the first time she'd seen a one on the streets of Horwich. The other was a burly man probably in his late forties, a cigarette dangling from his mouth, and greasy thinning hair. He shook his head with seeming despair when he saw how narrow the stairs were. He took the cigarette from his mouth and shook his head in Nick's direction. 'We'll never get this lot up these bloody stairs, mate.'

'Well, the bloke who lived here before had a sodding great brass bed with a metal base, so you'll just have to give it a go, won't you?' Nick wasn't taking any nonsense from this older bloke who thought he knew better than Nick.

'Well, we can but try. Come on you, time to shift your lazy black arse,' he said to his companion.

Kathy, standing at the top of the stairs, heard him. 'There's no need for that. He's a man like you, except his skin's a different colour.' Annoyance made her snap.

The young West Indian gave her a wide smile. 'Thank you, Miss, but I can take it. He dunt mean anyt'ing by it. I say same to him ony I call him honky.' His voice had a charming lilt to it that fascinated Kathy.

To her surprise, the older man laughed and clapped his companion on the back. 'So you should, lad, so you should. Give as good as you get. You're learning. Now let's get this bloody bed up these stairs.' And, between them, with much cursing from the older man, they did and left shortly after, a ten bob note in the older man's pocket. 'For a drink between you,' Nick had said though Kathy doubted the West Indian lad would see a drink in front of him, whatever the banter between them.

The bed stood now, both ends and the base, which folded in half, under the bedroom window, the mattress, in a protective plastic covering, against the adjoining wall. Awed, they both looked at it and Nick snaked an arm round her waist. 'Seeing it makes me realise the enormity of what'll be happening to us a few weeks from now.'

'I know. Who'd have thought it a few years ago?' Very much on her mind was the thought that this so very nearly hadn't happened.

Always quick to pick up on her mood, he said, 'You know, much as I regret what happened with Sally, I can only be glad that things worked out the way they have.'

She turned in the circle of his arm. 'How do you feel when you see her now, especially with Phil?'

'Still a bit guilty, if I'm honest. What happened between me and her wasn't my proudest moment but I can't help but be glad that she's found happiness with Phil.'

'I'm glad that you admit to still feeling that way. I might have thought less of you if you'd been able to shrug it off.'

They kissed and clung to each other for some moments longer then reluctantly returned to their rapidly cooling mugs of tea and by now lukewarm meat pies.

After finishing off their dinner, they both returned to their respective painting jobs but although nothing was said, they were both very much aware of the new bed. Deliberately, they'd left it in pieces for the moment, saying that it would be easier to move when they were wall-papering, but the fact that it was there was at the back of their minds. They didn't speak much, instead concentrating on the task in hand.

In the end, Nick threw down his brush making a distinct splodge on the already-painted splattered floorboards. 'It's no sodding use,' he said. 'I can't concentrate thinking about that bloody bed. What about us at least christening the mattress?'

She put her own brush down with a slow deliberate movement. 'What did you have in mind, Nick Roberts?'

'You know very well what's on my mind,' he said, grabbing hold of her hand and pulling her through to the bedroom.

Afterwards, they lay snuggled together on the mattress, now minus its plastic cover, sleepily content. Apart from their paint-splattered overalls, they hadn't bothered to remove their clothing, they'd been too impatient for one thing. Without any heating in the flat until the new Flavel Debonair gas fire they'd bought was fitted and only a faint hint of heat rising from the large gas-powered heater in the workshop, it would have been too cold. With no opportunity to make love since Christmas, their love-making today had been feverish and hurried. 'Sorry it was so quick, love,' Nick said now.

'It doesn't matter, we'll have plenty of opportunity for leisured love-making in another few weeks.' She was convincing herself as much as Nick.

'Stroke of luck me having a rubber johnny with me though.' Ever since the slip-up with Sally, he'd been aware of how easy it was to conceive and, on the few occasions they had made love, he'd worn protective sheaths. 'It was an old one though so hope it did the job.' Kathy hoped so too. The last thing they needed at this late stage in their arrangements was for Kathy to become pregnant. To fall for a baby now would mean Kathy having to leave work and losing her wage.

'It wouldn't have been the end of the world if I'd become pregnant. We'd have managed somehow. Everyone else does,' she pointed out, though she was hoping it wouldn't come to that.

'It's not what we want though is it? With Mac letting us have this flat, we've got the opportunity to get on our feet a bit before thinking about a mortgage,' Nick reasoned. 'With a bit of luck, before that happens, Mac will have finally decided about making me a partner.' This was something Mac had been talking about for some time but so far no firm decision had been made. It had taken him long enough to get around to buying his house.

'Is it time to get moving again?' Kathy said, becoming conscious that the cold was creeping into her bones. 'Get some more work done?'

He sighed. 'Do we have to?'

She laughed. 'The decorating won't finish itself, you know.'

'I bet Anthony Armstrong-Jones isn't having to decorate their new home,' he grumbled. 'You can be sure they'll have employed the best of decorators.'

To widespread surprise, an engagement had been announced between Princess Margaret and the society photographer, Anthony Armstrong-Jones. In fact the wedding was due to take place the week after their own, to much more pomp and ceremony she was sure. And it was to be televised too. 'You're probably right. In fact, I think I remember reading somewhere that his uncle is a wildly successful interior designer. Hardly in the same league as us. So, come on, lazy-bones.' She nudged him into action.

'No rest for the wicked,' he sighed but did as she said.

* * *

Kathy had been bitterly disappointed that the news editor had chosen to go for Edwards' account of the fire in Bank Street a few weeks back, merely adding her words about the loss of the fireman to Edwards' work and giving him the by-line. The more descriptive piece she'd written when Edwards had told her to shove off had not been published at all. She'd even gone behind the news editor's back and approached Matthew Bleakley to see if he might be interested. Perhaps out of loyalty to a long-standing colleague, he'd said that, although it was beautifully written, he didn't have a space for it in any of his columns. She'd been on her way out of his office when he said, 'You know, something atmospheric like this might suit Mary Stott at the Manchester Guardian.'

At the mention of Mary Stott's name, Kathy had felt a surge of excitement. Mrs Stott had long been a heroine to hers for having made her name in journalism at a time when it was extremely rare. She'd been

Women's Editor at the Manchester Guardian for a couple of years or more now and had made the Mainly for Women page very much her own, with vibrant articles that didn't necessarily include the usual 'women's' content of fashion, knitting and cookery. Instead, she covered more controversial subjects in her own forthright style. Better still, she strongly believed in letting the voice of the ordinary woman on the street to be heard by encouraging them to send in their own opinions and, if they were suitable, publishing them.

'Do you think she might interested?' she had asked.

'She might do if you include a little more about your own feelings and impressions rather than straight reporting,' Mr Bleakley said.

'I'll certainly give it a try and thank you. You've always been so supportive and helpful.'

'When you write, mention me and send her my regards,' he added as she opened the door of his office.

She looked at him in surprise. 'Oh, do you know her then?'

He grinned and said, 'Very well. We were reporters together here on the Bolton Evening News.'

Kathy gaped at him. 'I didn't know she'd worked here. When was that then?'

'Let me see. It would have been during the Depression. Probably early 1930s. She was only here a couple of years because there wasn't much doing round Bolton then. It was a grim sort of a place in those days, as it was everywhere. From here, she went to work for the Co-operative Press in Manchester.'

That night Kathy had composed a brief introductory letter, sneakily typed it up the following day when the office hit one of its relatively quiet periods and sent it, with her amended description of the fire, to the Women's Editor at the Manchester Guardian.

Now, today, waiting on her desk was an envelope embossed with the legend 'Manchester Guardian.' She stared at it before opening it with trembling fingers. To her surprise, it was a hand-written note from Mrs Stott herself. 'Dear Miss Armstrong,' it read. 'I was most impressed – and more than a little moved – by the piece you'd written about the recent tragic fire in Bolton and wonder if you could arrange to come and see me some time. Please telephone my editorial assistant, Fiona, on the above telephone number to arrange a mutually convenient time.'

Kathy's excitement rose on reading the letter. Did it sound as though Mary Stott might want to offer her a job? Going to work for the Guardian would mean a longer travelling time, involving not only the bus into Bolton but then a train to Manchester. It wasn't impossible; many people did make the journey into Manchester, only fifteen miles or so from Bolton, to work. But what a boost to her career that would be, working for the prestigious regional daily paper that was the Manchester Guardian. Not to mention it being one in the eye for her male colleagues. Oh, she'd enjoy that!

When, later that day, she told her mother about the letter and the possibilities it might open up for her, Vera bubbled over with excitement. 'Oh, love, just think of it. My daughter going to work for the Manchester Guardian. Your Dad would have been that proud of you.' She seemed to have forgotten that she'd been against the idea of Kathy going into journalism initially.

Clamping down on her own excitement, she thought it would be wise to calm her mother down before she boasted to all her friends and neighbours. 'It's not a foregone conclusion, Mum. Mrs Stott's simply asked me to go and see her.'

'I know that but it does sound promising, doesn't it?'

When she met Nick at the flat later, he didn't seem so enthusiastic. 'I'm pleased for you, of course I am, but surely it'd mean you putting in a lot of extra hours, not to mention travelling time.'

'So, after we're married, it would be ok for you to just 'nip downstairs to finish that job off' but not ok for me to take a chance at the Guardian?' She couldn't help the sharpness creeping into her voice.

He pulled her against his paint-smeared overalls, laughing now. 'You've got a point there but let's not argue about it now, eh? As you said yourself, it might not come to owt.' He tilted her chin upwards and looked into her eyes. 'Whatever happens, love, you'll have my support. You know I've never been one for keeping the little woman at home like some men.'

She travelled to Manchester the following week, her stomach full of dancing butterflies, her mouth so dry she wondered if she'd be able to speak when she finally got to meet the legendary Mary Stott. She'd gone on shopping trips to Manchester many times and knew the city well so finding the imposing Guardian offices in Cross Street was no problem. On being given instructions on how to find Mary Stott's office by a receptionist on the front desk, she made her way up the rather grand staircase to the third floor. There, tucked away down an unimposing corridor, was the office of the Women's Editor.

'Come in,' called a cheerful voice. She entered to be greeted by a woman in late middle-age, tall-ish, slim, with short bobbed greying hair and wearing thick spectacles.

'Mrs Stott? I'm Kathy Armstrong.' Kathy went forward nervously, holding out her hand.

The older woman had a no-nonsense hand-shake. 'Ah, yes, they said you were on your way. But please, call me Mary.' She waved Kathy to a chair near her desk and swung her own seat round to face her visitor. 'So, you know Matthew Bleakley. He's an old chum of mine.'

'Yes, he told me.'

'I gather from your letter you've done work for him from time to time.'

'Yes, I do theatre reviews occasionally and anecdotal stuff for the Town Topics feature.'

'But, I'm guessing, not much in the way of actual reporting,' Mary Stott said, a shrewd look on her face. At Kathy's nod of assent, Mary laughed and said, 'Same old story, eh? Sending you to all the duff jobs while the men get the cream of the crop. Used

Anne L Harvey

to drive me mad too, not being taken seriously. Not mention being paid a higher percentage than women.' The older woman looked at Kathy over the top of her glasses.

'I only found that out recently,' Kathy admitted.

'There's an accepted belief that whatever work a woman does, it is less skilled than a man's, leaving women feeling undervalued. That's one of the reasons I've tried to widen the scope of the women's page at the Guardian, to give women more empowerment.' She went on to describe some of the items she'd covered recently as well as mentioning certain articles she'd included from independent contributors. 'I was very impressed with your observations about the fire,' she went on, 'and you made me feel as if I'd actually been there. But this is an impressionist piece. What happened to the original report?'

Kathy explained that she'd done most of the actual reporting only for it to be taken over by Edwards, who'd got the by-line.

Mrs Stott tutted. 'That's so typical. Well, I'd definitely like to include what you've written soon, if that's ok?'

Excitement washed over Kathy. 'That would be lovely. Thank you.'

'The drawback is that we don't actually pay for such items but you'd get a prominent place and a by-line so it may well be picked up by one of the big newspapers,' the older woman went on.

'I don't mind that. It'd be an honour to be published by the Manchester Guardian,' Kathy was quick to say.

'You're a good writer and deserve to do well, my dear. I don't know if you came here hoping I'd be able to offer you a job but unfortunately I'm not in a position to do so. In fact, apart from my small editorial team, I don't have any journalists working for me at all. However, if I'm asked to send anyone to cover an event, particularly if it's over your way, I'll let you know.' Mrs Stott shuffled some papers she had on her desk together and Kathy guessed that the interview was drawing to a close.

Striving to hide her disappointment that there wasn't a job in the offing, she said, 'Whatever you can offer would be appreciated.'

The paper shuffling paused. 'I've just had a thought. You might like to work on something that highlights the difference in pay between men and women and why you think that's unreasonable given that they're doing the same job. I can see that it rankled with you.' She brandished Kathy's article that she'd obviously been looking for. 'In the meantime, if you write any more pieces like this one, do send them in. I'd grateful for anything I can get my hands on. Now, as you've come all this way, how about a cup of tea?'

Kathy travelled back to Horwich in a daze that afternoon, going over the stimulating and delightful conversation she'd had with Mary Stott again and again. She couldn't wait to get home to the flat to tell Nick. Then it dawned on her, she'd begun to think of the flat as home. Nick would be pleased about that too.

CHAPTER 15

I t had now been some time since Joyce and Dave had broken up, but she was missing him as much if not more than ever. She felt as if she was living in some kind of never-ending dream, one that had no substance. This suspended-from-reality feeling reminded her of the time they'd been forbidden to see each other by their respective families. For weeks then, she'd haunted the streets of Horwich hoping for a glimpse of him and had eventually been rewarded. She'd tried that this time too, hoping to bump into him on the long familiar streets but this time, it was as though he'd vanished. Maybe he was deliberately keeping out of the way.

For this reason, the subject of weddings, either Kathy and Nick's or Eileen's, was something she consciously tried to avoid. Unfortunately, it was all Eileen could talk about during their dinner-time chats. Once Jud had seen sense and withdrawn his opposition, the planning had gone ahead rapidly. Not that Joyce could blame her. Getting married was, after all, a big thing in her life. She was at it again today and Joyce was only half listening when something the other girl had said registered more fully with her. 'Sorry, Eileen, what did you say?'

'I asked if you'd like to come to the wedding. We're not having much of a do, the actual wedding is at St Catherine's, then at Ken's parents' house,' she said, breathless with excitement, 'but I'd love it if you could be there.'

Joyce's heart sank. 'Oh, Eileen, I would love to have come but it'd be impossible with your Jud being there.'

Eileen seemed puzzled. 'Why, what do you mean?'

'You do know the circumstances of him being sent down, don't you?'

'I know it were about the fight between Jud and his mates and your boyfriend.'

'But you don't know the reason behind the fight?'

She shook her head. 'I never took much notice at the time, sorry.'

'Jud had been mithering me for months to go out with him and because I wouldn't, he ...' She stopped, not wanting to tell Eileen that Jud had suggested that he and Dave should share Joyce, a suggestion too far for Dave. '...Picked a fight with Dave. But there were three of them and together, they charged him, he fell and cracked his head open.'

Eileen clapped her hand to her mouth. 'Oh, Joyce, I'm sorry. I didn't know owt like that. Though knowing what our Jud's like, I'm not surprised. And, of course, I do see why you can't come. Shame though,

I'd have loved you to have been there.'

To change the subject, Joyce said, 'Did you manage to sort out what your living arrangements were going to be?'

Her face fell. 'There's no way round it. For the time being, Ken's going to have to carry on living at home. With Mam in the front room, Jud in one bedroom and me and May in the other, there's no room for him to move in with us.'

'Couldn't you go and live with him and his family?'

'He's one of a big family and his oldest brother and wife already are already lodging in their front room so there's no room. Besides,' she said, 'that'd leave our May on her own ...' her face flooded with colour before she hurried on, '... and that wouldn't be fair on May. And I'm still needed to help look after Mam.'

'And it'd be too much to ask Jud to lend a hand.'

She laughed, her blush receding. 'You're joking, right? No, for the moment, we'll just have to put up with the way things are.'

'Not the perfect start for your married life though, is it?'

'I'm sure we'll find a way to be together occasionally.' She arched a knowing eyebrow at Joyce and laughter bubbled in her voice as she said, 'How do you think I got pregnant in the first place?'

* * *

Although it was now mid-March, spring seemed to be as far away as ever and Joyce was glad to get home from work. Even though she'd worn gloves and boots, her fingers and toes were tingling as they thawed out in the welcoming warmth of the front room. With Mam seeing to the tea in the kitchen, her Dad upstairs in the bathroom, Derek doing homework in his bedroom, only Lucy was there, curled up on the sofa reading a book. She willingly made room for Joyce but protested when Joyce put a cold hand to her face. 'Give over, Joyce! You're freezing.'

Joyce removed her hand and laughed. 'What are you reading?'

'Black Beauty. It's ever so sad in parts though.'

'I thought that too but it works out all right for Beauty in the end.'

They heard voices in the kitchen and minutes later, Nick wandered in. 'Bloody hell, it's cowd out there.' He bent to put his hands on either side of Lucy's face and she shrieked in protest. 'Ow, Nick, you're even colder than Joyce!'

'Give us a cuddle then. That'll warm me up.' He made a grab for her, laughing as she tried to wriggle away from him.

He plonked himself in his Dad's chair and thrust his hands towards the fire. 'Where's Dad then?' he asked of no-one in particular.

'Upstairs, I think.' At that moment came the sound of the toilet flushing. 'Sounds like he's been in the loo. Better shift yourself out of his chair,' Joyce pointed out.

'Nah, he won't mind for once.' He was grinning as he said it and Joyce knew he was doing it to wind her up. Danny hated anyone sitting in his chair, especially at the end of the working day. She sniffed. Anyone would think he was the only one who worked. 'Wanting to invite trouble, are you?' she said. 'Talking of trouble, did you know Jud Simcox were out of gaol?'

Nick sat forward, immediately interested. 'How'd you know that? You haven't bumped into him, have you?' There was no love lost between Nick and Jud even though they'd known each other since they were lads.

'I've got quite friendly with Eileen, his and Sally's sister, and she told me a while ago. I must have forgot to mention it before, I can't think why.' She knew why though, she'd too much on her mind, namely missing Dave.

'Has he been causing them any bother?'

'Only the usual, trying to bully everyone.'

Nick snorted. 'I'm surprised he didn't get sorted out by that tough lot in Strangeways.'

'Eileen did say he'd had his sentence extended because of some trouble but she didn't know what and Jud weren't saying.'

'Will you promise to let me know if he causes you any bother?' He gave her a look that said more than words ever could. 'I've a score to settle with him over what he did to Bragger – Dave.'

Joyce looked at her brother warily. Although

his voice was quiet, she knew that he meant every word of it.

From the kitchen came a shout from Mam that tea was ready. Joyce nudged Lucy who was still absorbed in her book and they followed Nick out of the front room. Derek clattered down the stairs closely followed by Danny, tucking his work shirt into his trousers, a copy of the Bolton Evening News under his arm. No wild guess then as to where her Dad had been, on the toilet, reading his paper. As they sat down to a plate of corned beef hash with baked beans, Derek and Lucy jostled each other playfully, secure in their easy-going friendship. It hadn't always been so. When Brian was alive, he and Derek had been more like twins, doing everything together. Brian's death had made a huge hole in Derek's life and for a while he'd been completely lost. It had been the then shy, timid Lucy who'd filled the gap by demanding that her big brother teach her how to play football.

Other than the occasional reminder to Derek from Mam not to wolf his food down and the clatter of cutlery on rapidly emptying plates, there was little sound. It wasn't until the plates had been cleared that conversation started up. 'Give us a fag, Nick, will you? I seem to have left mine upstairs,' Danny said. Joyce, brewing tea in the background, gave wry smile. It was a standard excuse. Her Dad was always cadging cigarettes.

Nick reluctantly shoved the packet of Players Navy Cut over. 'Our Joyce has just told me that Sally's brother, Jud, is out of prison,' Nick said, taking a cigarette for himself.

'It's a wonder he can show his face in Horwich again after what he did to Dave,' Danny harrumphed.

Joyce felt a sudden rush of affection for her lummox of a Dad for sticking up for Dave. From being against their secret relationship, her parents had grown to like Dave and had been as appalled as anyone when he'd developed epilepsy as a result of his injury.

'Don't suppose he'll have any scruples about coming back to Horwich. He'll be swaggering round same as he's always done,' Nick said, lighting both their cigarettes.

'Are you off out tonight, Joyce?' Mam asked as Joyce passed round mugs of tea. 'Only if you're not, I'd like you and Lucy to try on your bridesmaid outfits.' Mam was a dab hand with a sewing machine and had offered to make all the bridesmaid's outfits, much to Kathy's delight.

Fat chance, Joyce thought. As she'd promised herself, she'd made a conscious effort to get in touch with her old mates, Sheila, Brenda and Maureen, but they were all courting seriously themselves now and not much interested in meeting up, reinforcing Joyce's feeling of isolation. 'No, I'm not but what about Carole?' Joyce asked now. Carole was Kathy's best friend and chief bridesmaid who lived somewhere down at the bottom of Brazeley. 'Won't she need to try hers on too?'

'Will you ask Kathy to contact her, Nick? Happen she can come up at the weekend for her fitting,'

Mam said, turning back her attention to the two girls. 'In the meantime, as you're both here, I can be cracking on with yours.'

They'd all gone shopping together to Bolton a few weeks ago, Kathy insisting Nick's mother came too so that she could advise on a suitable material. It would have been more difficult for Mam had it not been an easy fabric to work with. In the end, they'd all liked a dark pink brocade embossed with a flowery pattern that seemed to shimmer in certain lights. The helpful assistant in the Co-op Department Store had cut the fabric into separate bundles so that each of them, even Lucy, was able to carry home a not-too heavy parcel. After their exhausting shopping expedition, Kathy had treated them all to a bit of dinner in Percival's in the Market Hall.

Mam had been making the dresses ever since, working for an hour or so in the evenings, longer at the weekends and even Lucy was becoming excited with the near-complete dresses. They hung now on either side of the bulky old-fashioned wardrobe in Mam and Dad's room. Joyce hadn't seen them for a day or two and she was stunned when Mam removed the old sheet that covered them. As they couldn't be certain of the weather at the end of April, Kathy had chosen a pattern with long narrow sleeves and a high neck which Joyce had, at first, thought a little plain. Now, though, with the tight-fitting bodice arrowed to a point at the front of the heavily-gathered full-length skirt, the material shimmered even in the dim light coming from the ceiling light in Mam and Dad's room. 'Oh, Mam, they're gorgeous,' Joyce whispered. Lucy, it seemed, was speechless, merely gaping at her dress and reaching out a tentative hand to touch it.

'I hope your hands are clean, young lady,' Mam said sharply and Lucy snatched her hand back guiltily. 'You'd better go and wash them before you try it on. Joyce, you can be trying yours on.'

Within minutes, it was sliding over her head and falling in folds to the floor. Mam looked at it critically, her head cocked to one side. 'Mm, I think the sleeves need to be a little tighter. And maybe the bodice too.' Reaching for a tin of pins nearby, she took in what seemed to Joyce to be a minute pinch of material on the sleeves and bodice.

Lucy returned at that point and stopped, a stunned look on her face, when she saw Joyce in her dress. 'Oh, Joyce, you look lovely. Can you imagine how you'd feel if it were you getting married?'

Joyce's heart plummeted with Lucy's words and she felt the threatening thickness at the back of her throat. 'Well, no chance of that for a while yet,' she said, making a determined effort to gulp the tears back.

'Can I be a bridesmaid for you when you do? I wouldn't mind wearing this dress again.'

Mam glanced quickly at Joyce as she carefully helped her off with the dress and replaced it back on its hanger. 'The rate you're growing, young lady, it'll be too small for you by next year, never mind whenever Joyce does get married. Right, come on, young lady. Your turn now.'

After she'd dressed again, Joyce sat on Mam and Dad's bed, trying to ignore the lingering old-sprout smell of her father's socks that lingered in the bedroom, while Lucy tried her dress on. It fitted her perfectly and the gawky nine-year-old was transformed into a lovely young girl. Already, Joyce could see a budding elfin-like beauty forming her sister. 'Oh, Lucy, sweetheart. You look gorgeous.'

'Doesn't she just?' Mam gloated. 'Like a proper little girl.'

'Yuk! Take it off,' she said, pulling a comical face at both of them.

'Perfect. Doesn't need any alterations,' Mam said, as she helped Lucy out of the dress.

'Can I go and play out for a bit, Mam?' she pleaded now.

'Off you go but think on you're back by half past seven. I don't want to have to come looking for you again.' As Joyce rose to leave with her younger sister, Mam laid a restraining hand on her arm. 'Stay a minute, Joyce, I want a word with you.'

Joyce sat on the bed again while Mam wrapped both dresses back up into the old sheet. 'Now then, love, what's up?'

Joyce squirmed. Trust Mam not to miss anything. 'Nowt, Mam. Why should you think there's summat up?'

Mam indicated the dresses back on the side of the wardrobe. 'You've lost weight since I started making these dresses and you're a lot quieter since you and Dave split up.'

Suddenly, it became too much for her and she burst into tears. Mam joined her on the bed and put an arm round her shoulders. 'I knew there were summat. Are you going to tell me what's up?'

She gulped back the tears and said, 'Me and Dave's split up because we were never going to be able to marry.'

'Why ever not? Is it because he's a Catholic?'

'No. Dave's been told that epileptics aren't allowed to marry.'

Mam's mouth fell open. 'I never heard owt so bloody daft in all my life. Who thought that one up?'

'Apparently, it's some law or other.'

'Well, I knew it were often thought in the olden days that anyone having a fit were demon-possessed and ought to be locked up, but not to be able to marry is downright cruel.' Joyce nodded and her mother continued, 'Listen, love, if that's really true, then you and he should go away somewhere and live together.' Joyce looked at her mother in amazement. 'I mean it, love. You shouldn't let your lives be ruined by some stupid old law.'

'That's what I suggested to Dave but he weren't having that. It's getting wed or nowt for him.'

'Well, you've got to admire him for that,' Mam conceded. 'Is there any way you can find out if what Dave's heard is true?'

'I've tried, Mam, but I can't find owt at the library. I told Sally about it at Christmas and she said she knew someone who might be able to find out but she hasn't come back to me yet. Every day I've looked for a letter but I don't like to pester.'

'No, you can't do that. In the meantime, you must try to carry on as best you can. Happen things will work out in the end. Now give us a cuddle.'

As Joyce reached over and hugged her mother, she wished Mam could make it all come right for them as she'd so often done in the past when they were little. 'Oh, Mam, I do love you.'

'Yes, well, that's enough of that now,' her mother said, obviously uncomfortable with the conversation. 'It's time I were getting on with these alterations.'

CHAPTER 16

Stepping outside after the warm and welcoming atmosphere of The Fawkes Arms, Sally shivered in the bitter cold of the March afternoon. As always in this village on the edge of the North Yorks Moors, the wind had a biting edge to it. She'd be glad to get back to the cosiness of Pear Tree cottage today.

She found the door to the cottage locked. Strange, as Phoebe always left it on the latch during the day so that either one of her neighbours could call in. Puzzled, she rummaged in her bag for her key. 'Phoebe?' she called out as she entered through the small kitchen. There was no answer. 'Phoebe, where are you? It's Sally.'

In answer, there was a groan from the adjoining sitting room. Throwing her bag onto the kitchen table, she made her way into the room, finding it icy cold and Phoebe lying on the settee, shivering under a blanket. Yet her forehead when Sally touched it, was hot and she guessed that Phoebe had a temperature. 'Sally? Is that you, love?' the old lady said in response to Sally's cold hand.

'It is, Phoebe. Are you ill?'

'Flu, I think,' she whispered, her voice a rasp. 'I

feel awful. Can you get me an extra blanket from upstairs? And perhaps do me another hot water bottle. This one's cold long since.' She struggled to produce it from under the covers and handed it over.

Sally flew upstairs and grabbed an eiderdown and a pillow from Phoebe's bed. Tucking it round Phoebe, she said, 'Why didn't you stoke the fire, Phoebe? It's freezing outside and not much better in here.'

The old woman waved a hand in the direction of the now dead fire. 'I tried, Sally, love, but I felt too ill. It was all I could do to get myself a hot water bottle.'

'I'm going to get a fire going first, then I'm off back to the pub to phone for a doctor.' Sally busied herself with finishing what Phoebe had started.

'No, don't trouble the doctor.' Phoebe still had the pre-National Health Service attitude that you shouldn't call the doctor out unless it was absolutely necessary. 'I'll be all right in a day or two.'

With the firewood now well alight, Sally piled coals on top. 'I don't think you will, Phoebe. I think you've got summat a bit more serious than flu.' She didn't like to point out that Phoebe was an old woman and because of that an illness like flu should be treated more seriously. Phoebe tried protesting but Sally was adamant and, once the coal had started to catch, she ran back to the pub.

Fortunately, Sid, the landlord was still wiping the surfaces down and grasped the seriousness of the situation quickly. 'Phoebe Harris isn't one as is sick a lot so I reckon it must be bad. Is it the doctor in Thirsk, Sally?' he said, already reaching for the phone. At her nod, he started dialling and said, 'You go back to her, love. I'll explain to the doctor now you've given me the details.'

Back at the house, Sally set the kettle to boil in the kitchen and went through to check if Phoebe was all right. The fire was well alight now and already the room was warmer. Phoebe had dozed off but already she looked a little better and the shivering seemed to have eased. Moments later, the kettle started whistling and she went through to the kitchen to fill the hot water bottle, which she slid under the blanket and eiderdown, then settled down to wait for the doctor to arrive, glancing from time to time at Phoebe.

By the time he arrived, she had become restless, trying to throw the eiderdown off and Sally guessed that she'd developed a fever. After examining Phoebe, he said, 'I'm going to have to get her into hospital, young lady. I'm afraid it's a nasty chest infection, possibly pneumonia. Are you her daughter? Granddaughter?'

'No, I'm just a friend, we've lodged with her since my husband ...' it still gave her a thrill to say those words ... 'was posted to the air base.'

'Am I right in thinking that she has a daughter?'

'Yes, but she lives in Australia.'

He shook his head in exasperation. 'These young ones! Leaving their elderly parents to manage by themselves while they go gallivanting to the other

Anne L Harvey

side of the world.' His attitude, like Phoebe's, spoke of another time, another era. 'She shouldn't be left on her own, you know. She's 86 and crippled with arthritis.'

'I'm always here during the night and first thing in the morning and her neighbours are very good about keeping an eye on her,' Sally pointed out, stung that he'd made it sound as if Phoebe had been neglected.

'Are you going to be around until the ambulance gets here?'

'Yes, I'll be here.'

'In that case, I'll leave you to it. Is there a phone box nearby?'

'No, but you can ring from the pub. Sid's very obliging and he knows about Phoebe being ill. It were him who phoned the surgery.'

It was nearly dark by the time the ambulance arrived and by then, Phoebe seemed delirious. Sensing Sally's distress, one of the ambulance attendants patted her arm, saying, 'Don't worry, love. We'll soon have your Gran settled in the hospital.'

'She's not my Gran, she's our landlady,' Sally said again.

'Hubby in the RAF, is he?' he said with a grin. 'Are you coming in the ambulance with us to the hospital?'

Going to the hospital with Phoebe, she felt guilty that Phil would have to fend for himself this evening but there was little she could do, other than leave him a note of explanation. She also asked him to ring Rachel, one of Phoebe's nieces, who acted as Phoebe's next-of-kin with daughter Nancy being in Australia. A few years older than Sally, she visited her aunt regularly and Sally liked her.

When she did get back from the hospital a few hours later and apologised to Phil for not having his tea ready, he said, 'Sally, love, you should know by now that I'm not like that. I were more bothered about what had happened to poor old Phoebe than having my tea on the table. How is she anyway?'

'Poorly, very poorly. The hospital confirmed that it was pneumonia,' Sally said, divesting herself of her coat. 'They're going to keep her in for a few days. Did you manage to get in touch with Rachel?'

'I did and she said she'd ring the hospital herself and let them in Australia know.'

Hanging her coat on the hook behind the kitchen door, Sally said, 'Will beans on toast be all right tonight?'

'I've got a better idea. Why don't you put your feet up and I'll get you a brew. While you're having that I'll do us an Egg Banjo.'

'A what?'

'It's a military special. A runny fried egg served between two thick pieces of bread, preferably served with summat called Gunfire.'

She gaped at him. 'You're making this up.'

'I'm not. It's been the staple diet of Tommies for a long time, but widely adopted by the other services.'

'But why Banjo? And what's Gunfire?'

He laughed. 'Because the egg's inclined to drip down your front and the action of mopping it up with your fingers mimics the action of playing a banjo.' He demonstrated this with his own fingers. 'And Gunfire's a heady mixture of black tea and rum. Said to stem from the time when the original Tommies were going over the top in World War I to give them courage.'

'Well, I think I'll give the Gunfire a miss but the Egg Banjo sounds delicious.'

'Right, Madam, one Egg Banjo coming up. Not forgetting a cuppa.'

Phil found some barm cakes, or bread cakes as they called them in Yorkshire, in the bread bin and the fried egg, suitably runny, tasted as delicious as her taste buds had anticipated. She managed to avoid it dripping down the front of her blouse but couldn't stop it dribbling down her chin. Phil didn't have quite so much luck; his landed as a blob on his shirt.

As they were washing up together, Phil said, 'With the fuss about Phoebe, I forgot to tell you. I've finally had a letter from Fred.'

'After all this time. How did he know where you were based?'

'I had another go at writing to his home address. Until today, he'd never replied. He reckons he hadn't liked to because – and you'll never believe this – he's been going out with Pam.'

Sally stared at him. 'Pam, your old girlfriend?'

'The one and only. It seems he'd been in love with her when she and I were going out together.'

'He hid that well,' she said, picking up another plate from the draining board, 'but how did they get together?'

'Here, read the letter for yourself.' He wiped his hands on a nearby towel and passed her a somewhat crumpled envelope. 'Sorry, it's been in my pocket since this morning.'

She tucked the plates back in the kitchenette and took the letter from him.

'Dear Phil and Sally,' she read.

'I've never been much of a letter writer so sorry for not replying to yours before now. Fact is, I didn't know how to tell you but me and your ex Pam have been going out together for the past couple of years. Here's how it happened.

Remember me taking photos at your wedding? Well, when I had them developed, I found that I'd taken accidentally taken a shot of the people outside the church and among them was Pam. You'd never have noticed her. She was hidden away at the back of the crowd but as I took the photo, someone must have moved aside. She looked so sad. I managed to get in touch with her through her Dad's building firm and asked her to meet me to see how she was getting on. We started meeting occasionally for a coffee then a drink in the evenings but then, as you know, I had to come back home to run the business after Dad had his stroke. I thought that would be that even though we agreed to write to each other. Then, she came to stay for a weekend and she told me how much she'd missed me. Well, one thing led to another and fact is, we've just got engaged and she's moving down to Wales when we get married next year. I reckon she must really love me to do that because I remember you telling me that she told you she could never move away from Blackpool because of her family. It's that that's convinced me she really loves me otherwise I might have always wondered if I was second best. And I can tell you now that I've always been in love with her. It used to really annoy me because I could tell you weren't as keen as she was and I knew I wouldn't have been like that with her.

Pam knows I'm writing this and says to tell you that finishing with her as you did was the best thing you could have done for her. She sends her love to both of you and hopes you're as happy as we are. We'd really love it if you come to the wedding but will understand if you feel it might be a bit awkward.

All the best
Fred.'

'Well, that's a bit of a surprise,' Sally said, folding the letter and putting it back in the envelope. 'I'm glad though. I always liked Fred. Pam too, come to that.'

'It all makes sense now because Fred did used to nag me about getting in touch if I hadn't seen her for a while. Come to think of it,' he mused, 'I used to tease him about it, never realising he might have feelings for her himself. As he used to tease me about seeing you instead of Pam.'

'And did you?'

'I did,' he said, looking uncomfortable. 'To my shame. But then, often she couldn't come out because they'd got some family get-together. If you remember, she was part of a big family.'

Didn't you tell me that Fred's got a big family too? That'll help,' Sally said, yawning so wide, tears came to her eyes.

Phil stood and pulled her to her feet. 'Come on

to bed, love, you're worn out.'

* * *

Sally managed to visit Phoebe a couple of times during the week the old lady remained in hospital. Initially the staff had been worried about letting her home with having no relatives nearby but Sally said she'd be glad to look after her and would arrange the next door neighbours to keep an eye on Phoebe whenever she was at work. So the old lady arrived home in the same way she left, in the back of an ambulance. She was still pale and drawn but a smile lit her face when she saw the lively fire dancing in the grate and the sofa made comfortable with cushions and a rug awaiting her. 'Oh, Sally, I can't tell you how lovely it is to be home. And you've made it all so welcoming,' she said as the ambulance men carefully lifted her on to the sofa and tucked the rug around her.

'Thank you, dears,' she said to the two men, 'you've been so kind.'

'All part of the job, love,' said the older one of the two, burly man with a friendly, open face.

'Would you like a brew before you go?' Sally asked.

'A brew?' the other man asked.

'Sorry, I mean a cup of tea,' Sally said. Even after two years of living in Yorkshire, she'd only just remembered that here tea was mashed, not brewed as in Lancashire.

'Thanks, love, but no. Got to get back to work.'

'Such lovely men, so kind,' Phoebe said, forgetting she'd said the same thing only a moment ago. 'It was the same in hospital. Nothing was too much trouble.'

Busying herself in making the tea in the china teapot Phoebe preferred, Sally said, 'Well, you were very poorly for a day or two.'

'I don't remember too much about it, to be honest. I seemed to be drifting in and out of consciousness for the first few days. I do remember you coming to visit me though. Bless you, so good of you.'

Sally pulled the well-used tea trolley closer to Phoebe so that she could reach it more easily. 'I didn't mind, Phoebe. And I'm more than happy to be looking after you until you've fully recovered.'

'Hopefully, it'll not be too long before I'm back on my feet.' As Phoebe reached out for the cup of tea Sally was holding out to her, she couldn't help but notice the slight tremor in her slender fingers or the way the cup rattled against the saucer.

'Would you like me to put your tea into a mug for you, make it easier for you to hold?' Sally asked her gently.

'Perhaps it would be for the best, Sally,' Phoebe said, handing the cup and saucer back. 'Such a shame as I do so love tea in a cup and saucer. Always tastes so much better, I think.'

Over the coming days, it became obvious to Sally, and Phil too, when he was around, that the pneumonia had really taken its toll on Phoebe Harris' ageing body. Sally had to help her up the stairs and to get into bed, promising to come to her in the night if she needed help. Then, in the morning, the process was reversed. Every day she was thankful for that small bathroom under the rafters instead of having to take Phoebe to an outside toilet.

Sally couldn't help comparing the grateful thanks Phoebe bestowed on Sally's efforts to that of the endless complaints and sparse words of thanks from her own mother. Yet in a way, she felt like she was contributing to Phoebe's well-being. The old lady did grow stronger with each day that passed but both Sally and Phil noticed that she was getting a little confused. There was one time when she came home from work to find Phoebe had managed to get up the stairs and get undressed by herself. When Sally gently asked her why, she'd replied, 'Well, it was getting dark so I thought it was bedtime.' The day had indeed been a dark one and heavy rain in the early afternoon had made it darker still.

Cuddled together on the sofa later that evening, she and Phil discussed the situation when Phoebe had been settled in bed. Fortunately, she was very biddable and went along with everything that Sally suggested.

'It looks like Phoebe's care's going to fall on you, love, though I'll help where I can,' Phil said.

'I don't mind as she's such a dear old thing and she's not much trouble.'

'Maybe we should have a quiet chat with Rachel next time she visits.'

The opportunity arose a couple of days later when Rachel herself arrived on the doorstep, red-cheeked from the cold, her hair hidden under a woollen hat. 'Hello, Sally. I hope you don't mind but I've got the afternoon off and thought I'd come and visit Auntie Phoebe.'

'Not at all. Come on in out of the cold and I'll make you a drink. You look as if you need it.'

'Thank you, that'd be very welcome.' Rachel took off her hat and ruffled her fingers through her dark brown curls to fluff them up. 'I know I've only come from York but you forget how cold it gets up here.' She bent to kiss her aunt on the cheek. 'Hello, Auntie Phoebe.'

Phoebe looked at her visitor, confusion flitting briefly across her face, then her eyes cleared. 'Oh, Rachel, how lovely you've come to see me. Sally, this is my niece Rachel, my younger sister's girl.'

Rachel, registering the confusing remark, gave Sally a questioning look. Sally mouthed 'later' to which Rachel nodded.

Phoebe perked up considerably during her niece's visit and she chatted happily away while Sally stayed quietly in the background, brewing tea and serving up some scones that Phoebe had managed to make earlier. She stayed more than an hour, leaving only so that she didn't miss the last bus back to York and promising to come over again as soon as she could. As she was leaving and with Phoebe dozing in the chair again, Sally outlined Phoebe's deterioration since her illness. 'Thanks for explaining, Sally. I'll let

Nancy know. We really appreciate you stepping in to look after Auntie Phoebe this way but if you feel you need to take a break, let me know and I'll arrange to take some time off work to cover for you.'

Relief flooded through Sally. 'In that case, could you possibly manage to cover for me next weekend? Only my younger sister, Eileen, is getting married and I'd begun to think I wouldn't be able to go. My husband, Phil, would help but obviously his duties up at the base would prevent him from being here for several hours a day.'

'I'd be delighted to step in. When did you want to go?'

Between them, they arranged that Rachel would come over on the Friday morning and stay until the Tuesday evening when Sally would be back. It also meant that Sally could take over looking after Mam while Eileen and Ken managed at least have a couple of days on their own in Blackpool, where they'd be staying at the Shangri-La, Betty and Bob's boarding house.

Before she left for Horwich, there was a letter from the Reverend Marchant with some good news for Joyce and Dave. Sally was jubilant and couldn't wait to tell them some time over the weekend.

* * *

When Sally reached the house in Horwich late on Friday afternoon, she could tell immediately that tensions in the Simcox household were running high. Jud was being particularly awkward, Eileen reported, picking on both her and May for the slightest thing and winding Mam up so that she was constantly complaining. 'I wished they'd kept him in prison for a bit longer,' Eileen said, on the point of tears. Out of duty, she'd asked him to give her away but he still hadn't committed himself to doing so. He'd taken against Ken and was barely speaking to him. Ken, being good-natured, had merely shrugged, saying that he could take it.

Jud was coming down hardest of all on poor May, using every opportunity to taunt her about Norman and what a slut she was for going out with him. Listening to all that Eileen had to report, Sally was horrified. Apparently, Jud no longer saw his two mates from the old days, Bill Stephens and Jim Murphy, who'd been released from prison earlier and were said to be reformed characters. Instead, he travelled to Manchester a couple of days a week to meet up with a couple of mates he'd met in prison which Eileen thought didn't bode well for the future. He seemed to be losing whatever bit of decency he'd had previously. It was as if prison had hardened him even further.

She had evidence of his behaviour when he strolled into the house around seven o'clock that evening. He glared at her, contempt in his eyes. 'What are you doing here?' he said.

'I've come to support my sister at her wedding,' she said, determined not to let him rile her.

'You should have stayed away, kept that bastard Phil Roberts warm in bed, where you belong.' Then, as if a thought struck him, he said, 'He's not come with you, has he?'

'No, he couldn't get a pass.' That wasn't strictly true. They'd talked about it and decided that it would be better if he stayed away. Sally hated that he couldn't come, it was all going to be so difficult without him by her side.

'Best thing he could have done.' He turned to Eileen. 'Have you saved me any tea?'

She nodded in the direction of the range. 'It's in the warming oven.' As he went towards the oven, she called out a warning, 'Use a towel or summat to hold it ...'

Too late, he made to pull the plate out then yelled as he realised how hot it was and dropped the whole lot on the floor where it lay, a glutinous mess. 'Now look what you've made me do,' he yelled, raising a hand as if to strike Eileen.

Sally moved quickly and stood between them so that she was only inches away from him. 'Stop that, Jud. It was your own fault for not using your common sense.'

He turned away in disgust. 'One of you get that lot cleared up.' As May scuttled away to the scullery for a dustpan and brush, 'he added, 'is there owt else for me tea?'

Before Eileen could say anything, Sally said, 'No, there's not. You'll have to go hungry tonight.'

He snorted. 'I'll be buggered if I'll do that. I'm

off up the Lane to get some fish and chips and happen a pint or two.' Once again, he stormed out of the house to the sound of Mam's plaintive voice from the front room. 'Jud, is that you?'

Eileen and May looked at each other, too shaken from Jud's latest onslaught, to go. 'I'll go,' Sally sighed.

'Sally?' Mam seemed pathetically glad to see her. 'Was that Jud I heard just now?'

'Yes, but he's gone out again.'

'He hardly ever comes to see me now,' she grumbled, 'good job I've got you girls.'

'One or the other of us'll always be here for you, Mam,' Sally reassured her, a lump in her throat.

CHAPTER 17

J oyce slipped into St Catherine's Church after Eileen and Jud, who was giving her away, had walked down the aisle, and took a seat right at the back. Eileen's intended, a tall, gangly lad, freshly shaven and scrubbed, looked round as Eileen approached. Joyce's heart went out to him, he looked so young yet so proud. Eileen, too, looked young and girlish in the short white dress Joyce knew she'd borrowed from another weaver, there'd being no money to spare to buy a new one. They were both only twenty after all.

The only bridesmaid, whom Joyce only vaguely remembered from the Senior School was the third sister, May, standing slightly to Eileen's rear. She was wearing a spring yellow dress, also borrowed, Joyce guessed, accounting for the slight tightness in certain places. Sally sat with a small group of men and women possibly aunts and uncles but there were few guests on either side. Mrs Simcox was not present. The family had taken the decision not to tell her about the wedding. Eileen had said that anything out of the ordinary was inclined to throw her into hysterical confusion. A kindly neighbour from over the road was sitting with her to keep her company.

Inevitably, the service itself, with its solemn and moving words, brought tears to Joyce's eyes, knowing that they would never be spoken about herself and Dave. As soon as the newly married couple moved to the vestry to sign the register, Joyce slipped out of the church and hid herself among the small group of onlookers that invariably gathered at the sight of a wedding, making sure she stayed well out of sight. As the couple came out of the church, followed by the guests, one of them started taking photos with a Kodak Brownie 127. Jud was being chivvied, reluctantly from the sour look on his face, into a family group shot. Even at this distance, the sight of him made her shudder. A surge of anger coursed through her for all that Dave had had suffered at the man's hands. How dare he look the same, even down to wearing the no-longer fashionable and decidedly shabby Teddy boy suit?

At that moment, Sally, dressed in a hyacinth blue dress and a dark jacket caught sight of her and half raised her hand in greeting. Hesitantly, Joyce returned the greeting, not wanting to draw Jud's attention to her. Sally tapped the bridesmaid on the shoulder, exchanging a word with her, then hung back as the wedding party moved on. When they'd turned round the corner out of sight, she came across. 'Joyce, what are you doing here?' she said, giving her a quick hug.

'With passing letters backwards and forwards,

your Eileen and I have got quite friendly. She'd actually asked me to come to the wedding ...,' she hesitated before continuing, '...but I thought it was better not to. Under the circumstances.'

'Jud you mean. Yes, I wouldn't have put it past him to make a scene.'

'I still wanted to see her though which is why I've been keeping out of sight either at the back of the church or out here.'

'I'm glad you did because I've got summat to tell you.'

Joyce's heart lurched with anticipation. Or was that apprehension? 'You've heard back from your friend then?'

'I have and its good news.' Sally's smile stretched across her face as she said it.

Joyce gasped and put a hand to her chest. 'You mean there's a chance me and Dave could get married?'

'Yes but I can't explain now. I have to get back. And I don't want to come up to your house and blurt out the news in front of everyone so can you meet me some time tomorrow?'

They quickly made arrangements to meet the following afternoon and as Sally walked away, Joyce called after her, 'Tell Eileen I came, will you, and that she looked lovely.' She lingered outside the church for some minutes longer, fizzing with excitement. She couldn't wait until tomorrow to find out what Sally's good news was. She didn't say anything to her mother when she got home. In any case, she and Dad were

glued to the television watching the Grand National from Aintree, being televised for the first time. Her Dad's face was a mixture of emotions as he watched the horses hurtle round the course and over the hazardous jumps. And Mam was almost as bad, wincing and covering her eyes when one of the horses fell and the jockey rolled into a ball to protect himself.

Not only did Joyce find it difficult to sleep that night but it seemed as if the hours dragged the following day until it was time to meet Sally. They'd agreed to meet at Ferretti's Ice Cream shop and her former workmate was already there when Joyce entered. Sally's face dropped when she saw that was she was alone. 'Oh, Dave not with you then?'

She plonked herself down opposite Sally. 'I haven't seen him since we broke up.'

'I thought you might have called at his house to tell him I had some good news,' Sally said. 'I was looking forward to seeing his face.'

'Sorry to disappoint you, Sally, but I wanted to hear what you had to say first, be sure of my facts before I went to see him,' Joyce explained.

'Never mind.' Sally produced an official looking letter from her handbag. 'Well, it seems that it's a bit of a myth about epileptics not being able to marry, arising from the wording of an old law, the Marriage Act of 1937.'

Joyce sagged in relief against the chair. 'Thank God, but how did you find that out?'

Sally looked a little uncomfortable. 'Through someone I met while I were working in Blackpool. His brother's a solicitor and this is a copy of his letter. It's a bit full of jargon but it's important that you have the evidence should anyone query it. The myth apparently arose out of a clause in the Act which ...' here she paused then began reading from the letter, '... decreed that a marriage could be annulled if it was discovered that one of the parties in the marriage had hidden the fact that he or she was subject to recurrent fits of insanity or epilepsy'. She tapped the letter in her hand. 'The Act says nowt about not being able to marry.'

Joyce reached across and clasped the hand holding the letter. 'Oh, Sally love, I can't begin to tell you how much this means to me. Wait till I tell Dave.'

'Well, having given you the good news, I'd better get back to see to Mam,' Sally said, folding the letter and handing it to Joyce. 'I'm staying for a couple of days so's Eileen and Ken can have some time to themselves. Our May's gone out and I don't want Mam to be on her own for long.'

'How is your Mam?' Joyce asked.

'Much the same really. Still forgetful, still complaining,' she said, pulling a rueful face, 'and still thinking the sun shines out of Jud's backside.'

A shudder went through Joyce. 'He's not changed then?'

'If anything, he seems to be more arrogant, like he's cock o'the north. One thing we've learnt is that if we stand up to him as a group, he's inclined to back down.'

'Same as all bullies then,' Joyce said.

Sally rose to her feet. 'I know Phil would only

be too happy to have a go at him.'

Joyce nodded. 'And probably Nick as well.'

After Sally had gone, Joyce sat in stunned silence for some moments contemplating what to do next. One thing was for sure, she needed to see Dave and there was no time like the present. Clutching the precious letter, she left Ferretti's and starting walking towards the Yates' house in Wright Street. Moments later, she was outside the front door where she found herself hesitating. What would his reaction be to seeing her on his doorstep? Suppose he wasn't in? She hadn't thought of that. Before she could have any more doubts, she knocked on the door.

It was opened a couple of minute later by Phyllis Yates and her face lit up when she saw who was standing there. 'Joyce, love, I'm that glad to see you. Come in, come in.'

'Is Dave in?'

She lifted her eyes to the ceiling and Joyce could hear the muffled sound of music. 'He's upstairs in his room. Spends a lot of time there now, he does.'

'Can I see him?'

'You certainly can but before I give him a shout, I want a word.'

In the cosy kitchen, with a glowing fire in the range, comfy armchairs and battered kitchen table, so typical of these kind of terraced houses, she turned to Joyce. 'Now, lass, I don't know what went wrong between the two of you and it's none of my business, but he's been that miserable this past couple of months since you broke up. Is there no way it can be sorted out?'

'I hope so. That's what I want to see him about.'

'Then let's not waste any more time talking.' She went to the bottom of the stairs which descended straight into the kitchen. 'Dave, there's someone here to see you.' She had to yell to make herself heard over Bobby Darin belting out 'Dream Lover.'

The music stopped abruptly and seconds later, Dave clattered downstairs. When he saw her standing there, a mixture of emotions flitted across his face. Delight, uncertainty, then back to delight. He looked thinner too, his eyes were haunted and dark and her heart went out to him. She wanted nothing more than to throw herself into his arms.

He must have been thinking the same for he took a step towards her then, hesitating, said, concern in his voice, 'What's up, Joyce? There's nowt wrong with your Nick, is there? Or anyone else come to that?'

'No, it's you I've come to see.' She had a vague impression of Phyllis disappearing either into the front room or upstairs but she only had eyes for Dave.

He shook his head. 'Joyce love, there's no point. We've said all there is to say.'

'Before you say owt else, read this letter.' She thrust the letter, warm now from being clutched in her hand, towards him.

He took it, obviously puzzled, read the contents of the letter then, shaking his head, read it again. Watching him, it was as if a light had been switched on and began to glow brighter as the implications hit home. 'Does this mean … that we can get married after all?'

'It does,' she said, laughing.

'But how did you find out? Who is this chap?' he said, tapping the letter. She told him how it had been Sally, appealing to some unknown friend, who'd found out on their behalf. With a whoop, he put the letter down on the table and grabbed hold of Joyce, twirling her round and round until she was dizzy. 'That's bloody marvellous! We can make that trip into Bolton to buy a ring. Finally.'

The enormity of what they were about to do hit her with a force that made her feel momentarily hesitant. 'If you're sure.'

'Never been more sure of owt in my life,' he said. 'It's a funny thing but when I thought we wouldn't be able to get married, I realised how much I did want to spend the rest of my life with you.' He confirmed that statement with a searing kiss that made her go weak at the knees.

Still in his arms, she looked up at him. 'There's summat we still need to sort out, summat we should happen have talked about before.'

'What else can there be, love?'

'I know we've vaguely discussed plans for a future together but we've yet to talk about religion.'

'You mean because I'm a Catholic?'

She nodded. 'I know your Mam's a staunch Catholic, how would she feel about us getting married in a Protestant church? Or even a Register Office?'

'She probably wouldn't be happy,' he admitted.

'Would you be willing to convert?'

'Would I have to do that?'

'Personally, I don't give a damn about the Roman Catholic faith. It always seems like a lot of mumbo jumbo to me. But you're right, it would upset my Mam if I weren't married in a Catholic church.'

'Or if any children we had weren't brought up as Catholics,' she pointed out.

'Bugger, I hadn't thought about that.'

'Well, I think it's summat we should look into before we go any further,' Joyce said, with determination.

'What, before we even buy an engagement ring?' His boyish enthusiasm of moments ago had vanished and his disappointment was evident in the tone of his voice.

'Dave, we've had so much uncertainty recently that it's only right that we get this sorted first.'

'Whatever the outcome, it's not going to stop us getting married,' he said, a look of determination on his face. 'If you're not happy about conversion, then we'll get married wherever you want. Mam would just have to accept it.'

'I don't want to hurt her any more than needs be,' Joyce said, 'she's been through enough these past few years, first of all your Dad dying suddenly, then all that's happened with you. Why don't we actually see how she feels about it?'

'Good idea.' He looked round the room as if only just realising she wasn't there. 'Mam, where are you? We need to talk to you.'

'There's no need to shout. I've only been in the front room,' she said as she came through the door and seated herself in one of the armchairs, holding her hands to the fire. Joyce guessed it must have been cold in the front room and felt guilty for being so wrapped up with each other, they hadn't noticed.

'We've been talking, Mam, and we'd like your opinion on summat,' Dave said.

She turned in surprise at his remark. 'Well, that'd be a change. You don't usually listen to owt I've got to say.' She was laughing as she said it.

'Well, this is important,' he said. He pulled himself a chair from the table behind him while Joyce sat in the armchair opposite Phyllis.

'I'm all ears.'

'Fact is, Mam, we want to get married.'

'About time too, if you ask me,' she harrumphed. 'I've been expecting an engagement for some time.'

'With this epilepsy, it hasn't been as straightforward as it could have been.'

'Why not?'

Briefly, Dave explained what he'd heard and their devastation on finding out they might not be able to marry, finishing his explanation with what Sally had found out. Phillis sat back in her chair, an expression of disgust on her face. 'Well, I never heard anything so daft in all my life but I'm getting the impression that there's more.'

'There's the question of religion, Mrs Yates. I'm not a Catholic, Dave is,' Joyce pointed out.

'I know, that were one of the reasons I was so against your going out together in the first place,' Phyllis said. 'Would you be willing to convert?'

'I'm not particularly religious but then neither is Dave but I might be willing to consider it, depending on what were involved.'

Mrs Yates looked thoughtful before replying. 'I've had a lot of time to think about it especially since the accident and we found out about the epilepsy. Dave, do you remember that daft idea I had about you becoming a priest?'

He laughed at the reminder. 'Don't I just? Nowt were ever more unlikely.'

She gave him a withering look. 'I don't need your sarcastic remarks, my lad.'

'Sorry, Mam.' He pretended to subside into a cringing heap.

'Oh, you!' she said, waving an irritable hand in his direction. 'If you remember, I talked to Father Mack about it and he pointed out that to become a priest it had to be a definite call from God and you clearly hadn't had that. I think the same thing applies to conversion. Joyce, you need to feel an urgent need to become a Catholic not just because you feel you ought to.'

Relief surged through Joyce and she reached across to clasp the older woman's hand. 'Thank you, Phyllis. I would have gone through with it if it meant being able to marry Dave but I know my heart wouldn't have been in it.'

'You do believe in God though, don't you?'

Joyce squirmed, a little uncomfortable. People tended not to talk about their beliefs. 'Yes, I suppose so. As much as anyone else does anyroad.'

'That'll do for me,' Phyllis said, relaxing back into the armchair. 'In the grand scheme of things, that's what counts. So, tell me now, what are your plans?'

'We don't have any definite ones yet, Mam. Until today, we didn't dare make any. But now we know, we are going to get engaged,' Dave said, looking at Joyce with eager excitement. 'Then save up to get married, I suppose, a couple of years down the line.'

'Don't waste too much time, love, life's too short,' Phyllis said, a bleak look on her face, 'as I found out. Me and your Dad thought we'd got years ahead of us. And you know you'd be quite welcome to come and live here with me.'

Dave gave Joyce a look that said, 'No way!' making her smile but merely said to his mother, 'Thanks for the offer, Mam, but we're a long way off that yet.'

CHAPTER 18

O n a blowy blustery day in early April, when clouds were scudding across a bright blue sky, Kathy was in Bolton on a special errand. She was picking up her wedding dress and would be trying it on for the final time. She and her mother had come to Bolton soon after Christmas, initially intending to simply have a look around but when they'd seen this one, they'd both known it was the right one. A high-necked long-sleeved design in creamy satin, it was cut away on the bodice so that her shoulders and arms were covered only by delicate lace. The skirt was slim at the front but full at the back and bunched into a tasteful bow at the base of her back. When she'd seen the price of it, she gasped but her Mum had pooh-poohed her protests away by saying, 'We'd been saving up for this, love, and it's what your Dad would have wanted.'

She'd filled up then, realising how much it would have meant to her Dad to have been there, to have been able to give her away, and had to wipe away a tear with the hankie Mum had whipped out of her bag. 'Thanks, Mum,' she managed to whisper.

'It's beautiful and I love it.' It had already been a good fit but the seamstress, when she was called, advised Kathy to leave the final fitting until shortly before the wedding itself as prospective brides nearly always lost weight and it might need taking in a little. It didn't; it was a perfect fit.

Even with windblown hair and a minimum of make-up, she was unable to believe that the vision of loveliness reflected in the full-length mirror of Whitakers' Bridal Department, was really her. 'Are you happy with it, dear?' the assistant, a fifty-something so well-upholstered that she had to be wearing a corset, something even her mother no longer wore, preferring instead an elasticated pull-on girdle.

She swept up a handful of the skirt and swirled it with her hand in front of the mirror. 'More than happy,' she said.

'When is your wedding, by the way?'

'The end of this month.'

'Oh, a spring wedding, how lovely,' the woman gushed.

'April showers permitting,' Kathy reminded her.

'Of course, of course. Now will you be taking it with you today or leaving it with us?'

'I'll take it if I may,' she said.

She'd intended doing some other shopping but when she saw the enormous box-like bag the dress had been packed in, she decided to head home. As she was making her way to where she'd parked the car, she heard a voice behind her. 'Kathy?'

Not immediately recognising who the voice belonged to, she turned, her face clearing when she saw who it was. 'John! What are you doing in England?'

She and John Talbot had been courting for a few months back in 1956 but, after finishing with him because she was in love with Nick, he'd gone to Australia. They hadn't kept in touch.

His good-looking face saddened. 'I've had to come back for my Dad's funeral. He died suddenly, a heart attack, a couple of weeks back.'

'Oh, John, I am sorry. Your Dad was a lovely man. How's your Mum taking it?'

'You know Mum, she's bearing up but I think underneath she's devastated.' From several visits to the Talbot home for the ritual of Sunday tea, she'd come to know and like the fatherly Marcus Talbot while Celia, John's mother, had never really seemed to take to Kathy. Not that she ever said as much, it was merely a feeling that Mrs Talbot didn't think she was good enough for her precious son. Still, she wouldn't wish the grief of losing her husband on her.

'Anyway, it's lovely to see you. Have you time to go for a coffee or something, give us chance to catch up with each other?' John said now.

Kathy glanced at her watch. 'I don't see why not.'

'What about going to La Casa Blanca for old time's sake,' he said. Kathy was glad then that she hadn't gone much further as the popular coffee bar was only a few hundred yards behind her.

'Oh, I haven't been in there for ages,' she said. 'Usually, it's a quick cup of tea and a piece of fruit cake in the Market Hall these days.'

'How very plebian of you, Kathy,' he said and, although there was a teasing note in his voice, Kathy couldn't help but be reminded of how often he'd tried to put down her and her ways down in the past.

'I'm usually too busy with work to do much else,' she said, more sharply than she'd intended. 'And they serve a better cup of tea. Cheaper too.'

He was immediately contrite. 'Sorry, Kathy, I didn't mean sound so condescending. If anything I was trying to be funny,' he said, then, his innate good manners coming to the fore, he gestured to the large carrier bag in her hand. 'Let me carry that for you.'

She was reluctant to let go of the bag with its precious cargo but decided it would be churlish to refuse so handed it to him. Besides, the yards and yards of fabric it contained made it heavy and her hand was red and ridged where she'd been gripping it, even after only a short time.

'I don't know what you've got in here, Kathy, but it's a lot heavier than it looks,' he said as he took the large package off her.

She hesitated, wondering what to say but he'd have to know some time. Taking a deep breath, she said, 'It's my wedding dress.'

He stopped and turned to her, a look of astonishment on his face. 'When are you getting married?'

'Soon. The end of this month.'

'Who's the lucky guy?'

Again, she hesitated before replying. 'Nick Roberts.'

She'd guessed he'd be shocked when she told him. What she wasn't prepared for was his laughter. 'Well, well, well,' he said eventually, 'the big-headed Teddy boy. I don't know why I'm surprised. He always did fancy the pants off you.'

'John!' She couldn't pretend she was shocked. She'd known that Nick fancied her at the time, of course, as she'd been attracted to him though she'd tried hard to ignore it for a long time. 'Now are we going for this coffee or not?'

'Of course. Then you can tell me how it all came about.'

As they turned into Old Hall Lane, she said, 'There's not much to tell really. Everything seemed to fall into place. Oh, and he's not a Teddy boy any more. He's a partner in a successful garage.' She was able to say that with relief for, after months of dithering, Mac had finally made Nick a partner in the business and the papers cementing their successful working relationship had been signed only a few days ago. It would mean slightly more money too as Nick would be entitled to a share of any profits.

'Good on him, then,' John said though she suspected it was said through gritted teeth. He and Nick had hated each other and what each had represented and had come blows at least once. 'Seriously, Kathy, I'm glad for you, if that's what you want.'

The coffee bar, with ubiquitous posters of Spanish bullfighters, Chianti bottles hanging strategically around the walls and hissing espresso machine, was much the same. It was busy as usual but they managed to squeeze into a table for two, the carrier wedged awkwardly between them. 'Tell me, how's the job going? Did you eventually get to be a reporter?' Her wish of becoming a reporter had been a bone of contention between them at the time, he believing that it was an unrealistic ambition, dismissing it as nothing but 'a silly girlish dream.'

'I did, thank you, and I love it. You were right about one thing, though,' she conceded, 'I do tend to get palmed off with the more girly jobs, flower shows, bonny baby contests, that sort of thing.'

He didn't comment immediately because at that moment, a harassed and red-cheeked waitress came to their table and, after asking her what she wanted, he gave the waitress their order. 'So, has it still been worthwhile?'

'Yes, because I've been doing other things as well, theatre reviews for instance. I get a by-line for that, by the way. And did you hear about the recent fire in Bank Street?'

'Yes, I did. Mum told me about it. Tragic that was.'

'I covered it at the time and, although what went into the newspaper was covered by one of the more senior reporters, my piece about it was published in the Manchester Guardian. And the Women's Page editor, Mary Stott, has asked me for more pieces like that.'

He pursed his lips and nodded, in approval. 'Oh,

well done, I'm glad for you. I know I was a bit off-putting at the time and I'm sorry for that.'

'What about you? Do you like it in Australia?'

Immediately, he was all enthusiasm. 'Oh, I love it, absolutely love it. It's such a different way of life, the sun, the beaches, the barbecues ...'

'The beer?'

He laughed. 'Yes, that too. Nothing tastes better than an ice cold beer at a beach barbecue. Do you know, nearly everyone celebrates Christmas Day down on the beach?'

Did she detect a slight Australian twang to his speech? After all, he'd been there well over two years now. And he certainly had a tan. It suited his fair colouring and looks. 'How can the beer be that cold with all the heat?'

'Everyone has cool bags. Can't beat it.'

'While over here, hardly anyone has a refrigerator.'

'That's why Australia's such a go ahead country. Britain's a stick-in-the-mud sort of a place.'

She was indignant on her country's behalf. 'I happen to like it.'

He laughed again and reached over to lay his hand on hers where it lay on the table. 'Sorry, I'm doing it again, aren't I? I'm much more aware now of how I tend to patronise people, thanks to you, and I do try not to do it. Drawing my attention to it was one of the best things you ever did for me.' He withdrew his hand and leaned back in his seat. 'How are your parents, by the way?'

Kathy's face clouded over. 'My Dad died of cancer over two years ago.'

Genuine concern was on his face. 'Oh, I'm sorry about that. I know how close you were to your Dad. How's your mother taken it?'

'Surprisingly well considering. She's become very involved with our local church, St Elizabeth's, particularly since they're trying to have a new one built. The one they have at the moment was built as a Mission Church at the end of the last century.'

'One of those tin tabernacles, eh?'

'It used to be apparently. Now it's got a wooden exterior, black and white timbered but it's seen better days.'

'So, tell me, have you and ...' She guessed it stuck in his throat to say the name. '...Nick got somewhere to live?'

'Yes, a flat above the garage where Nick works. Mac, who owns the garage, has bought a house and has let us have the flat. We've been busy decorating it.'

'Bad, was it?'

She grimaced. 'You can say that again. It hadn't had anything done to it for a long time, certainly while Mac's been there, which wasn't long after the war. What about you? Where do you live?'

'I've got a decent apartment in a fairly good district of Sydney.'

'And your job? How's that going?'

'I can't complain. I got my chartered accountancy through the company I'm with but the trouble is, under the terms of that, I've got to stay with them for a certain number of years. When that's over, I shall move on to somewhere else. Might even try Melbourne.'

Their cappuccinos had arrived while they were talking and, while she was sipping it, she listened to John enthusing about his new life in Australia. She couldn't help recalling how, when they'd been going out together, he'd sprung the news on her that he wanted to emigrate there and how horrified she'd been at the idea. Now, listening to him, she began to see the attraction. Many people were now taking advantage of the £10 immigration scheme to make a new life for themselves and it was proving very popular. Yet she still couldn't imagine moving there herself. Somehow, Christmas on the beach didn't sound that appealing to her. She preferred frost on the ground and cosying up with Nick in front of a warm fire as they'd done last Christmas. She had a sudden longing to be doing just that instead of listening to John boasting. When he paused for breath, she glanced at her watch and said, 'Sorry, John, I'd better be going but it was great to catch up with you again.'

'No regrets, Kathy?'

She looked him straight in the eyes. 'None whatsoever, John.'

'Strangely enough, I've none myself now. Fact is, it was probably as well that it happened the way it did,' he said, sounding sincere. 'And I've met someone, an Aussie girl, and I think it's going to work out between us.' Was she imagining it or did that added remark sound a little defensive? 'Of course that'll mean definitely settling in Australia.'

'Then I'm very glad for you,' she said, with genuine pleasure.

Outside the coffee bar, he handed her the bag containing her wedding dress and said, 'I really do wish you all the best, Kathy. You deserve it.'

'Thanks, John, and the same to you.'

'A hug for old time's sake?'

Being hampered with the bag, she could only put one arm round him but his arms came round her with a fierceness that surprised her. 'Goodbye Kathy,' he said, with a hint of catch in his voice. Then he turned abruptly and walked off in the direction of the Town Hall. As she walked to the car park, she found her own eyes welling up. What she'd felt for John had been, at least initially, something special. Had Nick not been on the scene at the time, they might have made a go of it. As it was, well, she'd got a wedding to prepare for.

* * *

'You'll never guess who I bumped into this morning?' Kathy said, as she wiped out the inside of the kitchenette. It had been Mac's but they'd decided to use it until such time as they could afford proper kitchen furniture. She'd seen pictures of fitted kitchens with proper worktops across in magazines and, while she might dream of owning such a kitchen one day, for the moment, on a limited budget, they would make do with what they had.

Nick was putting shelves up in the sitting room and, from the momentary delay before he answered, she guessed he'd had to remove screws from his mouth to do so. 'Not a clue,' he said.

'John Talbot.' She rubbed hard at a particularly stubborn stain – vinegar? brown sauce? – before deciding it wasn't going to shift and sighed. Mac hadn't been too particular about such things.

To her surprise, Nick appeared in the doorway, a screwdriver in his hand and a look of thunder on his face. 'That stuck-up prat! What's he doing here? I thought he'd gone to Australia.'

Although she felt nothing for John now, she instinctively wanted to stick up for him. 'That's a bit hard, Nick. He's over here because his father's died.'

'Oh, sorry to hear that,' he had the grace to say, 'but I can't help it. He always did rile me up. Still I wouldn't wish that on him.'

'As I remember, you were both as bad as each other,' she pointed out. 'Acting like schoolboys whenever you ran across each other.'

He laughed. 'I reckon it was the mating instinct. Like two stags trying to show off in front of the females.'

'And I seem to remember saying to John that I didn't particularly like being treated like a prize cow.'

'You never did!'

'I did. After you two had nearly come to blows that time at Rivington Pike.'

'How's he doing over there, anyhow?'

'He seems to be enjoying it. He was full of what his life was like. If I'm honest, he was a bit smug about it.'

He sidled up to her and took her in his arms. 'No regrets, then?'

She reached up to give him a quick kiss. 'None whatsoever.'

'You've got a pretty poor bargain opting for me instead of him. A motor mechanic with dirt permanently under his fingernails,' he said, holding his battered and grimy hands out for her inspection.

'And with one part of his mind on that job he wants to finish,' she teased. 'I know when I'm well off. With John, I'd have always been having to watch my p's and q's, especially when visiting his Mum. With you, I can just be myself. Besides,' she said, 'you're the one that I want to spend the rest of my life with.'

Giving her a lingering kiss, he moved as if to return to the shelves, then said, 'What were you doing in Bolton this morning anyway?'

'Collecting my wedding dress.'

His eyebrows quirked upwards. 'You kept that quiet. I didn't even know you'd bought one.'

'Mum and I went to choose one a while ago now. It had to be ordered first of all then altered to fit if necessary so it's all taken time.'

'Are you going to let me see it?' he teased

'No, you'll just have to wait till I walk up the aisle.'

He made as if to go back into the sitting room

then turned and said, 'Did you tell him you were getting wed, by the way?'

'He asked me what was in the large bag I was carrying so I told him,' she said, 'and who I was marrying.'

'Oh, nice one! I'd like to have been there,' he chortled. 'What was his reaction?'

'Same as you, he laughed. 'That big-headed Teddy boy' he called you. And that he'd always known you fancied me.'

'Well, he were right, weren't he? I were sure you'd never be interested in me though. A labourer on a building site as I were then.'

'Oh, I was. I just had to fight against it, believing it would never come to anything.'

'And here we are, over two years later, on the point of getting wed.' He held out his hand, reaching towards her. 'Come to bed, Kathy,' and she guessed that he needed the reassurance of her love after her meeting with John.

CHAPTER 19

Sally's mouth was dry and her heart seemed to be pounding in her chest as she approached the air base. Knowing that her symptoms were signs of anxiety did nothing to calm her nerves. The reason? Squadron Leader Thompson's wife, Jenny, had sent her a note via Phil asking her to come to an informal get-together, a sherry morning, as she described it, with other officers' wives one Friday morning in early April. She'd had to read the note twice to make sure she'd not misread it. 'But why have they invited me? I'm not an officer's wife,' she said to Phil.

He was as mystified as she was. 'I don't know, love, but you can't not go, you do know that, don't you?'

'I've been a service wife long enough to know that,' she said, sighing. It was more or less a command. To refuse without a valid reason could be wrongly interpreted by Phil's superiors and she couldn't risk that happening. She knew that her behaviour at social events would be judged as much as Phil's performance carrying out his duties. Although she wouldn't say so to Phil, she felt that the whole rigmarole was unfair but as a long-standing norm, she knew better than to try and kick against it.

How to dress was another problem. Wearing trousers was out of the question. She'd been given that advice quite early on by another serviceman's wife and didn't need reminding. In the end, she wore one of her good old faithful black pencil skirts, a pale blue blouse which matched her eyes and a darker blue jacket that she could discard once she reached her destination.

Approaching the Officers' Patch, as it was known, she was surprised to find that each house, all with neat lawns and a low fence, was detached from the others, unlike the NCO's and servicemen's quarters, which all tended to be standard blocks. This informal get-together was to be held at the Thompson's quarter and it was Jenny herself who opened the door for her.

'Sally! How lovely to see you again. Let me take your jacket.' Jenny was wearing a beautifully draped boucle dress in a lavender colour that suited her dark colouring.

As she shrugged her jacket off, Jenny handed it over to a youngish woman hovering in the background whom she recognised as a serviceman's wife she'd met at one of the more informal events she'd gone to. She couldn't help but be embarrassed but the woman gave her a friendly smile and a slight shrug of the shoulders as if to say, 'Don't worry, it happens.' Skivvying for officers' wives to eke out service pay was an accepted occupation for servicemen's wives but she was glad she'd chosen to work outside the base instead. Again, Sally wondered what she, a lowly NCO's wife, was doing here and could only hope she didn't make a fool of herself, a feeling reinforced when she saw several groups of women standing around chattering, all with sherry glasses in their hands. Almost all of them were wearing dresses in a wide range of colours, styles and quality. She felt positively dowdy at the side of them but, automatically straightening her shoulders, she marched in behind Jenny, determined that she wouldn't let Phil down.

Jenny led her to where various bottles of sherry and several empty glasses stood on a table nearby. 'Now, Sally, what would you prefer, dry, medium or sweet?'

She hesitated, not wanting to betray her ignorance, then said, almost in a whisper, 'I've never had a sherry before, Jenny. What do you suggest? I don't want to get tiddly.'

Jenny gave her arm a reassuring pat. 'Very wise. I'd go for a medium one then. Personally, I find the sweet too sickly and you might find the dry a bit, well, too dry. And,' she said, in an aside, 'go steady with it. It might seem innocuous but it can pack a punch.'

Sally smiled. 'Thanks for the advice.'

Jenny returned the smile. 'On the other hand, if you're nervous, it might give you Dutch courage. I remember a time once, when I had toothache, being told that sherry was good for killing the pain. It was but only because I got so drunk that I didn't care. Of course, that was before I met my husband.' Sally found herself liking Jenny even more. 'Now, being the hostess, I do need to circulate, Sally, but please do try to make yourself known to people,' she said, as she wandered away.

To prevent the panic that was threatening her at the thought of having to do so, she pretended an interest in her surroundings. The Thompsons' house was definitely of a higher quality than the NCO's quarters she'd seen. The rooms were bigger, for one thing, the fittings seemed to be of a better standard and there was even a carpet on the floor. The furniture, of course, would be the Thompsons' own but she could tell it was of good quality.

'Hello, my dear, and who are you?' Sally turned and found herself face to face with the frumpily dressed woman whom she recognised as the wife of the new CO.

'I'm Flight Sergeant Roberts' wife, Sally, Ma'am,' she said, panic drying her throat and resisting the urge to curtsey.

'Pleased to meet you, Sally,' the older woman said, with a warm friendly smile on her face and holding out her hand. 'I'm the Wing Commander's wife but there's no need to be so formal. You can call me Deidre. I haven't seen you around the base. Are you in quarters?'

Sally shook her head. 'No, my husband were – was too young to qualify. We're lodging with a lovely old lady in one of the cottages in the village.'

Deidre harrumphed. 'An absolute nonsense of a rule, in my opinion. As if you can discourage young people marrying,' she said, her eyes twinkling. 'I don't suppose it would have stopped you, would it?'

Sally laughed, feeling instantly at ease. 'I don't think so. Once we knew Phil was going to be posted, we got married so that we could be together. We didn't realise until later that we wouldn't qualify for either quarters or the marriage allowance.'

'Oh, my dear, how do you manage financially?' the CO's wife asked, concern in her eyes.

'I managed to get a job in the pub in the village so that I can help out financially.'

'Good for you, my dear girl. I bet that didn't go down well in certain quarters.'

'Some people do seem to disapprove,' Sally said, responding to the twinkle in the older woman's eyes by feeling much more at ease.

Deidre took an appreciative sip of her sherry. 'I believe your husband was one of those instrumental in setting up the current administrative procedures when the base was opened as a training school.'

'Yes, he was. He's very good at things like that.'

'Well, between you and me, I can tell you that my husband was very impressed with the system and the efficiency with which it's being run.'

Sally felt a glow of pleasure at her words. 'He did have similar experience at RAF Kirkham which has a high turnover of trainees similar to here.'

'Remind me, what Kirkham's used for?'

'Armament training.'

'Ah yes, I remember now. Now, I don't know about you but I could do with another drink,' Deidre said, holding up her empty glass. 'Then I think we'd better circulate but, don't worry, I'll introduce you to some of the other wives.'

When Sally looked down at her own glass, to her surprise, it was empty even though she'd only sipped it from time to time. It had relaxed her though and she thought she could manage another one before becoming tiddly and duly followed Deidre over to the drinks table. Over the next hour or so, she was introduced to various wives, almost all of them being introduced as so-and-so's wives which amused her yet irked too. It was as if they had no lives of their own. From time to time Deidre excused herself to talk to other women but Jenny was never far away so Sally didn't feel particularly isolated. By and large, everyone seemed likable, but there was one woman, a sharp-featured thirty-something, a Flight Lieutenant's wife, whom she didn't like at all. 'Oh, you're one of the Flight Sergeants' wives, aren't you?' she said, on being introduced, a snooty look on her face.

Sally winced at the inferred appendage to Phil but said, 'Yes, I'm Sally Roberts.'

The other woman didn't offer her own name. 'And am I right in thinking you work behind the bar at The Fawkes Arms?'

'I do,' she said, bristling at the condescension in the woman's voice. 'It's honest work and, because we don't have quarters, it helps to pay our lodgings.' She wondered if the woman was jealous because of Deidre's interest in her.

The woman sniffed in obvious disdain, and moved away, without saying another word. Sally shrugged her shoulders and turned, to find a smiling Jenny behind her.

'I'm glad you didn't let her get to you, Sally. Fiona Carter can be a pain in the whatsit sometimes.'

Sally giggled at the remark. 'I had the feeling that she might be jealous though I don't know what of.'

Jenny drew her away to a quiet corner by a window which looked out over a neatly trimmed back lawn. 'It's possible she is. She's ambitious for her husband but he's a third rate officer who's taken years to get to the rank of Flight Lieutenant whereas she's probably heard how highly regarded your Phil is. In fact,' she said softly, making sure no one was nearby, 'I was particularly asked to invite you today.'

So it was as they were suspected, she was being judged. The Wing Commander's wife's probing questions suddenly made sense. 'Deidre?' she hazarded.

'I can't say but you must know by now that the way a wife behaves is judged as well as how efficient the serviceman is,' she said, 'as well as her ability to cope with new postings every few years.'

'I guessed as much.'

'What I can say is that your husband is being considered as future officer material. Not immediately, of course.' Sally already knew that because Phil had seen the tell-tale 'POT,' potential officer training, on his file a few years ago.

'Thank you for tipping me the wink,' Sally said. She couldn't wait to tell Phil but knew she'd have to wait until later when he came off duty.

Several of the women were decidedly tiddly by the time the gathering broke up and Sally was pleased she'd decided to stick to two glasses of sherry. Even so, she was glad of the fresh air on the walk back to the village, as she felt decidedly sleepy. When she got back to the cottage, Phoebe had succumbed to a doze in her chair, something she was prone to do since her illness, her head tilted at an awkward angle and Sally was reminded of her Mam being in a similar position. She tiptoed about so as not to wake the old woman and sat down in the other armchair. It was then she noticed the yellow telegram envelope addressed to her propped on the mantelpiece. With a feeling of dread, she quickly ripped open the envelope and read the staccato words typed there, sinking into the chair as the news hit her.

'Oh, I see you've found your telegram.' She looked up to see Phoebe watching her. 'Not bad news, I hope?'

'It is, I'm afraid. My Mam's had another stroke, a massive one this time.'

'And?'

'She's dead, Phoebe.' Her voice broke as she dissolved into tears.

* * *

The sheer logistics of organising a funeral at long distance proved to be something of a nightmare and reluctantly she had to leave most of the arrangements
to Eileen and May. Predictably, Jud had had little or
no input, merely letting the girls 'get on with it,' Eileen reported. Fortunately, the cost was covered by a
good insurance policy their Dad had taken out with
the Prudential many years before and their usually
imprudent mother had kept up with the payments.
And, as a grave plot had been leased for their Dad,
she could be buried in the same grave. They'd never
been able to afford a gravestone for their Dad; all
that marked the grave from others was a memorial
urn bearing his name, now chipped and with weeds
sprouting from it.

Neither was it the best timing for a funeral.
With Nick and Kathy's wedding only a couple of
weeks away, Phil was unable to get any time off, probably a wise move with Jud being around. Sid, her
boss at The Fawkes Arms, wasn't too happy with her
asking for more time off especially as she'd booked
a few days holidays to coincide with the wedding
but, under the circumstances, he couldn't refuse especially as she promised to make up the time later.
Phoebe was so much better now that she insisted
she'd be alright and that there would be no need
for Rachel, her niece, to stay. Again, Phoebe's caring
neighbours promised to keep an eye on her throughout the day and, of course, Phil would be around at
some point depending on his duty roster.

So it was that Sally found herself making the tedious journey from North Yorkshire to Horwich once more. What made this one particularly difficult was the persistent rain. By the time she reached the house in Mary Street West, she was wet through, tired and thoroughly miserable. Her mood wasn't helped by walking into the middle of yet another row between Eileen and Jud. Eileen was standing, hands on hips, the bump of the baby clearly visible under her overall, almost face to face with a red-faced and clearly furious Jud. 'You'd no right to do that! It should have been my name on the rent book,' he was yelling.

Sally hid a smile. Phil's advice, that the two younger women put the tenancy of the house in their names as soon as possible, relayed in the welter of letters that had passed between the sisters, had been a sound one. She doubted any of them would have thought of it. Fortunately, Eileen had recently passed her 21st birthday so had been considered a responsible and reliable tenant, along with May, by the landlord.

'You weren't considered to be a suitable tenant, Jud, being a convicted criminal,' Eileen spat.

'And who were it that told him I'd just come out of prison? You, you poisonous cow!'

Sally thought it was time she intervened. 'What's going on here?'

Jud whirled round to face Sally. 'I should have thought that were obvious. I tried to get the tenancy in my name, as the eldest and a man, only to find my bitch of a sister has already beaten me to it.'

'Quite right too. It were my idea that she did that,' Sally said. No need for Jud to know it had been Phil's suggestion. That would only add fuel to the flame of his anger.

He snorted. 'Might have known you'd be at the back of it. Well, I'm not having it. It's not fair.'

'Then let me remind you of a few facts,' she said, struggling to free herself from her wet mackintosh. 'At the moment, you're out of work and not contributing to the running of this house, which both Eileen and May are. And,' she said, 'with a criminal record, your future employment prospects aren't looking good.'

He reeled back. 'Bloody hell, woman, you know how to rub it in, don't you?'

She draped her mac over the back of a kitchen chair. 'You should have thought of all that before you started beating people up, causing serious injuries. Long lasting ones too.'

'What do you mean?'

'Has no-one told you? Dave – Bragger – Yates has developed epilepsy and the doctors thinks it could stem from his head injury.'

He had the grace to look uncomfortable. 'I didn't know that.'

She took the towel May handed to her and patted her hair dry. 'Well, you do now. I hope you're proud of yourself.'

For a moment, he looked unsure of what to do and say next until finally, he shrugged his shoulders into his jacket on the back of another chair and said,

'I'm off out. I've got summat to sort out so don't wait up for me.'

'You'd better not come back sozzled. It's Mam's funeral tomorrow,' Eileen called after him as he disappeared out of the door.

In the silence that followed his departure, the three of them looked at each other then Eileen said, 'I didn't think he'd take the news about us taking over the tenancy so easily.'

'Neither did I,' Sally admitted. 'Although the news about Dave Yates did seem to knock him sideways a bit.'

'Have you noticed? He always tends to run off when we stand up to him,' Eileen said.

'I don't trust him. He's up to summat,' May said, looking thoughtful.

Sally sighed. 'Let's put him out of our minds for the moment. Tell me in more detail what happened with Mam.'

'I took her a brew in after tea, like always, and found her ... ' here May faltered before taking a deep breath then continuing, '... slumped sideways in her chair, sort of breathing funny and with her bottom denture half hanging out of her mouth and I yelled for Eileen.'

Eileen, her eyes full of tears at the memory, continued the story. 'I could tell straight away summat were up so I shot off to Mrs Pritchard's to phone for the doctor. But it were too late. By the time he got here, she were dead.' She fell silent while she wiped her tears. 'I know she were a splutter muck and all that but she were still our Mam.'

'I know, love,' Sally said, reaching to hug her two sisters. 'If you're owt like me, the pair of you, you suddenly realised how much you'd miss her.'

'Do you realise,' May said, 'we're now orphans?'

That set the trio giggling. 'Well, at least we won't have to go in an orphanage,' Sally said, 'and we've still got each other,'

The rain had cleared the following day but there was still a dampish feel to the air and Sally shivered a little in the coldness of St Catherine's church as the funeral service began. Jud was on the other side of her, a little bleary eyed and with his somewhat crumpled Teddy boy suit which he still insisted on wearing, but at least he was there. He hadn't come home the night before and they'd half-hoped he wouldn't turn up. Only a handful of people had come along to the funeral, mostly neighbours having a nosy, though dear Mrs Pritchard was there, in the pew behind. When he'd been alive, their father had discouraged visitors to the house and Mam had rarely ventured out, so she'd had few friends. What a sad little life she'd had, Sally reflected, and suddenly felt sorry for her mother. She'd always thought of her as being old but it was a shock to discover that she'd only been 49.

It was an even smaller gathering at Ridgmont Cemetery as their mother was laid to rest in the newly opened grave of their father but Sally still invited them back to the house for the usual post-funeral get-together. Even so, the house seemed empty without Mam's calls for cups of tea or the 'po' as called the chamber pot she'd used. Jud, for some reason of his own, chose to make himself pleasant to everyone and, remembering May's concerns, Sally found herself wondering what he was up to. She hadn't long to find out. A white-faced May sought her out as she was in the scullery washing some cups. 'Sally, I think our Jud's done summat to Norman.'

'What do you mean, love?'

'He's just asked me how my boyfriend was which I thought were a bit odd. When I said I hadn't seen him for a day or two, he said, "Well, I think you'll find he's blacker than ever."'

Sally gritted her teeth. 'Where is he? I'll ask him what he meant.'

'You can't. When I asked him to explain, he laughed and buggered off again,' she said, a bleak look on her face. 'I'll just have to wait until I see Norman.'

The day after the funeral, she was on her way back to Lindrick, tired, drained and more than a little fed-up with the goings-on with Jud. Because of all the rain the other day, a couple of the roads were flooded so it was later than it should have been when she finally reached the cottage. The light from the curtained windows was a more than welcome sight. As she opened the door, Phil rose to greet her but it was an unusually dishevelled Phil, tie askew, the neck button on his shirt undone, his face showing signs of strain.

She sensed immediately that something was very wrong. 'Phil, what's up?' It was then that she noticed Phoebe's chair was empty. 'Where's Phoebe? Has she been taken ill again or what?'

'When I got home, I found her in her chair, a smile on her face, a cup of cold tea on the hearth at the side of her. She were dead, Sally, love.'

For Sally, after the emotion of the last two days, it was too much. She fell into his arms, weeping. For loss of her Mam and for poor kind motherly Phoebe.

CHAPTER 20

J oyce was queuing with her work-mates to brew-up at the cistern on the Monday morning of Easter week. Weavers stood patiently in line, glad of a chance to chat in the comparative quietness of the warp shed, bearing their own mugs and a brew, usually consisting of a teaspoon of tea and sugar in a twist of greaseproof paper. As she reached the front of the queue, a voice close by said, 'Joyce?'

She turned to find a clearly distressed Eileen by her side. 'Eileen, what are you doing here?'

'I sneaked out saying I needed the lavvy,' she said, patting her slight bump. 'I can't stay or I'll be missed.'

Something about the desperation in her voice filled Joyce with dread.

'Summat's obviously upset you so give me a sec while I brew up.' She held her mug out and turned the tap on, careful not to stand too close as the huge cistern had a nasty habit of spitting. With her steaming mug in her hand, she steered Eileen away from her nosy work-mates to stand by a stack of pleasantly oily smelling warp drums. 'Now, what's up? It's about

Anne L Harvey

Jud, isn't it?'

'Yes, he says he's going to get everybody who's ruined his life.'

'Ruined his life!' Joyce said through gritted teeth. If anyone's life had been ruined, it was Dave's – and so very nearly hers. 'I know he's your brother, love, but he's brought it all on himself.'

'We know that but he's got worse since Mam died, acting like he's lord and master of the house.'

The queue at the cistern was dwindling rapidly, signally the end of brew time, and Eileen still needed to get back upstairs. 'Look, you'd better get back or you're not going to get a brew yourself. We'll talk about it at dinner time.'

'Make sure you save a place for me if you're there first and I'll tell you all about it,' the other girl said, looking round to be sure none of the supervisors were about and darting away.

Because of a last minute problem with one of her looms, Joyce was a few minutes later than usual so Eileen had already bagged a table and was waving at her frantically from across the canteen. At the counter, Joyce opted for the easiest thing she could see, sausage, chips and beans and, grabbing some cutlery, went to sit down with Eileen. 'Right, now tell me what's going on with your Jud.'

Between mouthfuls of food, Joyce learned that Jud was furious that he wasn't able to take over the tenancy of the house and had been taking his frustration out on both of them. 'He weren't too bad while our Sally were still there but once she'd gone back, he turned really nasty,' Eileen said.

'Has he been thumping you again?'

Eileen lifted her hair to show a bruise on her forehead. 'Aye, he did that because I answered him back. Pushed me against the door jamb. And he has May in tears most days, taunting her about her black boyfriend.' She stopped as if to take a deep breath. 'And that's not all. Someone's beaten Norman up and we think it were Jud.'

Her bald statement stopped Joyce's fork half way to her mouth. 'Oh, no! Was he badly hurt?'

'Fortunately not. Whoever did it seems to have made sure he didn't end up in hospital but May said he were a bit of a mess, black eyes, bruises, you know the sort of thing.'

'What makes you think it were Jud?'

'Apparently, a couple of lads got Norman down an alleyway one night so he couldn't see who his attackers were. And that's the sort of thing our Jud would do, isn't it? That way he couldn't be caught and bunged in gaol again. He dreads that more than owt.'

'Not daft, is he?'

'No, he seems to have picked a lot of dodgy stuff like that in prison. Me and May thought you should know in case he tries summat on with you or Dave.'

The seeping dread she knew so well crept back into Joyce's bones. She hoped he'd forgotten his obsession with her but she knew what he was like. Once he'd latched on to something or someone, he didn't let go. 'Thanks, Eileen, for letting me know. I'll make sure we're careful.

'Now,' she said, 'how's things working out with Ken now your Mam's gone? You'll have more room now, won't you, so has he been able to move in with you?'

A sadness filled her eyes. 'We daren't risk it while Jud's the way he is. He's no time for Ken, you see. Tries to put him down every time he sees him. I've suggested that Jud move into the front room so that me and Ken could have Mam's bedroom upstairs but Jud won't have it. Says he wants Mam's old room.'

'Sounds like he's just being awkward for the sake of it,' Joyce said. 'Couldn't you and Ken have the front room, make it a sort of sitting room for yourselves? That'd seem to make sense.'

'But that'd leave May upstairs at the mercy of ...' Eileen flushed and looked down at her empty plate.

Joyce twigged what Eileen was implying the second she saw the other girl's fiery face and was embarrassed herself before asking, 'Has he ... you know ... tried summat on?'

'Sort of ... but in the past we've always made sure we've stuck together.'

While calling Jud a right bastard under her breath, she said, 'So, unless something changes, you're stuck with the situation as it is.'

'Fraid so.'

Joyce remained deep in thought all afternoon wondering what any of them could do to stop Jud Simcox ruining more lives. She was still in thoughtful mood at home that evening, staring into the fire, and wishing Jud into the middle of it. 'What's up, our kid?' came Nick's voice as he plumped beside her on the sofa. 'I thought you and Dave had managed to sort yourselves out but you still look down in the dumps.'

'I am a bit,' she said, 'but it's nowt to do with me and Dave. Not directly, that is.'

'Well, spit it out. Maybe your big brother can sort it.'

'I wish you could.' She told him what Eileen had told her that day while keeping to herself the curl of suspicion as to what nasty business he would get up to with his sisters if he could.

'Bastard!' he said, through gritted teeth. 'I thought being in prison with all the nasty big boys would have sorted him out but it doesn't sound like it.'

'If anything, he sounds to have come out harder and meaner than ever. He's making those girls' lives a misery. And he lashes out at them given half a chance.' She told him about the bruise to Eileen's temple where he'd pushed her against a door jamb. 'And Eileen thinks he's the one who gave Mary's West Indian boyfriend a good-hiding a few days ago.'

Nick's face was bleak as he listened but he remained silent for a moment before saying with quiet authority, 'I think it's time we sorted him out good and proper.'

Remembering how badly Nick had been beaten up by Jud and his mates a couple of years ago, she wished she hadn't said anything now. 'Nick, don't do owt daft, will you, not before your wedding?'

'Sometimes, Joyce, you have to do summat instead of standing by while people like him get away with it. But don't worry, I won't tackle him on my own. I don't trust him for one thing. In the meantime, love,' he said, giving her a stern look, 'you and Dave must watch your backs at all times.'

'We will, don't worry.'

Dave was angry too when she told him that night as they queued to see Tommy Steele in 'Tommy The Toreador' at the Picture House. 'I think Nick's right. It's time we stood up to him.'

'How can you do that? He seems to be lying low at the moment. The only time I've seen him was at Eileen's wedding.' She remembered the sick feeling she'd experienced when she'd seen him and a shiver ran through her.

They'd reached the front of the queue by now and as Dave bought two tickets from the box office, he said, 'Didn't you tell me that he seems to spend a lot of time in Manchester these days? Happen he's palled up with some blokes he met in prison.'

She sniffed. 'Knowing Jud, they'll be rough types and he'll be up to no good.'

'It'd better if he cleared off there and left Horwich permanently.'

'Even though he's their brother, I don't think any of the sisters would be sorry to see him go. Eileen said even her Mam had started to realise what he were like and he'd always been the apple of her eye before.' This last was said in a whisper as the cinema lights dimmed and the introductory music to first feature started playing.

Friday of that week was Good Friday. Even though it was now mid-April, the weather was cold and with a raw damp feel to it, as if it might rain later. The weather wasn't putting off people from Horwich and surrounding areas, young and old alike, making the annual trek to the top of Rivington Pike on Good Friday. The tradition had been going for so long that the origins of it were lost in time. Not that it mattered, it was something people did, whatever the weather and today was no exception. There were still hundreds of people making the trek as Joyce and Dave started the arduous climb from the back of Rivington and Blackrod Grammar School. She couldn't help remembering the time three years ago when she'd done this with her mates, Sheila, Maureen and Brenda. That day, when Dave had come up behind her at the summit and pointed out Blackpool Tower and the sea beyond, had been the first indication that he might be interested in her. That particular memory was especially poignant because, since they'd got back together, they were treasuring every moment of being in each other's company, almost as if might be their last.

About half way up, as Dave was pulling her up a particularly steep bit and laughing at her struggles, a familiar voice spoke behind them. 'Well, if it isn't the young lovebirds, Bragger Yates and Joyce Roberts.'

Jud Simcox! Dave's hand tightened on hers as he pulled her the last bit until she stood beside him, his arm protectively round her shoulders. 'Bugger off, Jud! Haven't you heard, two's company, three's a crowd?' he said, his lips tight.

'Oh, I don't know, if Joyce was included, a three-some sounds good,' Jud sneered.

Dave's body, at the side of her, tensed. 'You suggested that once before. It weren't a good idea then. It's even more disgusting now after all that's happened.'

'Think you're up to taking me on for it, are you? You and that loony head of yours?' With his forefinger, he executed the familiar and derogatory circling gesture by his forehead.

Immediately, Joyce wanted to leap to Dave's defence but instinct told her that, with his post-epilepsy lack of self-esteem, it would make Dave feel worse so she said nothing even though she had to clamp her lips together to do so. But it seemed Dave didn't need her help for he said, 'Loony head or not, I'm willing to take you on any time you like. I notice you've no mates with you this time. Billy-no-mates now, are you?'

For a brief second, a haunted look passed over Jud's face, then he said, 'Nah, it'd be no fun tackling a spastic. Any time you fancy a real man, Joyce, I'm ready and willing.'

This time she couldn't stop herself. Yanking herself out of Dave's grasp, she lashed out and slapped Jud across the face so hard her fingers stung and his head whipped back a little. 'He's more of a man than you'll ever be, you bastard. As for fancying you, in your dreams! For me, it'd be my worst nightmare.'

To her annoyance, he merely laughed and sauntered away, seemingly taking the steepness in his stride. 'I'd like to try and change your mind, Joyce,' he called over his shoulder. 'I like a bit of sparkiness in a woman.'

Dave made as if to go after him but Joyce pulled him back. 'No, Dave. Leave him be. He's not worth it.'

With a ferocity that made her step back, he shrugged her arm away and said, 'Don't ever do that to me again, Joyce!'

'What?' She looked at him perplexed, not understanding his harshness.

He stood before her, his body rigid, his arms clenched tight by his side. 'Intervene like that. Like you have to protect me. It makes me feel even more inadequate than ever.'

She was immediately contrite. 'I'm sorry, love. I didn't think of that. I were just trying to put him in his place.'

'If we're going to make a success of things between us, you have to let me protect you as well as myself if the need arises,' he said, a note of decisiveness in his voice. 'I need to feel that I'm in control of situations like that. Not like a bloody wimp who's got a dodgy brain.'

She put out a tentative hand to his cold face, unsure what she should say or do next. 'I'm truly sorry, Dave, love. I can see what you mean.'

The rigidity went from his body and, reaching out for her hand, he pulled her towards him. 'I'm sorry, too, for shouting at you.'

Somehow the incident had taken the shine off the day and after eventually making it to the top of the hill where the Pike was located and finding the view obscured by clouds and a definite feel of rain in the air, they made their way back down through the Bungalow grounds. The wild and overgrown but much-loved Chinese gardens that had once been in the grounds of Lord Leverhulme's country home must have been beautiful in their day and Joyce thought how sad it was that they were so neglected. Somehow the melancholy air the gardens exuded seemed to match the thoughtful mood that had lingered between herself and Dave. Once again, Jud Simcox had managed to spoil things.

CHAPTER 21

The four men sitting round a table in the Long Pull pub on Lee Lane were deep in conversation and all had serious looks on their faces. Yet they had met up with the intention of celebrating the wedding of one of them the following day. Pint glasses, the contents barely touched, stood on the table before them and the atmosphere was thick with smoke from cigarettes and the older man's pipe. 'So,' Nick said, 'Jud Simcox. He's caused problems for all of us, one way or another, so what can we do about him?'

'Short of killing him, do you mean?' Dave said with a grimace. He had just been telling the group about his latest altercation with Jud on the Good Friday trek to Rivington Pike.

Nick snorted 'Well, I'm certainly not prepared to hang for the likes of him, no matter what he's done.'

'I agree, he's a nasty piece of work but not worth the death penalty,' Phil, who was in civvies, commented.

Mac used the pipe as a pointer. 'Nor do any of you want to be getting yourselves into bother with the police which rules out giving him a right good seeing to.' He puffed on the pipe then took it out again to say, 'Not that he doesn't deserve it.'

Phil lifted his glass from the table and took a long gulp of his beer, wiped his mouth with the back of his hand, then said, 'Sally reckons that when the three of them, Sally and her sisters, tackle him, he always backs down. Well,' he waved his arm round the group, 'there's three of us.'

'He did that with me when me and Sally ...' Nick said, then turning to Phil, continued, '... sorry to remind you, Phil ... when Sally were pregnant. He sort of ran out of steam.'

'Aye, I remember you telling me that, Nick,' Mac said, pipe waving in Nick's direction.

'So if the three of us were to tackle him,' Dave said, pointing to Nick and Phil, 'you reckon we might make him back off permanently?'

'It's worth a try,' Phil said. 'I'm up for it if you two are.'

Both Nick and Dave murmured in agreement and Mac said, 'And you can count me in. That makes four.'

Nick reached across and put his hand on the older man's shoulder. 'Nay, Mac. You keep out of it. You can keep a watch out for us, if you will.'

'Any ideas how and where we should do it?' Dave said.

'Preferably tonight, if we can find him, as Phil's here with us. More weight with the three of us. It might be months before he can get home again,' Nick said.

'I definitely want to be there. I've a personal score I want to settle with him,' Phil said, with a grim set to his mouth.

'I didn't realise you'd had any run-ins with him, Phil.' Nick said.

He seemed to hesitate before replying then said, 'Not personally, but for one thing, he's been making my sisters-in-laws' lives a misery since he came out of prison. But what about you, Nick?'

'I've still not forgotten that beating him and his mates gave me when he cost me the best Teddy boy suit I ever had,' he said, grinning. 'Plus, there's that time he grabbed Kathy in Coffin Alley and I had to butt in. That were no bad thing, as it happens, seeing as it eventually led to me and her getting together.'

'But it's Dave here who's suffered at his hands more than any of you,' Mac reminded them. 'That in itself would be reason enough to go after him.'

'So, how do we go about it then?' Phil asked.

'Get him on his own some time?' was Dave's suggestion.

'Sally did say he seemed to be a bit of a loner since he came home,' Phil said. 'The girls reckon he cops off to Manchester at every opportunity.'

'Looks like tonight's the night then, lads. Jud's just come in.' Mac nodded his head in the direction of the bar where they could see Jud drumming his fingers impatiently on the bar counter, while the landlord continued serving another customer.

Nick looked from one to the other of them. 'What do you say, should we tackle him?'

'The sooner the better,' Dave said, already clenching his fists while Phil simply said, 'Count me in.'

'Best wait until he goes for a pee,' suggested Mac.

They hadn't long to wait. Jud had downed only half his pint before he put it on the bar counter, said something to the landlord, then disappearing out of the door to where the toilets were. As one, they rose and followed him. The narrow corridor led to both the gents and ladies' toilets then on to the back door and the yard. When he came out, still wriggling his wrinkled drainpipe trousers into place, they were waiting for him. He backed away when he saw the purposeful look on their faces. 'Whoa, what's this? Some sort of welcoming committee?'

'Summat like that,' Nick said. 'We've a score or two to settle with you.'

'So you've come mob-handed,' Jud said, flicking his eyes over the three of them.

'We've decided that we've had enough or your nastiness to our nearest and dearest,' Phil said.

Jud laughed. 'You and whose army?' He made as if to push past them to return to the bar but they joined arms and stepped forward, forcing him to re-treat against the back door. Realising he'd no way past the three of them, he turned and opened the door, obviously intending to make his escape through the yard and out onto the street. Quickly, Dave out-man-oeuvred him by standing in front of the back gate. 'Think you can stop me, loony head?' Jud snarled.

'I can have a good try,' Dave said, folding his arms.

'Dave's the one who's suffered more than most from your bully-boy tactics. He's got to live with the consequences of your actions every day for the rest of his life,' Nick pointed out. 'What do you have to say to that?'

'I didn't know he were going get that epilepsy, did I?' He shifted his weight from one foot to the other. 'And there's no proof that were down to me.'

'I've been told it's more likely than not,' Dave said.

'And what about knocking your sisters about, eh? Following in your old man's footsteps, are you? Make you feel more of a man, does it?' Phil said.

'They deserve it, the daft cows. Anyroad, a man can do what he wants in his own home.'

'Except it isn't your house, is it?' Phil continued. A look of fury and resentment passed across Jud's face, 'And what about beating up young May's boyfriend?'

'You've no proof that were down to me,' Jud blustered. 'Way I heard it, it could have been anyone. Coloureds are allus getting knocked about.'

'Bears your stamp all over it, Jud. Then, there's your persistent pestering of my kid sister.' Nick said. 'You were at it again on Good Friday, I hear. Well, all that's got to stop right now.'

'Yeah? How you going to stop me?'

The three of them looked to each other and took a step forward, forcing him even further back against the back wall. 'By giving you a good hiding you won't forget in a hurry,' Nick said.

'You wouldn't risk that, not when you're getting married. Tomorrow, isn't it?'

'Some things are worth the risk,' Nick said, taking another step towards him.

Then, almost quicker than the eye could see, Jud was facing them a flick knife in his hand. 'Come on then, who's going to be first?' He jabbed it towards each of them, one after the other. They could do little else other than retreat a step back. 'Not so sure of yourself now, are you? Being in the nick taught me a useful lesson or two, like how to take care of meself.'

Phil waited until the knife was jabbed towards him again then grabbed Jud's knife arm and twisted it behind Jud's back so that he was forced against the wall. Then with his other hand, Phil bent the fingers holding the knife back so that Jud cried out in pain and the knife clattered harmlessly to the floor, where he kicked it out of harm's way. 'That's for what you did to Sally all those years ago,' he said quietly so that only Jud could hear. 'And tried to do with your other sisters.' To make sure Jud had got the message, Phil bent his fingers back even further, forcing a scream from Jud.

'Bloody hell, Phil! Where'd you learn that?' Nick said, his mouth gaping wide in surprise.

Phil grinned. 'Just because I'm a pen pusher in the RAF, doesn't mean we aren't taught the basics of unarmed combat.' Tightening his grip on Jud, he said, 'Now what do we do with him?'

From Dave came a strangled groan and he fell to the floor shaking, obviously in the throes of a fit. Immediately, Phil let Jud go and dropped to his knees to see to Dave, loosening his tie, and earning an involuntary kick from Dave as he did so.

As Nick knelt too, he looked up at Jud and said, 'Take a look at what you've done, Jud. I hope you're proud of your handiwork.'

The colour fled from Jud's face and, backing away, he looked on in horror at Dave writhing on the floor, his limbs and face contorted. 'I didn't know ... I didn't realise ...' he stuttered.

'Well you do now. Do everybody in Horwich a favour, Jud, and bugger off somewhere else.' Nick waved in the direction of the back gate. 'You're not worth bothering about. Dave's more important right now.'

Jud took him at his word and fled through the back gate into the night, stooping to pick up the knife he'd been forced to drop.

'What can we do, Phil? Do you know?' Nick asked, concern in his voice.

Phil shook his head. 'I don't think we can do much except make sure he doesn't hurt himself on owt. Happen it'll not last more than a few minutes.'

Even as he spoke, the juddering of Dave's body slowed and moments later, he went limp. His eyes opened and he looked from one to the other. 'Nick? Phil? Did I have another fit?'

'You did, mate, but you're ok now,' Nick said, helping him to sit upright, with Phil at his back. Together, they propped him against the back yard wall.

Dave stared round the yard with heavy eyes. 'Jud?'

'He's gone. I reckon seeing you having a fit frightened him more than owt we could have done.'

Dave managed a rueful smile. 'It weren't intentional.'

The back door opened to let Mac into the yard. 'Everything alright here? I heard a scream and thought I'd better come and check.'

'Dave's had a fit and it scared the shit out of Jud. He's buggered off,' Nick said as he and Phil managed to get Dave standing, one of his arms around each of their shoulders.

'You alright, lad?' Mac asked Dave, peering into his eyes.

'I am now, Mac. Thanks to these two here.'

Mac turned to Nick. 'Best thing you can do is get him home. He'll be tired.'

'How do you know that, Mac?'

'During the war, we had a lad with us, a conscript, who was subject to fits. He ought to have been exempt but him and his folks had always kept it quiet. Fortunately, the fits mostly happened at night so between us we coped and managed to hide it from everyone else. He'd have been locked up otherwise.'

'I do feel a bit buggered to be honest,' admitted Dave.

'Come on, then, let's get you home,' Phil said.

As they were walking towards Dave's house, he said to Phil, 'Just before I started fitting, I saw what you did to Jud. How'd you learn that?'

'Everyone's taught to be combat ready. Between you and me though, it were the first time I've ever done it outside of a training exercise. Good job Jud didn't know that,' he admitted, leaving the three of them chortling with laughter and struggling to stay upright.

CHAPTER 22

It was still early when Kathy woke on the morning of her wedding. Her first thought was to wonder what the weather had brought. Leaping from her bed, she opened the curtains and peered anxiously out of the window. Thankfully, it looked to be a bright, clear day with an intermittent sun and clouds scudding across the sky. She hoped that didn't mean it was windy. Her headdress wasn't as stable as she'd expected and she'd visions of the froth of artificial flowers and lace floating away from her. She'd just climbed back into bed when her mother came in carrying a cup of tea with a biscuit on the saucer.

'Morning, Kathy love. Did you sleep well?'

'Thanks Mum,' Kathy said, taking the cup from her. 'I woke up a few times thinking it was time to get up.'

'Not surprising really. How are you feeling now?'

'As if I've got a couple of butterflies dancing round each other in my stomach, you know, the way they do on a summers' day.'

Vera laughed. 'You and your imagination! Now there's no particular rush, you've plenty of time.'

Kathy knew from past experience that her mother's remark was a hint that she didn't have much time to dawdle.

She settled back against the pillows, sipping her tea and nibbling the biscuit, wondering how Nick was getting on, whether he'd be a little bit hungover from going out with Phil and Dave the night before, even though he'd promised her he'd be careful. She'd once been to a wedding where the groom was the worse for wear after a night out with his mates. It hadn't been a pretty sight especially as the bride had a look of thunder on her face that didn't bode well for the groom on their wedding night. Dreamily, she looked at her wedding dress, covered at the moment with an old sheet, hanging on the back of her bedroom door, thinking back over the past few years and all that had happened between her and Nick. Hard to believe that finally they were getting married.

She must have fallen asleep again because the next thing she knew, Mum was shouting up the stairs, 'Are you up yet, Kathy? Don't forget you've got the hairdressers in an hour. And you've to get a bath and have some breakfast before then.' Kathy thrust the covers aside, thankful that she'd put her cup on the bedside table before dozing off. From that point on, it was all go and she'd no time to think about her nervousness. Briefly, she gave a thought to the Roberts' household, wondering how they were coping with everyone wanting the bathroom at once, with Nick's Dad, Danny, probably being the loudest of them all.

As she arrived back at the house from having her hair done her Uncle Don, her mother's elder brother, and his wife, Babs, were arriving by car from Cheshire, along with Auntie Liz, the one who'd fallen at Christmas. Kathy and her mother had thought long and hard about who could give her away but in end Uncle Don had been asked. It made sense. She'd always been fond of her jolly uncle. True, he had the knack of saying the wrong thing at the wrong time, making everyone laugh, including himself. Her cousins would be going straight to the church, no doubt calling in the pub on the way there, if she knew anything about them.

Seeing her aunts and uncle pile out of the car outside the house, the butterflies in her stomach started up again, this time doing either a rhumba or a tango, she didn't know which. With only an hour or so to go before she was due at church, it was now time to finish getting ready. Her friend Carole, who was to be her chief bridesmaid, arrived as Kathy was greeting her relations. Leaving them to her mother, Kathy gave Carole a quick hug, hampered a little by the large carrier Carole had containing her own bridesmaid's dress. 'Thanks for being here for me, love,' Kathy said.

'I'm happy to help. By the way, the postman gave me this letter on my way up the path,' she said, handing Kathy an envelope.

Kathy gasped as she took it from her. 'Oh, it's from the Manchester Guardian. I wonder if it's about an article I submitted recently.' In the background, her mother was fussing round her uncle and the aunts. Having so many people in the far-from-large sitting room made it seem crowded and she didn't want to open her letter in front of everyone. 'Let's go to my bedroom and start getting ready.'

'Good idea,' Carole said. 'And you can open your letter. I can see that you're dying to.'

The two girls had been friends since they'd been at commercial college together but with both of them courting they hadn't seen as much of each other as they would have liked. When they did meet up, it was as if they'd never been apart. Carole was engaged to a lovely lad called Ian and they were due to be married later this year when Kathy would return the honour by being her maid of honour.

In the quiet of Kathy's bedroom, she sat on the bed, while Carole removed her bridesmaid's dress to hang on the door alongside Kathy's dress. 'Is it good news?' Carole said, nodding to the opened letter in Kathy's hand.

'The best,' Kathy said. 'Remember me telling you about how unfair I thought it was that I wasn't being paid anywhere near as much as the male reporters though we were doing the same work?'

'I do. I did a bit of investigating where I work too. The same thing's happening there. The male clerks are being paid more than the women even though the work is virtually the same.'

'Well, I did some more research. Would you believe, it's a system that goes back to biblical times? Even as far back as the First World War, when women first started taking the jobs men had vacated to join up, a group of women bus conductors went on strike in an attempt to get the same war bonus as the male conductors. They got it too.'

Carole sat down beside Kathy. 'I never knew that. Good for them.'

'Apparently, the reasoning behind the fact that is that men need a higher wage in order to raise a family. That a man's wage should be enough to support his wife and their children.'

'Presumably that explains why so many men don't want their wives to go out to work. To their way of thinking, it would look like the man couldn't support the family.'

'Precisely. It also has the effect of making women dependant on the man for everything.'

Carole laughed. 'Ah, the fragile male ego!'

'Anyway, I wrote a lengthy article about it, justifying why I thought it was unfair and this letter from Mary Stott, the Women's Editor, is confirmation that she's going to publish it.'

'Oh, I'm that thrilled for you, Kathy,' Carole said.

'Thanks, love. It's a big step forward for me. To be taken seriously about such an important social issue.' Then she giggled. 'I can't imagine my male workmates will be too thrilled.' Already she was planning to delve deeper into the subject. After the wedding of course.

The two girls continued chatting while they made their preparations, stopping to giggle occasionally over some remembered episode in their past, as they applied make-up or titivated their hair. Kathy had chosen to wear her hair up in a modest beehive style pinned at the back in a French pleat and was now wondering if it had been a mistake. It felt unnatural to her and she'd have been happier if she'd worn her hair loose in its usual style. Too late to change it now.

Her mother's voice from the bottom of the stairs interrupted their gossip. 'Kathy, are you and Carole nearly ready? If not, you'd better get a move on. The car to pick me, Carole and the aunties will be here shortly then coming back for you and your Uncle Don.' Perhaps understandably, her mother sounded anxious.

The two girls looked at each other in consternation but got cracking immediately, Kathy helping Carole to slip into her bridesmaid's dress first then Carole slipping the wedding dress over her head.

'How are you feeling now, love? Carole asked, zipping her up at the back.

'Nervous now that it's nearly happening,' Kathy said, holding shaking hands out.

'You'll be OK, love. I'm sure it'll all go beautifully.'

Just then, there came another call from downstairs. 'Carole, the car's here.'

'Will you be alright if I go now?' Carole said.

Kathy made shooing gestures towards the door. 'Course I will. I'll have a few minutes to finish off before the car comes back.'

'OK love, I'm off then. See you at the church.' She gave Kathy a quick hug then went carefully downstairs, holding her dress up to stop herself tripping over the voluminous skirt.

As Kathy heard the car depart, leaving the house in silence, she realised in a start of panic that she should really have had Carole help her with her headdress. After fiddling with it herself for a couple of minutes, she had a last look round her bedroom. It was a mess but there was nothing she could do about that. Her mother would surely have something to say about it after the honeymoon but for now she flew downstairs in a flurry of satin and lace, clutching the headdress in her hand, forgetting in her panic to be careful. Fortunately, she reached the bottom without any slips or falls.

'Uncle Don,' she said as she dashed into the sitting room, 'I need your help.' She stopped in the doorway, concerned by the stunned look on her uncle's craggy face. 'What's the matter, Uncle Don? Don't you like it?' she asked, indicating her dress.

'Don't be daft, love. You look absolutely gorgeous.' His voice sounded choked up and she could see moisture in his eyes. 'Your Dad would have been so proud of you.'

For a moment, sadness filled her own heart as she thought of her lovely Dad. How she would have loved to have him here to give her away. But she'd no time for tears. 'Never mind that. Can you help me fix my headdress?'

He looked at her in surprise. 'Me? But I'm useless at things like that. I'm all fingers and thumbs according to your Auntie Babs.'

'Well, you're all I've got so let's see what we can

do between us.'

And they did though it still felt a little wonky to Kathy. Never mind, she'd get Carole to have another fiddle with it before they went into church. Then, there was no more time to think, the car to take them to church had arrived and as she stepped out of the house, she saw the usual small gathering of neighbours, Mrs Westbury among them, and other well-wishers. She waved to them and, with a thudding heart, wriggled her way into the car, gathering her skirts as she went. Uncle Don climbed in beside her and reached for the hand that wasn't holding the bouquet. 'Well, love, this is it. Ready?'

She turned to smile at him and squeezed his hand in return. 'As ready as I'll ever be. Let's go to a wedding.'

* * *

Sally had mixed feelings about Nick and Kathy's wedding. It wasn't that she retained any deep feelings for Nick; those had died when their baby had been stillborn. Yet it was decidedly weird staying in the same house where they were packed in like sardines. The sleeping arrangements alone had been a nightmare. And today, with everyone wanting the bathroom, it resembled a military operation with those most intimately involved using the bathroom first. As she watched everyone's preparations, it was almost as if she was divorced from the proceedings. After all, unlike the rest of the family, she'd no role in the actual wedding.

Instead, she made herself useful by helping Lucy and Joyce to get dressed. Lucy was excited and in a giddy mood but Joyce had been subdued since she'd been told by Nick and Phil about Dave having a fit while they'd been out celebrating last night and confessed to Sally that she was worrying about whether Dave would cope with the excitement of today. By the time their preparations were complete, the two young girls looked stunning, still-girlish Lucy with her fair hair and colouring contrasting to Joyce's slim height, dark eyes and hair. Joyce's hair had been a problem, inclined to spring from the sides of her head in wavy abandon as always but somehow, between them, they'd managed to tame it with plenty of Kirbygrips and the flowered headdress that Kathy had chosen.

All three were giggling over this when Phil shouted up the stairs, 'Sally, love. The car's arrived for me and Nick.' She flew downstairs, wanting to give him a kiss before they left, and he caught her in his arms as she reached the bottom. 'You look gorgeous, love,' he whispered in her ear. She was wearing her own hyacinth blue wedding dress and her dark blue jacket.

'You look pretty good yourself,' she whispered back, proud of how smart he looked in his best blues, cap in hand ready to don it for the march into church.

'How are you feeling?' he asked now, concern in his grey eyes. They were warily certain that she was pregnant, especially as her breasts had started to feel tender. She'd completely lost track of her period dates with all the grief of losing Phoebe so soon after losing her own mother. There was the consequent worry too about whether Nancy, Phoebe's daughter, would want to sell the cottage now that her mother had died. Finding somewhere to live could be a real problem as lodgings in the village were always at a premium and there was still another couple of years to go before they'd be eligible for quarters. Nancy had solved that problem for them. The cottage was to be the family's own eventual bolt-hole should they decide to return to the UK but in the meantime, she'd be happy for Sally and Phil to stay on to take care of things. Only then had Sally realised she was almost a month overdue. Fortunately morning sickness hadn't kicked in yet. She could imagine the chaos a mad dash to the bathroom would have caused this morning with so many people needing it.

She gave him a loving smile. 'I'm doing fine. Don't be worrying about me. You concentrate on your best man duties. Got the ring?'

He pretended a stricken look then patted his pockets in turn before grinning and saying, 'All taken care of.'

Nick appeared in the doorway of the front room. 'When you two have finished whispering sweet nothings, we need to get going,' he teased. Long gone was the Teddy boy image, the only reminder of that era being the Tony Curtis quiff of his hair. Instead, he was wearing a well-made suit that outlined the broadness of his shoulders and slimness of his waist. The Nick of her youth had gone to be replaced with a mature man. Then, with another brief hug for Sally from Phil, the two brothers were walking down the path to the waiting wedding car, accompanied by Derek, wearing his first grown-up suit. With him being so long-legged, he looked much smarter in long trousers than the short trousers lads of his age were expected to wear.

Phil's Mam and Dad were the next to be collected and Sally was to accompany them with Joyce and Lucy as bridesmaids being the last to be picked up along with Carole, Kathy's friend. Mrs Roberts' last words as they walked down the path was to remind Joyce to lock the door and leave the key under the plant pot by the front door. She was looking very smart in a dark pink dress with a matching loose-fitting jacket that she'd made herself and a wide-brimmed hat tipped to one side. Sally suspected that Danny's suit was one that hung in the wardrobe and didn't come out very often. It couldn't even have been his demob suit since he'd been in a reserved occupation at the Works during the war years. More used to wearing baggy trousers and a vest and shirt, he looked distinctly uncomfortable, wriggling his shoulders in the jacket and attempting to pull his trousers up, probably because they were a bit tight on the waist and kept slipping down over his belly. In the car, Mrs Roberts said, 'Do stop fidgeting, Danny. If your suit's uncomfortable, it's your own fault. You should have had a new suit.'

'What's the point?' he grumbled. 'I never wear it other than for weddings and funerals. In fact, last time I wore it were for our Brian's funeral.'

'All the more reason why you should have bought a new one,' Mrs Roberts said crisply. 'You needn't think you'll be wearing it for our Joyce's wedding.'

He laughed. 'Our Joyce won't be getting married for a while yet. She's far too young.'

'In case you'd forgotten, Danny, she turned twenty last month. And, yes, she will be getting married at some point and you'll be giving her away,' she said, then added in a firm voice. 'In a new suit.'

Sally hid a smile by inspecting her fingernails. Over the last couple of years, she'd grown fond of her mother-in-law, given that there'd been some initial hostility. She'd come to appreciate that her mother-in-law had a core of steel and there was little that she let Danny, or indeed any members of her family, get away with.

By now, the car was drawing up outside the entrance to the Parish Church and, as the chauffeur stopped the engine, she heard the bells ringing. The sound was a poignant one as with only a limited budget for their own wedding, she and Phil had had to do without. As the chauffeur opened the door to let his passengers out, Sally caught sight of her own sister among the small crowd who were waiting outside the church. Excusing herself to the Roberts', who continued down the path to the church, she went over. 'Eileen, what are you doing here?'

'I wanted to see the bride. And you, of course.' She seemed brighter somehow, the tension had gone from her eyes.

'Summat's happened. What is it?'

'Sally, you'll never guess! Jud's buggered off, says he's never coming back again.' The words came bubbling out of her sister's mouth.

Sally, too, felt the tension she hadn't realised was there seep out from her. 'Do you think he means it?'

'Well, he's certainly packed all his stuff in that old suitcase of Mam and Dad's as well as a couple of carrier bags I'd to find for him.'

'I wonder what brought that on.'

'I know he were out last night but he came back early, white as a sheet and subdued for him. He never even mentioned owt about my Ken being there and usually he always makes some snide comment, just went straight to bed. I reckon summat must have happened while he were out.'

'Phil and Nick went out with Bragger – Dave Yates – last night,' Sally mused. 'I wonder if they know anything.' Had there been more to the evening than they were letting on to Joyce and Sally over breakfast? It had been obvious when they came back that neither of them had had much to drink. But she'd thought then that might have been due to Dave having another fit.

'Looks as if the bridesmaids are arriving, love,' Eileen said, nodding to the approaching car. 'You'd better get yourself inside before the bride gets here. Before you go, though, will you and Phil come to our house tomorrow and have a bit of a get together with me, Ken and May? I've invited Norman too. It'll be a chance to get to know him.'

'Course we will. It'll be great for Phil to get to know you and May better too.' Previously, any meetings between Sally's family had usually taken place in a noisy pub and had usually been of short duration. Giving her sister a quick hug, she hastened up the path just as Joyce, Lucy and Carole stepped out of the car.

Stepping inside from the brightness of the day, she had to adjust her eyes to cope with the dimness of the old church. The organ was playing softly in the background and Derek was taking his usher duties seriously by waving her to the right side of the church as a member of the groom's family. As she passed him, Dave gave her a wink and a whispered, 'Hello, Sal.' She was pleased to see he had some colour in his cheeks though there were shadows under his eyes.

At the front of the pews, Nick and Phil were waiting, whiling away the time by whispering to each other. Again, she felt the surge of pride to see her husband in his RAF uniform. Behind her, she could hear the rustle of the bridesmaid's dresses as they entered the church and waited for Kathy and her uncle to arrive. In several of the pews, there was a goodly mix of people, probably aunts, uncles and various offspring, some of whom she'd met on a few occasions. Among them was the somewhat stern looking white-haired old man, Mary Roberts' father. He'd always scared her a bit but to her surprise, he turned as she passed and gave her a smile and a nod, which she acknowledged.

Perhaps hearing her heels clattering on the

Anne L Harvey

stone floor, Phil half-turned and blew her a kiss as she sat down in the pew where Mr and Mrs Roberts were already sitting. 'Don't the lads look smart?' Mrs Roberts nodded towards Nick and Phil as she leaned across Danny to say to her.

'They certainly do.' There was subdued chat, the odd laugh and much rustling among the people who had gathered to witness the wedding of Kathy and Nick and she guessed that, besides the invited guests, there would be work colleagues and friends of the pair. As she turned to look around, she caught the eye of Mac, Nick's one-time boss and now partner, who was sitting a couple of rows behind her and nodded to her. She returned the gesture. At some unseen signal, the organ burst forth with the bridal march, which meant that Kathy and her uncle had arrived. In common with everyone else, she turned to watch as Kathy walked steadily and slowly, on the arm of the older man, down the aisle towards Nick, who had half-turned to watch her. The look of adoration on his face when he saw a glowing Kathy approaching towards him told her everything she needed to know. She had made the right decision when she'd released Nick from his promise to marry her.

Then she noticed that Phil had turned too but he was looking at her not Kathy. The look on his own face spoke volumes and she knew, in that instant, that he'd guessed her thoughts. Instinctively and unnoticed by anyone else, she blew him a kiss and was rewarded by a loving smile.

'Dearly beloved,' the vicar began.

* * *

When the wedding party emerged from the church onto the porch, the fitful sun had lost any pretence of warmth and what had formerly been a breeze had become a cold wind that whipped the bride's and bridesmaids' dresses round their legs. Joyce had to grab Kathy's headdress to stop it floating away in the wind. Laughing, she managed to fix it more firmly onto Kathy's head and was rewarded with a whispered, 'Thanks, Joyce.' Then Kathy turned to face the small crowd that had gathered outside the porch to congratulate her and Nick, including, Joyce saw, Sally's sister, Eileen. She raised her hand in acknowledgement and Eileen waved back.

The photographer, a tall, thin bespectacled man, was standing outside with his professional-looking camera already on a tripod. Close by were a couple of sturdy equipment cases. 'Can I start off with the happy couple?' he said.

By the time the seemingly interminable photographs had been taken, Joyce was shivering. Lucy was too, and Joyce pulled her close in an attempt to warm the girl's thin body. 'Won't be long now, love,' she said.

'Wish he'd hurry up,' Lucy grumbled. 'Why does he have to take so many photographs?'

'I think it's so that he can pick the best ones for Kathy and Nick's wedding album,' Joyce soothed even though she sympathised with Lucy.

'Most of the guests have gone to the pub anyway,' Lucy said, nodding to the few guests who'd stuck it out by the church porch.

Lucy was right. It was really only the closest relations that had remained. Almost all the cousins from both sides of the family had disappeared in the direction of the Black Bull. Carole, the chief bridesmaid, was fussing around with Kathy's head-dress which was threatening to come adrift again, the flimsy veil swirling round her head and making them both laugh.

'What did you reckon to being a bridesmaid then?' Joyce asked now.

'S'alright, I suppose. Too much waiting around if you ask me, especially for the photographs,' she said, grimacing in the direction of the photographer, who thankfully seemed to be packing away his gear.

'Happen we should be grateful that Kathy and Nick weren't getting married in the winter,' Joyce sad. Already the newly married couple were walking down the path towards the gate marking the entrance to the church where the remaining guests and onlookers had now gathered, eager to dump the contents of the boxes of confetti they held on the newly married couple.

Although the Black Bull was only a few hundred yards down the road, the cars were waiting for the wedding party to convey them there and they all were glad of the warmth of the car. 'I don't know about you two, but I thought that photographer was going to go on forever,' Carole said as they sat in the back seat of the car, Lucy wedged between them. 'And I'm dying to wee.'

Lucy giggled. 'So am I.'

'And me,' said Joyce.

'Kathy whispered to me when I was trying to fix her headdress that she was too,' Carole said. Perhaps relieved that the seemingly interminable photographs were out of the way, the three of them ended up in fits of laughter until Carole said, 'Stop it or I'm going to wet myself,' which only made them laugh more.

In the upstairs room of the Black Bull where the reception was to be held, there seemed to be more waiting around while the introductory formalities were dealt with. Their need for the toilet eased, Lucy whispered, 'What are we waiting for now, Joyce?'

Joyce was as mystified as Lucy was. 'I don't rightly know,' she said, as Dave approached them. Beyond a word or two when they'd first entered church and immediately afterwards, the pair hadn't had much chance to chat. He reached out and put his arm round her, pulling her towards him,

'Hello, love. Nick told me about last night. How are you feeling now?' she asked, then could have kicked herself. He hated her fussing round him.

'Fine, no problems at all – that I know about.' Though the fits were largely controlled by the drugs he was taking, every now and then, like last night, he got caught out with one. Prior to the wedding, he'd admitted that he'd been worried that the excitement of the day might bring one on and was desperate to avoid that if possible so as not to spoilt Kathy and Nick's wedding day.

Finally, they were seated at the top table, with guests arranged at various tables round the room. Ushers Dave and Derek had been seated at one of the front tables but all Joyce could see were the backs of their heads. Sally, sitting at the same table, was the only one facing her and catching Joyce's eye, yawned with an exaggerated hand over her mouth, as if indicating boredom and making Joyce giggle. Seeing the frequent loving looks Kathy and Nick were exchanging made Joyce wish she and Dave could have been nearer each other. As it was, only the bridal party plus her own parents and Kathy's Mum were seated at the top table. Mam looked both proud and tearful while Kathy's Mam merely looked sad, no doubt missing her husband's presence. Although the meal of prawn cocktail, roast chicken with all the trimmings, followed by fruit trifle, was good, it seemed to take a long time to clear the dishes away between each course and Joyce only had a fidgety Lucy on one side and Kathy's Uncle Don, admittedly a lovely man, on the other to talk to. Carole was seated on the other side of Kathy and Nick.

Then it was time for the speeches. Fortunately, they helped to pass the time. First off, it was Kathy's Uncle Don telling everyone how honoured he was to be standing in for the late Mr Armstrong and how proud he would have been to see his beautiful daughter marrying such a successful young man, a partner in a business no less. Nick sort of spluttered into his napkin while Kathy nudged him with her elbow, struggling to hide a giggle herself. No doubt they were both remembering Nick's Teddy boy days when all that mattered was having a good time in the pubs and dance halls. Phil, as best man, followed with a surprisingly witty, occasionally suggestive, speech delivered with a mature confidence. Joyce felt a surge of pride for her smartly uniformed older brother. Glancing at Sally at the table in front her, she could tell that she was feeling the same.

Next came Nick. Out of his pocket he took out what looked like a thick wodge of papers and pretended to scan through them, ah-hemming several times and mouthing words as if he was still practising his speech. This continued for a couple of minutes and several people, not knowing Nick, looked at each other in concern. Joyce knew him better than that. She was right. In a dramatic gesture, he threw the papers on the floor and she could immediately see that they were all blank. 'First of all, I'd like to thank the bridesmaids.' He turned to Carole, sat to his left. 'Carole, a dear friend to both my wife and myself, who played a large part in getting us back together, thank you from the bottom of my heart.' Then, turning to his right, he said, 'And my two beautiful sisters, Joyce and Lucy. I'm so proud of you both.' In turn, he raised his glass to all three girls, one by one. Putting the glass back on the table, he continued, 'Now I'd like to tell you a story,' he began. Several of the guests groaned and rose as if to leave before laughing and sitting down again. 'About ten years ago, a shy, gawky schoolgirl started coming to St Catherine's Youth Club, looking as if she'd run a mile if you so much as spoke to her.' Kathy, at his side, coloured and hid her face in her hands. Joyce, who'd heard the story before, knew what was coming next. 'As time passed, I noticed that she kept popping up wherever I was. In fact, my mates ribbed me about it. "It's that girl again, Nick. I reckon she's got a crush on you." It were quite embarrassing I can tell you. Yet she weren't doing me any harm and I could never bring myself to be rude to her.' By now, Kathy had removed her hands and looked as if she could kill him. Laughing, he put his hand down and touched the side of her face.

'I stopped going to the Youth Club, went into the Army to do my National Service and lost touch with her. Then, some four years ago, when we ran into each other again, I almost didn't recognise her. That shy gawky schoolgirl had become a stunningly attractive young woman and I think I was hooked from that moment. I'm not ashamed to say I even dreamt about her that night. Our path hasn't always been easy, as some of you know, and I nearly lost her to a young chap who could offer her far more than I ever could. Yet, for some reason, she chose me. Because she did so, I'm a better person and I shall be eternally grateful.' He picked up the glass in front of him and raised it in a toast. 'Ladies and gentleman, I give you my beautiful bride, Katherine.'

As one the guests rose and toasted Kathy. Her earlier embarrassment now gone, her face was now glowing with love and, as Nick reached down to kiss her lips, she slid her arm round his neck and pulled him closer, to the cheers of the guests. From her closeness to the couple, Joyce heard Nick say to Kathy, 'Do you forgive me, my love?' She didn't need to hear Kathy's reply. The look on her face said it all.

As the afternoon wore on towards evening, there were long periods of time where nothing seemed to be happening except for guests chatting among themselves. Whereas at first the bride's side didn't mix with the groom's side, as more booze was consumed, the two sides starting mingling. Her Dad was his usual ebullient self and seemed to always have a pint glass in his hand and was keeping company with Kathy's Uncle Don, both of them bellowing with laughter. Her own mother was sitting with Mrs Armstrong and a couple of ladies whom she presumed might be Kathy's Aunties, chattering away and seemingly perfectly at ease. Lucy, who'd made her boredom with the proceedings obvious earlier, had now made friends with a couple of younger male cousins of Kathy's and was busy tearing round the room with them, all traces of the earlier fairy-tale princess gone. Joyce guessed that for preference, the three of them would rather be outside kicking a ball around. Kathy had a couple of younger girl cousins but, as they were quite girly girls, Lucy had no time for them. Derek was talking to a slightly older lad, perhaps another one of Kathy's male cousins, and was looking more grown-up by the minute. Dave, sitting by her side, was discussing football with Ian, Carole's fiancé, causing Carole herself to pull a funny face at Joyce and saying, 'Some bits of a wedding do drag, don't they?'

'I were thinking how glad I was that Kathy

and Nick hadn't opted for a morning wedding,' Joyce said, laughing. 'You're getting married yourself soon, aren't you?'

'Yes, September for us. You and Dave must come to our evening do.'

'We'd love to, thank you.'

'Any sign of you and Dave – you know?'

Joyce shifted uncomfortably in her chair. 'Eventually we hope so. But you do know that Dave has epilepsy and that's thrown up a few difficulties.'

'I knew about the epilepsy, Kathy told me, but in what way are there difficulties?'

Joyce explained about the myth that epileptics weren't allowed to marry.

'Oh, no, that's awful! Carole said, looking truly shocked.

'And, of course, we'll still have to think things through very carefully. His diagnosis has caused us a lot of heartache.'

'I can see it's never going to be an easy path for you both but I'm sure that together you'll get through,' Carole consoled. 'I wish you both well whatever happens.'

While they'd been talking, the small band Kathy and Nick had arranged to play had set up in readiness for the evening's entertainment. The newly-married couple were going back to their new flat tonight and leaving tomorrow for a few days away, their destination a secret, so they were able to stay and join in the fun. The evening got off to a rollicking start with Kathy and Nick choosing to bop for their first dance as a married couple rather than a more sedate waltz or foxtrot. The band turned out to be rather good, playing a combination of rock and roll for the younger contingent and more sentimental numbers for the older guests, although many of the elderly guests, including her grandfather, had already left while several younger friends had arrived, invited specifically for the evening do.

A little later, Joyce was surprised to see a couple of policemen appear in the doorway. With a concerned look on his face, Nick wandered across to them but after a word or two and a laughing good-bye, the policemen left. Borrowing the microphone from the band leader, he said, 'Sorry for the interruption, folks, but it's a bit unfortunate that the police station is just opposite. They can't hear themselves think over there so we've been asked to try and keep the noise down.' His remark was met with a gale of laughter but the band leader did oblige by turning down the volume on the loud speakers. And someone wandered over to the windows which had been opened to let in some fresh air and closed them. The trouble then was that the atmosphere became stifling until someone propped open the entrance door. Even so, with so many bodies and the inevitable fug of cigarette smoke, it was almost unbearably hot especially after the more energetic dances such as the particularly lively Gay Gordons Joyce and Lucy had been doing.

Propping each other up, they were almost helpless with laughter as they came off the dance floor and

Joyce saw that Dave was deep in conversation with Kathy and Nick. She didn't think any more about it until Dave walked up to the leader of the band, had a word with him then took over the microphone.

'Ladies and gentlemen, can I have your attention for a few moments?' Intrigued by what Dave was going to say, Joyce sat up straighter. 'For those of you who don't know me, my name is David Yates and I've been a mate of Nick's for a good few years. Following a serious head injury a few years ago,' here Joyce guessed he was sparing Sally's feelings by not mentioning Jud, 'and a diagnosis of a serious illness, these have been difficult times for me. With me throughout that time has been Nick's sister, Joyce, the love of my life.' Shock coursed through Joyce and her hands started shaking. What was he up to? He'd said nothing to her about this. Surely he wasn't going to announce their own engagement? They'd talked about it at some length but decided to wait until after the wedding so as not to steal Nick and Kathy's thunder. 'The worst part for her was when, because of the head injury, I couldn't remember a thing about our previous relationship,' he continued. 'My first thought, when I realised she was there, was, "What's Nick's sister doing here?" I did start to remember bits, enough for us to make a new start but it was only after being diagnosed with epilepsy, that I remembered everything.' Joyce felt a surge of pride that he'd declared what his illness was, even knowing that some guests might not approve or understand, such was the prejudice against the disease.

He was looking at her now and holding out his hand. 'Joyce, love, come over here.'

Blushing furiously, she rose on trembling legs to join him at the front of the band and took the hand he was offering. 'A short time ago, we didn't think it would be possible for us to marry. Thankfully, this proved to be a misconception. We didn't want to say owt to our families earlier so as not to spoil things for Kathy and Nick but with their approval, I'd like to tell you all that Joyce and I are now officially engaged to be married.' With that, he produced the box containing the engagement ring they'd picked so lovingly a couple of weeks ago and, to her blushing pride, placed the solitaire diamond they'd chosen onto the third finger of her left hand. The cheering and clapping that greeted the news faded to a murmur as Dave kissed her, a kiss so deep with meaning and longing that she never wanted it to end. 'I promise you, love, that we will be married within the year,' he whispered, his lips caressing her ear, 'I don't know how yet but I don't want us to waste any more time.'

The moment had to end, of course, as they were surrounded by Mam, Dad, Lucy, even Derek thumping Dave on the back, all wanting to hug and kiss them both. Then, she realised that even Phyllis Yates was there, tears in her eyes, on the other side of Dave. She didn't know how that had happened, no doubt she'd find out later, but was glad that she'd been included in this lovely moment. She knew then that she'd found the only place in the world where she wanted to be, safe in the circle of Dave's sheltering arm, no matter what the uncertain future might hold.

AUTHOR NOTES

The fire at a Bank Street warehouse portrayed in this book is entirely fictional. It does, however, foreshadow the tragic fire at the Top Storey Club approximately a year later. I could have used artistic licence to bring that fire forward a year but, out of respect for those who lost loved ones during the sad event, I chose not to.

About the same time that I started writing this novel, I discovered the autobiography, **Forgetting's No Excuse,** of the renowned journalist and feminist **Mary Stott**. When I read that she had once worked at the **Bolton Evening News** in the 1930s, I knew I had to include her. It was a wonderful bonus as it meant Kathy might have more career development opportunities than she would otherwise have had.

I chose the setting of the North Yorkshire, a stunningly beautiful and wild area, as the base where Phil and Sally are posted, knowing that an RAF base was located there. As already mentioned, I decided to make my base fictional because of security concerns. This was reinforced when, to gain an idea of what living on an air base was like, I tried to access a couple of forums moderated by servicemen's wives. This proved impossible because the forums seemed to have ceased functioning several years ago. I believe this to have been a direct result of servicemen's wives being targeted by people intent on delivering a blow to the services. However, I have done my best to reflect an RAF wife's as I thought it might be at the time. This is, after all, a work of fiction.

If you have enjoyed reading this book, you might be interested in the two previous books in the series, Kathy and Nick's story in **A Suitable Young Man** and Sally and Phil's story in **Bittersweet Flight,** available across all Amazon websites or you can find them at my Amazon author page https://www.amazon.co.uk/-/e/B00FA20V2U

Made in the USA
Middletown, DE
13 December 2019